MW00782378

Hearts and Arrows

....

S.N. Moor

Copyright © 2024 by S.N. Moor

All rights reserved.

No part of this publication may be reproduced, distributed, or transmitted in any form or by any means, including photocopying, recording, or other electronic or mechanical methods, without the prior written permission of the publisher, except as permitted by U.S. copyright law. For permission requests, contact authorsnmoor@gmail.com

The story, all names, characters, and incidents portrayed in this production are fictitious. No identification with actual persons (living or deceased), places, buildings, and products is intended or should be inferred.

Contents

Hey Dad

THIS IS YOUR ONE and only page that you can read. Trust me. This book is not for you. I will write you a book you can read, but this is not it. Seriously. I don't even want you to read the dedication or the warnings. I will summarize this book for you and then you can put it on your shelf. If your friends ask about it, just ask if they know the definition of smut or what STFUATTCLAGG means. As a heads up, I will not be answering those questions for you, and I would recommend you *not* googling them either. Hello rabbit hole. I googled pressure test once and let's just say they weren't talking about cooking food. To this day, if someone says pressure testing an idea. NOPE! Walk away, because I will giggle which then starts a whole conversation on why I'm giggling. But I digress. If your friends cannot answer those two things, then they did not pass the test to read this book. Trust me. I am saving your friendships because if they read this unprepared... well, let's just say bunko night will be awkward AF. Wrapping up, this story is about a woman who was done wrong by her ex. Her best friend helps her get back out there and she meets some... male friends. These friends help her get her sparkle back. Go jazzhands! The end.

To all the smutty social media groups that give women a place to find the word porn that tickles their fancy without fear of judgement. Who create a safe space and don't yuck someone's yum. You are the cliterati, a group of well read, smuttaterians who always come through in a clutch. The ones, when someone asks for a rec on squid love, monster smut, feathers or three dicks, have books at the ready. You are a walking sexodex!
You are amazing and should be appreciated!

Warnings

This is a retelling of Cupid's Contract (published February 2023) but has been re-edited and includes 10 chapters from the men's POV to be more in line with the rest of the series.

This is a why choose holiday romance series that follows the group through the holidays (Valentines, Easter, Pride Month, Fourth of July, Thanksgiving, and Christmas). There is a standalone Halloween that is a paranormal retelling of Cupid's Contract/Hearts and Arrows that can be read in sequence or not (you will find Easter Eggs in Deal with a Djinn that have been planted throughout the series). If you like it spicy, like super spicy, then welcome, welcome. Find a seat, grab your toys, and prepare for a one-handed read.

Warnings:

There is attempted sexual assault (not by MMCs)

In this book you will find DVP, TP, sword crossing, anal, throat grabbing, dom/sub, praise, kick ass female, and a spunky fun-loving best friend, o-control, cinnamon roll, play with toys,

This is the first of a larger series where most books are around 225-250 pages. This one does end on a cliff or rather a mountain they have to overcome to get to the happy ending. :)

In the series you will find, all the above mentioned, plus bi-awakening, sex clubs, shibari, breath play, primal, cock-warming, medieval tongue chairs, comedic sexual encounters, STFUATOCLAGG, Crawl to me, and so much more.

EVERLEE - IT'S A CUPID PARTY

FUCK ME.

I glance across my display of battery-operated boyfriends, BOB for short, and they're all on life support. My favorite, the bright green one, with a large ripply shaft and little nubs on the end, is the worst off. My best friend, Lizzy, bought it for me when I was going through a monster smut phase. She thought it would make me feel like I was fucking a monster and it doesn't disappoint.

I guess I won't be using any of you tonight! Filled with irritation, mostly at myself for not planning better, I grab my phone off the dresser and flip it open to the Let's Mingle App. A pity party download I signed up for at Christmas. A one-year subscription all because I was sad, drunk, and the fucking ad rhymed. Jingle, Jingle, Let's Mingle!

I'm a sucker for ads that rhyme. And gift with purchase. It would explain why I have a bar cabinet full of random liqueurs and fifty different martini glasses. With all the festive promotions, Christmas is undoubtedly the prime time to buy alcohol.

Did I need them all?

No.

But I was sad and wanted to be drunk. My favorite is the no stem martini glass with a pair of beady eyes at the bottom looking at you. Seriously though, what was I thinking?

As soon as the app opens, the bubble beside my name turns green and my phone dings.

Eight new matches.

As my finger swipes across the screen, I search for someone who catches my eye, but find nothing. Frustrated, I close the app and dial Lizzy, who answers on the first ring.

"Hooker, you were supposed to call two hours ago!" she yells into the phone over the deafening bass thumping around her.

I pull the phone away from my ear for a second. "I'm calling now."

"Are you coming tonight?"

"I hope so." I look longingly at Bob, Bob, Bob, and Bob.

"What? To the Valentine's party!" she yells again, completely dismissing what I said before letting out a squeal. "Tony says you should totally come. He has a friend he wants you to meet."

I roll my eyes. That's the entire reason I don't want to go. I don't want to play third wheel at whatever club they're at. Not only do I think it's a stupid holiday created by jewelry companies to squeeze money out of men who are buying jewelry to apologize for not being present enough the rest of the year, but I don't want to be set up.

I'm old enough I should be in a stable, committed relationship, but that doesn't really seem like it's in the future for me. The longest relationship I've had was my last, which was fourteen months. I really thought we were going somewhere, and apparently, he did too, with three other women. It's been six months since our official break up, so now I've become the natural pet project for my best friend, Lizzy.

Her and Tony have been in a relationship for three months and one day. I know this because we had to go out yesterday to find a special outfit for their three-month anniversary. We ended up at Le Rousso's, the local kink shop, because she wanted something extra spicy. When she caught me looking at their vibrator collection, she tried to buy me another one, which I declined, but am now regretting. She then insisted I come to this Valentine's party tonight.

Hard pass.

I lied and said I had plans because I thought I did. I glare at my toys. Traitors!

"You know you don't have to set me up. I'm totally fine being single right now. I love the fact I'm getting to meet people."

"You were staring at a wall of dildos and vibrators yesterday. How many people could you be meeting?" Fortunately, she seems to have stepped outside because the music is quieter and she's no longer yelling.

"It's always good to have variety."

"Of men. Not dildos."

"I beg to disagree."

"Girl. Come on. I know you're not doing anything tonight. You hate this holiday, so come and hang out with your friends and get wasted."

"It's a Valentine's party. You want me to go to a party celebrating the holiday I hate?"

She laughs. "When you say it like that, it does sound bad! I want you to come hang out with your BFF at a dance club and possibly go home with someone new. I'm just trying to help you get some ass. Isn't that what a wing lady is supposed to do?"

"Fine. I'll be there soon. Text me the address."

"Wait. You need to dress up."

"Dress up?"

"Yea. It's a Cupid party."

"What the fuck is a Cupid party?"

She laughs again, the kind of laugh where you know you're fucked. The kind of laugh where your best friend just roped you into some wild shit they knew you wouldn't like, so they make you agree to come before they tell you all the details.

"Why am I still friends with you?"

"Because you love me and your life would be boring as hell without me in it."

I shake my head, trying to figure a way out of this. "I don't have an outfit."

"Boo boo, do you think I would let you come unprepared? Go get the big red box from under your bed."

"You're shitting me."

"I shit you not."

Putting the phone on speaker, I hastily walk to the edge of my bed, drop to my knees, and pull out a large box.

"Hurry. Open it! You're going to love it." She's nearly jumping through the phone with excitement.

"I doubt it."

"Stop, puss pants."

After I untie the red velvet bow, I cautiously remove the lid. I've learned over the years to approach gifts from Lizzy with caution. She loves those cards that burst open, which sort of matches her personality.

"What the fuck am I looking at?"

My fingers instinctively rub over the white feather trimmed bra and matching panties, white sheer slip looking thing and a pair of red wings.

"Is this a fucking sex party?"

She lets out a loud cackle like I caught her off guard. "No. No. No. Not really. But you have to dress up to get in."

"Like this?"

"Well, the men's match, but with no shirts on, obviously."

"Obviously."

I drop the items back into the box and rub my face.

"You ok, boo?"

"Why didn't you tell me it's a Cupid party?"

"Because you'd say no." She pauses for only a second. "Tony's friend is super-hot and looking forward to meeting you."

"Yay." My voice drips with sarcasm.

"Get your ass over here!" The music in the background gets louder, so she must have walked back inside.

"Fine. You owe me, though."

"You can repay me with your orgasms." She laughs out loud, the kind of laugh you only do when you're drunk and realize you said something wildly inappropriate, but you don't care.

"Bye and please don't drink too much."

The line goes dead.

I turn my gaze back to the box and pick the pieces up one at a time, letting them dangle in my hand, trying to figure out what in the fuck I'm doing.

Here goes nothing.

EVERLEE - OH, I'M NOT A HOOKER

THIRTY MINUTES LATER I'M waiting for my ride share to pull up, dressed in the skimpiest outfit I've worn in several years, with an inconspicuously conspicuous beige trench coat draped around me with a pair of red angel wings in my hand and six-inch red stilettos on.

The light blue, four-door sedan pulls up two minutes later with a woman as old as my grandmother driving, accompanied with her hair in rollers and a daisy patterned top on. I check the license plate with the app on my phone, along with the driver's picture.

Betty.

Of all the people I could have gotten, it would be a Betty. I'm certain I'm going to have the scripture read to me on the entire car ride to the club.

The back seat is cushiony and her car smells like rose petals, no doubt a spray she uses before she picks up each guest. She confirms the name of the club, then flips her blinker on and slowly pulls onto the road, casting several curious glances my way. This is going to be the most awkward twenty-minute ride of my life.

Lizzy sends a picture of her and Tony. Her large white wings glow against her light brown skin and dark hair, and Tony has her tucked under his arm, chest exposed, loving life. She looks so happy and I love that for her. I just don't love she's in the dating stage where she tries to replicate her happiness in my life. She's already told me she's going to marry this guy, which seems a bit premature, but she's certain. And one thing about Lizzy is she always gets her way. I look at the wings on the seat.

Case in point.

The three times I've met Tony, he seems over the moon with her too, so hopefully it works out. She's had some real assholes in the past, so I'd be ecstatic if she's found her Prince Charming.

"Big plans tonight?" Betty asks, breaking the silence, with a deep southern accent. Her hands move back and forth around the steering wheel like she's wringing out a wet cloth.

"A party." Keep it simple.

She nods and hums. Betty and I both seem to share the same wonderment about the party I'm going to.

"I did that once," she blurts without reservation.

"Go to a party?"

There is a brief pause before she speaks, and then she utters the words at a deliberate pace. "Yes. A *party*."

You little wild child Betty, I tease to myself.

"Then the cops were called."

"Oh." My neck jerks back in surprise. Shit.

"Yea. They caught me snorting coke off a penis."

My hand reaches for the door handle because I need something, anything, to grab onto. What the fuck, Betty? Not at all where I saw this story going.

"Sorry if that was too much. I just figured, you know... with you dressed like that... going to a party and all."

"No, no. All good." I pinch my arm to make sure I haven't somehow hit my head and I'm passed out at my house. "What... happened?" Dare I ask... Yes, I dare. I very fucking much dare. Betty has surprised me and now I need to know more about this party she was at.

She noticeably relaxes. "Well, I stopped going to parties. Scared me straight. I was rebelling against my father. He was our town's local preacher."

I swallow hard, then look around her car for hidden cameras, because I feel like I'm being punked right now. "So you never went to another party again because of the one?"

"Well, no. I wasn't allowed to."

"You weren't allowed to go to anymore parties? Can they do that?" I feel bad for Betty. One time getting caught snorting coke off a penis and bam! No more parties!

"Well, yea. I suppose they can." She shakes her head like I asked a stupid question, but there's clearly something I'm missing. "Anyway, I settled down and found a nice man who takes real good care of me now."

I look around again, my eyes scanning every corner, convinced that I must have overlooked the hidden cameras during my first pass. There have to be large chunks- important chunks- missing from her story.

"Is it just you? It's not safe to be going to *parties* alone."

Deep down, I can't shake the suspicion that "parties" is code for something else. "No. There's... I don't know how many people are there, but I'd have to guess a lot. It's at a club. I'm meeting my best friend there with her boyfriend."

"Oh, that's trouble," she huffs, shaking her head.

"What is?"

"You should never mix personal and business. That's what did me in."

Once again, my hand finds the door handle, because I feel like I'm about to continue on the rollercoaster of her story. "How so?" But I can't stop. I have to know more.

"Well, Darlene thought it'd be fun to have me over for a party for her and her boyfriend. They had a couple other friends over, but it was Darlene's boyfriend's birthday and she wanted to do something really special for him."

"Seems nice."

She huffs. "I told her. I said, Darlene. Now listen. This ain't a good idea. But Darlene she didn't listen. Put us two in a room together, turned the music on and, well, Darlene's boyfriend thought it was a different kind of present. I stripped for him and what not, had me about three beers too many and next thing you know." She hits the steering wheel. "You guessed it. Cock out, me on my knees snorting coke. Darlene's neighbors called the police on us and, apparently, Darlene's boyfriend had locked the door when I wasn't looking. So they bust in, thinking I was a hooker. I mean, I guess I kind of was, but only the one time and I never got paid." She adds, "Unless you count the coke and beers, but..." Her words fall off.

"Wow."

"Yea. Didn't speak to Darlene for a while after that. She was mad at me and I's mad at her."

"That was unfair to you."

"Heck yeah it was! I was just trying to do my friend a favor and whammo blammo."

"Whammo blammo for sure." Note to self: don't get locked in a room with Tony and snort coke off his cock.

The buildings passing by do little to stop my mind from reeling as I try to process the twists and turns of that conversation. When we pull up to the club a few minutes later, I step out of the car, but she calls me back.

"Listen here. I've left that life behind me, but if you need me, you keep my number handy. I'll come get you. Us ladies of the night have to stick together." She nods with a stone-cold serious look on her face.

She thinks I'm a hooker. "Oh. I'm not a hooker."

"Me either." She winks.

As Betty takes off down the road, I can't help but feel a wave of doubt wash over me, making me question what I'm doing here. Glancing at her business card in my hand, it feels like a lifeline I didn't know I needed, so I stuff it into my purse and look around.

I feel so ridiculous right now. It's been a while since I've dressed in anything one would call sexy and paraded around in front of a bunch of strangers after my ex shattered my confidence. I keep reminding myself that tonight is for Lizzy. I have to show her I'm ok, even if I don't fully believe it myself. Fake it, 'til you make it, right?

Valentine's Day is still four days away, but I already feel like it's suffocating me.

The long line of people standing against the brick wall does little to soothe my nerves. There are some dressed in more clothes than me, but most in less. Which is saying a lot since I'm wearing the equivalent of a feather bra and a sheer nighty. At least I was smart enough to wear a jacket. Most of the other people in line are bouncing up and down, huddled together, trying to fight off the winter wind that continues to bite.

"Everlee!" My name ricochets off the walls of the building, grabbing my attention.

Lizzy is standing behind a rather large bald bouncer in a black shirt, waving at me. Turning my head, I look at the long line of people, then back to her with my brows peaked on my forehead.

"Come over here!" she yells, bouncing up and down, likely more from excitement than temperature.

The short distance from the curb to her seems endless, with the disapproving eyes of the other waiting patrons burning holes into my back. The bouncer looks me up and down, then moves the rope out of the way. Two ladies next in line behind the rope let out some mangled groan and make a snide remark about us. Lizzy, being Lizzy, casually waves at them over her shoulder, then blows them a kiss before the door closes.

"What took you so long?"

"I had to get dressed and catch a ride. Not everyone lives down the street from the hot new club."

She bats her hand, ignoring me, and starts untying the knot on my jacket.

"Well, if I knew you felt this way about me," I tease, shrugging the jacket off.

"Girl, you know I'd fuck you. I just didn't think you'd go for it."

I blow a breath from my nose and catch her smile, before she turns and hands my jacket to the attendant at the front desk, grabbing a ticket from them.

"Here. Don't lose this."

Ticket number sixty-nine, with a bar code on the bottom. I chuckle. What are the odds? Sixty-nine has been a running joke with us forever. We set each other's thermostats to sixty-nine, may or may not have rounded a number or percentage to sixty-nine for work presentations, or given an extra tip to round up to sixty-nine dollars. General immature shenanigans, but it always makes us chuckle, and I love it.

"Put your wings on and fix your tits."

"What's wrong with my tits?" I slip the wings on and lift them up.

"Nothing now." She pats the top of them like bongos. "Girl, you are fire."

"How much have you had to drink?"

"Enough." She winks, grabbing my hand and leading me through the club.

Club Vixen recently open and seems like it could be a fun place. Most of the decor is glossy black tables and bar tops with neon-colored light beams shooting around the room. There are several floor-to-ceiling cages set up with people dancing in them and a few others which have swings hanging inside. I don't know if the people in the cages are employees or others just having fun, but the swings are calling my name. Give me a couple of drinks, and I know I'll be trying to sneak in.

A woman dressed in a black bra and matching underwear with black wings walks by carrying a tray of light pink shots. Lizzy grabs two glasses and hands me one.

"Free?"

"Your entry into the club covered all the costs."

"But I didn't pay."

"Tony did. He covered the party."

"Well, wasn't that nice of him," I say, knocking the drink back. The burn eases down my throat and into my chest. "So where is this friend of his?"

She points across the room to a group of people standing in a corner, but with all the feathers and everyone wearing white, pink, or red, they all sort of look the same. "He's super nice and cute, too."

"Will he make me come in the bathroom?" I laugh. "Sorry," I say after I bump into some guy walking past me.

Lizzy slaps my arm. "You dirty whore." She laughs.

"It was a valid question. I need to feel my twat tingle. I need that big dick energy tonight."

Lizzy is still laughing when we get over to the group. I recognize a few of the people from various parties they've had over the last couple of months, but really only know Lizzy.

"Everlee, Derek. Derek, Everlee," she introduces.

"Hi." He smiles, holding out his hand for a handshake.

He's attractive. Dark tan skin, green eyes and dark hair trimmed short. He's wearing a pair of red silk boxers with hearts all over them and a set of red wings.

"Hey love," a man says, placing his hand on my lower back.

Confused, I turn around, but don't recognize him. "Hi?"

"Can I buy you a drink?" He does that stupid little brow thing that I'm sure he thinks is sexy, but he looks like a douche.

"They're free dick wad. Keep moving. She's not interested," Lizzy interjects, and the guy scoffs before walking away, mumbling something under his breath.

My head snaps in her direction. "A bit aggressive, don't you think?"

"I don't need some horn dog on my hoe."

"I'm your hoe now?" A smile curls on my lips.

"It's the drinks, sorry. You know how possessive I become."

"I'd hate to see what you'd do if a girl came up to Tony."

"Oh, they won't," she says matter-of-factly.

"They won't?" A deep furrow forms on my brow as I struggle to understand.

"No. He's in white."

I look around the group and see most are in white, a few in pink, and a few others with red. "What don't I know, Lizzy?"

She smiles a wicked smile.

"Damn it, Lizzy! What did you not tell me?"

"You remember back in college when we used to go to those stoplight parties?"

My mind drifts back to memories, and everything clicks into place. "Let me guess. White off limits, pink maybe, and red is ready to bone?" Derek's face twists with shock, so I pull my lips in apology for the assumption.

"Pretty much."

"Damn it, Lizzy."

"You didn't tell her?" Tony asks, grabbing her arm, entering the conversation.

"You didn't tell Derek!" she snaps back.

Derek's lips pinch into a flat line, and he shakes his head.

A woman in black walks by carrying another tray of drinks, so I grab two off and knock one back, and offer the second to Derek.

"No thanks. I don't drink." The surprise is obvious on my face, so he quickly adds. "I drink. Just not shots... or liqueur... anymore."

"One time in Cabo, he had a few too many tequila shots," Tony adds, patting his chest and providing context.

Not wanting it to go to waste, and needing to take the edge off, I knock the other shot back before the conversation falls awkwardly quiet. I get the impression Derek is not super comfortable here and was probably lured out by Tony and Lizzy. Poor guy. I feel bad for him, but I need to get my feathers flicked and my candy licked, and I'm thinking he won't be the one to do it. I know it makes me sound needy, but damn it, it's been six months.

"Those shots are fantastic. They taste like those little sugary candy hearts." I lick the remnants off my top lip, trying to find another girl in black with a tray.

The room is bursting with energy as people dance to the beat, their movements illuminated by the flickering lights that fill the air. It's almost mesmerizing to watch.

A tingle prickles on the back of my neck and when I look up to the balcony above, I find a pair of electric blue eyes watching me. The man has feathery dark hair, strong jawline with a sexy five o'clock shadow, and is wearing all black. He has those smoldering fuck me eyes I hoped Derek was going to have, but Derek seems like a good guy. The guy you'd want to meet your parents, but not the kind who could rock your world in bed. A soft fuck kind of guy. Not saying he'd be bad, but there would be that thing missing.

CALLUM - SEEING RED

THE SCREENS IN MY office rotate through all the cameras we have up. It's our first big night and I want to make sure everything goes off without a hitch. Knox insisted we do a themed party for our big kick-off and initially, I thought it was just to fuck with Jax, because everything feathers, hearts, and wings would be things that would excite Knox and piss off Jax. But it actually seems to be working. There is a long line of people stretching almost to the corner of the building.

A woman jumping up and down near our bouncer grabs my attention. When I lean in closer, I recognize Tony's girlfriend. She seems to have a big personality, which is the opposite of what little I know about Tony. He and his firm helped with the design of Vixen, so he was on the friends and family list for opening. He decided to rent out a few tables in our VIP section upstairs, but it wasn't ready yet, so we sectioned off a place downstairs.

What is she doing? It looks like she's yelling at someone.

Switching the camera, I find a woman standing on the curb wearing a beige trench coat and holding a pair of red wings.

Red. She's single.

My chest tightens for a second, but I ignore it. She's pretty, but the guys and I agreed we were going to take a break from bringing anyone home right now. The last girl we fucked wanted more than we could or would give.

No. Right now, we just need to focus on Vixen. We have this and Emmett's restaurant, Bo La Vie, to keep us busy.

Work. Work is good for us.

Tony's girlfriend yells something else and is waving her hand over and stomping her foot. The other girl seems confused, looking at the line, then back to her friend. Interesting. Most girls would have been fine jumping the line without a thought for anyone else, but she seems to feel... guilty?

Cut it off, Callum. Get back to work.

When the girl walks towards the door, I flick the cameras back to rotating and lean back in my chair and stare at the office wall.

We did it. We opened our nightclub.

My eyes glance back down at the screen and I see red wing girl walking inside with her friend nearly pulling her jacket off her and handing it to the coat check. She slips her wings on and I can't help but notice even though she's smiling, it's not reaching her eyes. Why did she come to a club if she didn't want to be here? Why isn't she happy? More importantly, why in the fuck do I care?

Her friend pats the top of her breasts then grabs her hand. They're walking towards the main dance floor and I have to fight the urge to pull up the next camera to watch her. This is not me.

The buzzer on the office door beeps, pulling my attention, so I quickly flick off the camera and push to standing.

"Whatcha doin'? Watching something you shouldn't be?" Knox asks, nearly bouncing into the room with a smile spread across his face. If he were an animal, he'd be a kangaroo or maybe a golden retriever, not only because of his golden blonde hair, but his personality. He's always so happy, which I wouldn't expect knowing the shit he's gone through in his life.

"Nothing." As soon as the words are out of my mouth, I cringe because I spat the word out too fast, calling attention to it and Knox is a dog with a bone.

He claps his hands. "Something." He skips across the room and twists the screen around to look at the cameras. "Was it people having sex in the hall? On the dance floor?" He gasps, "In a corner? I hope not. I don't feel like cleaning up that shit."

"Nothing." This time I say the word slower and with more confidence. "How's it going out there?"

"Great, but I think we're out of Clasa Azul."

"What? How can we be out? We haven't been open for that long?"

"Some guy just bought a lot of shots... a lot of times."

"Why? We have free drinks floating around the floor?" I should be happy that he decided to spend God knows how much money on alcohol when he didn't have to, but seriously, we had three bottles. "Ok, let's look in the back and make sure. Maybe we can talk to Emmett and see if he can sell us one from Bo La Vie."

Knox and I walk out of the office and across the empty second floor. This was supposed to be open for our VIP, but the bar wasn't ready and we didn't want to manage running drinks up and down the stairs. I walk over to the railing and look down at the dance floor. So many people, but not the one I want to see. She should have made it to the floor by now. It's not a long hall.

"I'll be back. Check on the tequila and let me know."

"How brave of you... venturing down below." He throws his head back and laughs, before making an inappropriate gesture with his fingers and tongue.

"Really fucking mature," Jax snaps, walking over to stand with Knox.

Knox rolls his eyes and pats Jax on the back. "You're just mad that I was right, and this is a phenomenal success."

Knox turns in a circle with his arms spread wide like a boxer does in the ring just after they've won a fight.

"Fuck off," Jax shoves Knox, who laughs and bounces away.

The stairway to the main floor is narrow and the bass of the music sounds muffled as I make the transition.

When I get to the main floor, I do a quick sweep and find her knocking back one of Emmett's shots. He's been working on it over the last month, trying to perfect the flavor. It meant a lot of late nights on our rooftop bar at home sampling drink after drink to the point that looking at the drinks almost makes my throat close. They're delicious, but after about one hundred samples, I need a break.

Before I can stop myself, I'm walking in her direction. I'm not going to talk to her. I just want to see her. Hear her. Fuck, I sound like a stalker.

"Will he make me come in the bathroom?" She laughs, and not paying attention, bumps into me. "Sorry," she calls over her shoulder, but I keep walking, clenching and un-clenching my fist.

She's talking about having some guy make her come in the bathroom. Our bathroom? She came here to have sex with a man in our bathroom? Why is this bothering me so much? I don't even know her, so I have no right to be mad or jealous that she's here to hook up with some guy. I mean, it's a nightclub, so...

Is she really going to fuck him in the bathroom? I didn't think Red would do that.

Red?

Damn it! I huff out in frustration as I walk outside to say something to the bouncer. Anything, so I can pretend that my reason for walking downstairs was to see him and not get closer to some woman I don't even know.

A few minutes later, I'm back upstairs trying to keep myself busy. Anything, so I'm not standing at the railing wanting to find her again. Get it together, Callum, this is not who you are. You don't search out women; they come to you. Preferably on their knees, wearing nothing but a pair of high heels.

"Looks like we're going to run out of vodka tonight, the way people are knocking back E's drink," Jax says from the railing.

"Should have put a limit on it or something," I snap back, letting my frustrations get the better of me. Add vodka to the list of things that aren't perfect tonight.

"Yea, Tony's party seems to enjoy them," he says, pointing and before I can even think about what I'm doing, I'm looking over the railing and I see Red drinking another shot. She needs to slow down before she gets sick. I don't need her puking all over our floor. It's not the image I want Vixen to be known for.

Shit! As if sensing me, she turns around and looks right at me. Her eyes dance over my face and body, then narrow like she's trying to solve a puzzle. She doesn't look away like she expects me to, but I'm not. I don't look away or back down.

When I see her jaw twitch slightly, I suppress a smile, finding it amusing. She seems to have a fire in her eyes, causing my cock to twitch. I love the ones with the fiery spirit. They're a lot more fun to break when they're riding my cock and crying out my name.

A hand grips on my shoulder. "No go on the tequila. Emmett said Bo's should have one bottle we can grab."

My lips harden into a flat line and I unwillingly have to break my gaze from her. Gripping my hands on the rail, I blow out a slow breath before I look at Knox. "Let's see if we can grab another bottle or two of vodka, and call our distributor to see if they can increase our order for tomorrow's delivery."

EVERLEE - PINK DRINKS ARE DANGEROUS

MY HEART FEELS LIKE it is about to pound a hole through my chest. Those last few seconds with that man on the balcony were... my stomach clenches at the thought of what his hands could do to me.

Damn it, I'm horny.

"What are you looking at?" Lizzy asks, putting her cheek beside mine. "Oh, that's the owner's suite, and future VIP suite, up there."

"Owner's suite?" Makes sense that the guy in the suit would be an owner. His aura screamed power and the way he expected me to look away.

"Yea. Do you want to meet them?"

Shocked, I nearly stumble on my words. "No. Why? Do you know them?"

She laughs. "No. But Tony and Derek do. They helped design this place. I could talk to Tony."

"No. That's ok."

"Good. Tony said they're kind of weird."

"Weird?" Is it bad I'm intrigued? I glance back up at the balcony, but he's gone.

"Yea. He said there are four of them, but only one really talked to him. The others were... not standoffish... but I don't know."

"Maybe they were under a tight deadline to get the club open and they each had their own roles," I defend, garnering an odd look from her.

"Anyway..." she chuckles, turning us back around to the group. "We have this entire area." She waves her arm around to several seats and tables. "We are VIPs tonight, baby."

"Wooo!" I yell, feeling the spirits of St. Valentine- rather St. Rum and St. Vodka- flowing through me.

"Want to go dance?" Lizzy asks our little group of four.

Both of the boys politely decline with the look of panic on their faces. "Let's go." I grab Lizzy's hand and drag her to the packed dance floor. It's been a while since she and I went to a club and danced the night away.

On the way to the dance floor, I snatch us another shot off the passing tray and knock it back.

"You should probably slow down," Lizzy warns softly.

"You've had at least as many as I have." With my eyes closed, I surrender to the music, allowing my body to sway and the deep bass to reverberate within me.

"Yes, but we all know I handle my liquor way better than you. I don't need you ending up in one of those swings tonight."

My eyes pop open, and I stop dancing. "Do you think they'd let me?" I ask, way more excited than I should be.

"No, and don't even think about it." Her words carry the weight of parental disapproval, the scolding tone leaving no room for argument.

"Well, you're no fun." I frown.

"You're serious?" She stops dancing for a second, then laughs. "You're one wild bitch and I love it."

"Thanks."

"Anytime hooker."

Betty. "I won't snort coke off anyone's penis. I draw the line there." The music continues to flow through me as I shimmy my hips down and pop back up. "I guess technically that would be passed the line, so the line would be somewhere behind that. Or before that? And not the line of coke, obviously, because I'm not doing that."

"What in the actual fuck are you talking about?" She grabs my arm so I stop moving, with her brows pinched into a v on her forehead.

"Betty." My eyes blink slowly, like they weren't really open, while I try to focus on Lizzy's face. Shouldn't have had that last shot because it still feels like I'm moving.

"Who's Betty?"

I grab onto Lizzy's arms for both balance and ... well, balance. That's it, because I'm trying not to sway too much. "She was my driver here. She's found Jesus now, but apparently, she was not hookering for a friend and ended up doing blow off her BFF's boyfriend's dick." I laugh out loud as a thought hits me. "Do you think if she gave him head while there was coke on it, she could say she was blowing blow?"

Lizzy looks at me with a concerned smile on her face. "Let's go to the bar and get you some water."

"I'm fine." I'm not fine. The room is spinning, but I don't need her babying me. I'll admit I probably had too many shots too quick together, but I want to have fun tonight. I may not have wanted to be here at first, but once I commit, I'm all the way in. Which is why Rich hurt me so much. I was fucking committed. Planning out our future and babies and everything else. "Asshole."

"What?" Lizzy asks, pulling me across the club.

"Sorry. Inside thought slipped out." I lean in and whisper, "Hey if my boob slipped out, would you tell me?"

"Where did that-" She shakes her head, "Nevermind. Yes. Yes, I would tell you." Lizzy pushes her way through the crowd to an open spot at the bar and flags down a bartender. He's attractive with dark hair, dark eyes and a short-trimmed beard that's perfectly etched along his jawbone, wearing black pants and a nipple piercing. That's it.

"Can I get a glass of water and a menu?"

"We don't have food here."

"Nothing?"

The man's lips flatten as his gaze falls on me. I toss a flirtatious wave, wiggling my fingers in his direction.

"She going to be ok?" He nods in my direction.

"Yes. She-" I shake my head. "I'm going to be fine. Just keep those vixens-" I laugh out loud, realizing I didn't even mean to say that. "Sorry. I didn't mean... Nevermind. Just keep those delicious pink drinks away from me."

"That's my creation." He smiles pridefully.

"Well, you're going to hell sir, because those are delightful." I point my finger in the air.

He chuckles. "You're probably right, but not for that."

He pumps his eyebrows and a heat races through my body and I can feel my nipples harden under my bra.

He continues, "They also pack a punch. How many?"

"Three."

"Four," Lizzy corrects.

"No." I count back on my fingers. "Fuck. Yea. Four."

"I'll send someone out to get you some food."

"No, you don't have to." I bat my hand in the air and try to hide the astonishment on my face when the colors from the laser lights above causes ripples behind my hands. The rational part of my brain knows I hit the sauce a bit too heavy, too fast, is yelling at me to buckle up buttercup and sober up. I can't puke here tonight. I promised myself after the last time I threw up in a bar that I would never do it again. It was disgusting and yet I find myself back in this situation again because of my ex. I should take responsibility for my actions and again, the rational side of me knows that it's my fault I'm here, but the other side, the irrational, hurt, and angry side, would rather blame him because it's easier to feel anger than the other feelings.

"I think I do. If Callum found out my drink fucked up a lot of people, he'd kill me. So really, I'm doing it for myself, not you."

"Well, as long as you're being selfish." I wink.

He waves someone over and whispers something in their ear before pulling his card out of his pocket.

"You're over there?" He points across the club to where Tony and Derek are standing.

"Yea. How did you know?"

"I make it a point to keep an eye out on all the pretty ladies that could cause me trouble." He winks, grabbing a bottle of liquor for someone else's drink.

A smile curls on my lips. I was hesitant to come out tonight, but suddenly, I'm feeling a lot better about this decision. A fine ass guy is flirting with me. Me!

Emmett's eyes travel from me to something above me, and the smile drops from his face. Following his gaze, I see the man from earlier with the blue eyes, standing there looking down at us... me, again. In all my alcohol induced stupidity, I wink at him. His head tilts to the side like I've broken him. Is he a robot? He huffs before he walks off. Not a robot.

My pulse is beating fast in my chest. That man. I'm dying to know more about him. Who is he? Why he's staring at me? What his voice sounds like. Knowing the bartender would know, I turn, setting my sights on him. "Who was that?"

"Who?"

"That man up there looking at us."

His face falls. "That was Callum."

"Callum didn't look too happy." My stomach clenches when I say his name. Callum, I repeat. Unique name. Not one I've heard before, but it seems like it fits him. He's definitely not a Bill, or John, or even some weird name like Thaddeus.

The bartender looks down at the bar. "He's... an acquired taste. I have to go help some other patrons," he says before darting off, but then calls back, "I'll bring that food over though, Trouble." He tosses a quick wink at me, causing the butterflies in my stomach to dance.

EVERLEE - FUCKING ROMCOMS

LIZZY AND I ARE in a deep conversation about nipple piercings when I feel a cold tap on my shoulder. I turn around to find Callum, the mystery man from the second-floor balcony, standing behind the table with a bag of food in his hand. His intense stare is focused on me, with a hint of something else. Annoyance? Curiosity?

"Thank you." I stand up to reach for the bag, but trip over the shoes Lizzy left on the ground. In my tipsy... yes, tipsy, not drunk state, I fall towards Callum. It's like I'm in one of those fucking romcoms. Look at me clumsy bumsy, catch me if you can.

And he does. He not only catches me with one arm, but leans me back like we've choreographed a sexy dance routine, eyes locked, staring at one another. My skin is on fire under his touch and penetrating gaze. He definitely has that big dick energy with delicious fuck me eyes and I'm pretty sure my whole body is yelling pick me! Pick me!

"Everlee!" Lizzy shouts in shock. "Here." Lizzy steps forward to grab the bag out of his hand, breaking our trance. With his other hand free, he helps me stand upright. I wobble in place, staring at him, not because of the alcohol, but because he makes my head spin. Holy shit! He's tall and when I thought I was falling, my hands wrapped around his arms, his very muscular arms that he's hiding under that perfectly tailored suit.

His eyes narrow on mine. "You shouldn't drink so much, Everlee," he commands before turning around.

Before thinking, I sarcastically reply. "Yes, sir."

His head snaps around and there's a fire ignited in his eyes. My breasts swell and my stomach tightens as my breath hitches in my throat. Can I orgasm off a single look? Because fuck, I'm close.

When I look back up, he's gone. Vanished, like a ghost.

"Wow," Lizzy breathes.

"What?" I ask, hoping she hadn't seen me nearly melt into the floor.

"Nip nip did you good."

"What? Who?"

"I don't know his name, but the bartender bought you several gourmet sandwiches from Bo La Vie."

"Really?" I snatch the bag away from her and peek inside. Treating the sandwiches like golden bars, I carefully pull them out of the bag and lay them on the table, looking at my options.

I've been dying to try the new restaurant, but can never get a reservation. The fact I even have to make a reservation to get into a gourmet sandwich shop irritates me, but now I'm all too eager to try everything I can.

"Do you think nip nip would let me have a knife? I can cut these up and share."

"No. You don't need to share," Tony says.

Lizzy's eyebrows shoot sky high. "Don't listen to him. That's a great idea."

I know she wants to go there as badly as I do and won't let Tony stop her from trying the goods. As I make my way through the bustling dance floor, the vibrations of the music pulsate through my body. Finally, I reach the bar and eagerly wave my hand to get nip nip's attention. I really need to learn his name. He walks over, smiling. "I'm not serving you. You're cut off."

I pout. "I wasn't coming over for a drink, but now I want one."

He looks over my head again and I turn to find Callum in his usual spot, watching me. "What's with him?"

"Who?"

"Callum," I say in a deep and spooky voice.

He laughs, then stops. "What do you mean?"

"He's been standing up there most of the night watching... people." I don't want to presume and say me, but I definitely feel his eyes on me.

"Oh. He's just... watching everyone. Big night."

"Yea?"

"This is our first big opening. We had a soft opening before, but tonight's the big night."

"So, he's not always that uptight?"

He chuckles. "No, he is." He looks up at him again, then says nervously, "Well, I better get back to it."

"So, you really wouldn't serve me if I wanted a drink?"

He pulls his lips. "Callum's orders."

"Does he always get his way?" I mumble under my breath before I turn my gaze up to cast daggers at Callum. But he's gone. Refocusing on Nip nip, I say, "Well, I didn't want one. Just a knife."

His neck snaps back in surprise.

I laugh. "For the sandwiches. Speaking of which, you really didn't have to get me food and from Bo La Vie, of all places. Although, I'm not complaining. I've been wanting to try that place out for a while and haven't been able to get in."

"Really?" He seems shocked.

"Yea. Reservations are like a month out. How were you able to get food from there? Oh my gosh, do you want one? I can bring it over to you."

He chuckles. "I know the owner and no, you and your friends enjoy."

"How much do I owe you?"

"Nothing, but you also aren't getting a knife." He winks. "Now I really have to go."

"What's your name?" I call after him, but he only smiles. Dejected, I walk back to the group. "No knife."

"I love you thought he would just give you a knife to walk across a crowded club with."

"Yea, I didn't really think that through."

I pick up a Wagyu sandwich with truffle and Gruyère and take a bite. I'm pretty sure if it weren't for the thumping music, I would have thought I'd died. It's the best thing I've ever put in my mouth and that includes cock. And I love cock. Unfortunately, chances aren't looking great I'll be getting any of that tonight since Derek left. I can't blame him. We didn't really click, and he was getting hit on every two seconds. Aside from the first guy, no one else has tried to dance with me, which is a bit of a bummer. Almost like someone has warned them away from me, but who would do that? No one. Well, maybe Lizzy, but she wouldn't twat block me.

"Lizzy. Try this." I wave my sandwich in front of her face.

"No. You have to try this! It's a grilled cheese, but..." her eyes roll into the back of her head.

We trade sandwiches and both moan at the same time.

"Can I get some of that?" Tony asks, peeking over Lizzy's shoulder.

"No!" Lizzy and I both say at the same time.

We finish the sandwiches and decide to dance again. I'm feeling a lot more stable and less drunk, but I have a good buzz going. Part of me wants to test a theory to see if Callum has really cut me off. There's something about him that makes me want to push him. Is it because he seems so stiff? Do I want to see him break?

A prickly feeling tingles on the back of my neck, so I turn and find Callum's eyes on me again. If he's going to keep watching me, then I'll give him something to watch. With my back to Lizzy's chest, I sway my hips from side to side as our eyes lock again. I run my hands over my body, over my chest, through my hair, and then down between my legs. There is a fire in his eyes and I feel alive. Electrified.

"You're doing your fuck me dance," Lizzy says in my ear. "Whose attention are you trying to get?"

"No one." I let my hands drag over my breast.

"Liar, liar, panties on fire."

Turning around, I put both of my arms around Lizzy's neck and snake down her body and back up again.

"Well, whoever the poor bastard is, good luck to him. When's the last time you had a dick in you?"

"Lizzy!"

"It's an honest question. Vibrators and dildos are great, but they got nothing on a good dick."

"Hey, ladies. I saw you two over here dancing and thought you needed some company."

My gaze moves up and down the man who just walked over, then up to see Callum leaning forward on the railing watching us. Being the mature person I am, I wink at Callum, then put my arms around the man.

Break like a twig.

CALLUM - GET CONTROL

HER EYES DANCE LIKE fire when she catches me watching her again, and now I know she's playing with me. The little smirk she tossed my way before she slung her arms around the douchebag's neck. I've been watching him all night, moving from woman to woman, getting a little too handsy too quickly, and that was before he had another drink. One woman already smacked him and another male pinned his arm behind his back. He's the type of man that gives other men in clubs a bad rep and it makes my blood boil.

My hands grip the handrail even tighter, wishing it was that man's throat.

Jax.

I need to find Jax and have him throw that asshole out, because if I go down there, I'll rip his fucking cock off with my bare hands and shove it down his pathetic throat.

Jax is sitting in an empty booth typing away on his phone when I walk up to him. He glances up at me, then looks back at his phone, before his head slowly swivels back up to stare at me. His eyes widened in alarm and he stands, jaw set. "What's wrong?"

My fists clench and unclench. I need to get control of myself before I speak.

"Cal?"

"Dickbag McGhee is dancing with Red," Knox walks up, rolling up the cuff of his shirt.

"You named her Red?" Jax asks, puffing out a breath.

"You told him about Red?" Knox whines. "I thought it was just a me and you thing."

"He's serious? This is about Red?"

"Her name is Everlee."

"I don't give a fuck what her name is. We said no women right now. We're taking a break."

"I don't want to fuck her," I defend.

"No? Does your cock know that?" Jax nods his head at me, making me look down.

"I don't!"

Knox butts in, not helping. "I do. Fuck, she's hot. Like the kind of hot that doesn't know she's hot. She has a bit of fire, but also seems vulnerable."

"What the fuck?" Jax runs his fingers through his hair and turns in a circle. "Where's Emmett when I need him?"

"He's been downstairs... flirting with her."

Jax's eyes flash before he regains control. "He's a bartender. He flirts with everyone."

Knox laughs. "She told him he was going to hell. Love her already."

"You don't even know her. None of you do. Why are we even talking about her? Is this how this is going to be? Every time a hot chick comes into the club, we're going to swoon around her and want to fuck her?" Jax blows out an exasperated breath.

"You just admitted she's hot." Knox points his finger at Jax, who bats it away.

I try to bring the conversation back to my original point. "No. I don't want to fuck her. I'm just concerned the guy she's dancing with is going to hurt her or other women in this club. We need to get him out."

"He bought a membership tonight. You're going to revoke it?"

"Yes. Give back his money and send him on his way. If women don't feel safe here because of assholes like him, then word will spread. It's bad for business."

Jax's eyes, still hard, shift when he realizes it's less about Red and more about the asshat downstairs. "Fine. I'll get his paperwork printed off." He stomps towards the office and I walk back over to the handrail, but stand in the corner. I don't need her seeing me and trying to put on a show, only pressing dickbag further.

Lizzy is walking away from her when I get to my spot. Some friend she is. She has to see that the guy is up to no good and here she is, leaving her friend alone on the dance floor.

Irritation prickles under my skin like boiling water.

Dickface runs his grimy hands up her arms, over her shoulders, then down her back, where he plants them near her ass and pulls her to him with a dopey ass grin on his face. Her hands fly up to his chest to prevent her from colliding with him, and her face contorts. No doubt smelling all the alcohol that has to be pouring out of his body. She seems a lot more coherent since she's gotten food in her stomach and drank several glasses of water over the last hour.

He asks her a question, and she responds with Felicia. Over the years, I became adept at reading lips. She may not have said Felicia, but she sure as shit didn't say Everlee.

Did she give him a fake name because he's making her feel uncomfortable?

She looks up to where I was standing earlier. Is she looking for me?

His hands slide down to her ass and he asks, "Want to get out of here?"

She puts her hands on his chest, trying to create distance between them and subtly shakes her head no.

Good. Don't go anywhere with him.

The more I've seen of her tonight, the more I realized her comment about fucking a guy in the bathroom was a joke. She hasn't put herself out there like one would expect someone looking for a quick fuck would.

Dickface must have not liked that answer because his hands are now gripped on her upper arms and he presses his leg between hers.

She pushes away from him, stumbling a little and bumping into the couple behind her.

She levels her gaze at him, eyes set in anger, not fear. She's a fighter.

"Don't be a bitch," he spits. Even if I couldn't read lips, I would have been able to hear the faint echoes of the words above the noise.

My head snaps back to her and a modicum of relief pours in. She doesn't fly off at the handle, she's calculated. She's sizing him up with a level of confidence that brings some ease to me. When she says something back to him, she's quiet, eyes hard. I can't make it out because she's turned far enough away that I can only see the side of her face now.

Everlee's eyes lift, and I follow her gaze to Lizzy, whose gaze is locked onto her with unwavering intensity. Maybe she's a better friend than I gave her credit for. Lizzy struck me as the airhead type, but perhaps she was giving her friend some space.

Everlee throws her fingers in the air and signs for the bathroom. She knows ASL? Why? Is she deaf, or is Lizzy? Probably Lizzy. It would make sense why she's so loud.

It's been a long time since I've used ASL, but I still remember quite a bit. I learned it when I was younger because little Luca was mostly deaf. He got picked on a lot by kids at school because he could never hear the teachers, and it wasn't until he was in middle school, they learned he only had thirty percent of hearing in one ear and completely deaf in the other. I learned ASL with him, so he had someone to talk to.

My heart skips a beat when I see dickface following Everlee off the dance floor. I toss a glance at Lizzy and she's unaware because Tony is talking to her.

Damn it!

Pushing off the railing, I head for the stairs.

EVERLEE - WHEN THEY CAN'T HEAR THE WORD NO, PUT HIM IN HIS PLACE

WHEN I STEP INTO the bathroom, I press my back against the door and take a deep breath. I needed to put space between that stage five creeper outside, and me. He's getting a little too handsy and aggressive for my tastes.

When my pulse slows, I open my eyes and look around the bathroom. They're nice. Nicer than any other club I've been in. It's a lot of black, but more sophisticated, less goth. Along the walls are white pedestal sinks in front of oval mirrors with gold frames. It's like walking into a five-star hotel. Granted, this is their first night, so I'll have to check back in six months, or hell, even a month. But something tells me it will probably be the same. They seem to have a fine attention to detail.

A few minutes later, I'm walking out of the bathroom and my good friend Jordan is waiting in the dimly lit hall.

"Jordan," I huff, fists balling at my side.

"I'm sorry. I shouldn't have said those things."

"Can you be more specific? There were several things."

He rolls his eyes. "The bitch part."

"And..." I prompt. He looks at me, dumbfounded, so I help him out. "And for assuming I'm an easy piece of ass because I was having fun and dancing with my friend?"

"Yes, that too."

"Thank you." Just as I start to walk past him, he forcefully grabs onto my arm, causing me to halt in my tracks.

"Let go!" I try to jerk my arm away.

"I thought we made up. Aren't we supposed to kiss?" He pulls me closer to him.

"No." I push him away.

"Why are you playing hard to get?"

"I'm not." I try to pull my arm out of his grasp again, but his fingers only tighten.

"Come on, then." He swings me to the wall and presses his body against mine, pinning me in place. He leans in, putting his mouth on my neck with his forearm across my chest.

"Get. Off. Me." I jerk my knee between his legs and I'm fairly certain he's tasting his balls right now.

His forearm drops as he slumps over, sucking wind.

Stepping around him, I start walking down the hall when he grabs my wrist and jerks me backwards. "Wrong fucking move." He lashes out, voice hard as steel. "I tire of you women out here dancing like you do. Looking for attention. Then when you get it, you try to push it away. You asked for it, you're going to get it." He drags me down the hall and forces me into the ladies' room.

Fuck.

I tried to play nice with Jordan, but he seems to need something more direct. Unfortunately for him, when I was in college, there were a lot of girls getting attacked, so I took a self-defense class. I liked it so much I took karate and got my black belt.

When he stops moving, I raise my arm and crash it down on his, breaking his grip on my wrist. I run towards the door, but he slams it shut and pins me against it.

This motherfucker just doesn't give up. I bring my hands down on his arms, causing his elbows to bend and quickly use one hand to grab the back of his head, while my elbow crashes into the side of his cheek, swiping across his face. He grabs his nose as blood trickles down onto his chest, yelling a string of expletives at me. I push him off and walk into the hall only to find Callum standing there, frozen, like I'd surprised him.

His intense gaze travels from me to the door, which bursts open with a bloody Jordan climbing out of it, still pushing forward. Asshole doesn't know when to take a hint.

A smile tugs on Callum's lips before he calmly walks towards me, his hand outstretched. I slip mine into his and feel a heat radiate up my arm as he glides me behind him. He moves forward and grabs Jordan by the throat, jacking him up on the wall so his feet dangle. He leans in and whispers something, so quiet I don't even hear it, but the color drains from Jordan's face and his body goes limp.

A moment later, Jordan falls to the ground just as someone else walks up behind me. Another man dressed in black. I recognize him as the one from the balcony earlier that delivered some information to Callum. He's even more beautiful close up, with sandy blonde locks and hints of tattoos protruding from under his black button-down shirt.

"Shit, Callum. What did you do? It's our opening night."

"I did nothing, Knox. It was all her." He nods in my direction, and I feel a hint of pride in Callum's tone.

Knox turns to look at me, and his eyes nearly pop out of his head. "I stand corrected, my lady." He gives a slight bow, and I smile at him.

"Get him out of here and revoke his membership."

"What? Because of her? She better be glad I'm not pressing charges."

Rage boils uncontrollably within, and I march over to him and grab him by the collar, pressing him against the wall. "Press charges, you asshole. I dare you. You're a fucking pussy. It's assholes like you that make it so fucking difficult for women to go out and enjoy themselves. Even more astounding is that all the other people in this club were able to demonstrate some civility and resist the urge to assault a woman. You say it was my fault for dancing the way I was, but I say it's your fault. You were raised with a sense of entitlement and believe you can take whatever you want. News flash, you fucking can't!" I raise my fist, and he flinches before I push off him.

"Take him," Callum demands through set teeth, causing a tingle to raise up my spine.

Jordan bats his hand in the air before Knox leads him away.

"Come with me," Callum commands, his tone a hair softer than before.

I follow him down the hall to a hidden door just past the restroom. He pulls out a keycard on a retractable string and swipes it against the pad. When the panel turns green and buzzes, he pushes the door open, inviting me in with a gesture. I get the impression he's a man of few words.

The lights flicker on in the room and I notice we're in another bathroom. Perhaps the employees' restrooms, but they're not finished.

"The door is going to lock behind us for privacy, but I won't touch you without your consent. You are safe." His words sound rehearsed, like he's used them before.

I nod.

"I need to hear the words." His tone is soft, but final.

"Ok," I whisper.

He shrugs out of his jacket and pinches it on the upper corners, folding it in half and laying it on the couch. "Are you ok?" he asks, walking over to the sink. He rolls up his sleeves until the shirt stretches around his forearm, exposing several tattoos which stop just above his wrist.

He flips the water on and lets it run for a second before taking a rolled-up towel from a basket to the right of the sink and wetting it. I'm entranced. The way he moves, the way his muscles flex in his arms. The way his fingers expertly wring out the cloth.

My breathing slows and I have to take deeper breaths the longer I watch him. My head is dizzy as a tingle moves through my body, causing my stomach to clench.

"Do I have your permission to wipe the few scrapes on your face?"

I nod because his simple presence steals my breath.

"Everlee. I need your words." His words are just above a whisper.

Raising my chin to look up at him, my chest tightens at the sight. Damn, he is beautiful. "Yes, sir," I mumble, curious to see if it will get the same result as before.

His eyes ignite again, but he maintains his calm. He tilts his head to the side as if he's testing something and responds quietly. "Good girl."

There it is. I forget how to breathe for a second. That's the second time I've said that to him.

To anyone.

I had never... before... but. His hand gently grabs under my chin and holds it as he closes the distance between us. He's so close I can feel the heat radiating off him and smell his intoxicating scent. Fresh, citrus with a hint of musk. Our eyes, once more, lock in an intense gaze. They're mesmerizing in person, electric blue... and fuck. Sexy as hell. There are no other words to describe them. His other hand gently pats a scrape on my forehead, the sting lasting for only a second. My heart is pounding a hole out of my chest, the same time butterflies are erupting in my stomach. What is happening to me? I feel... lightheaded and woozy.

"My Cupid... in... armor."

Darkness swoops in like a raptor for its meal.

EVERLEE - DON'T PUSH THE INTERCOM BUTTON, WHEN YOU'RE GETTING YOURSELF OFF IN HIS SHOWER

THE SUN IS SHINING down on my face as my cheek brushes against the soft silk sheets.

Wait.

Where am I?

As I slowly open my eyes, an unfamiliar room comes into focus as the hazy blur from sleep fades away.

Where the hell am I?

Pinching my eyes closed, I try to remember the events from last night. Slowly, it starts coming back, piece by piece. The party, the dancing, the creep, the bathroom with Callum, then nothing.

My eyes shoot open. I'm in a large open room with a contemporary industrial feel. There is a brick accent wall, hardwood floors, exposed wooden beams, and floor to ceiling windows trimmed in black. There's a chair in the room's corner and a dresser along the opposite wall.

To my left is an open shower that's as large as my entire apartment with glass walls and a square shaped showerhead hanging on the end of a down rod. Just to the right of the shower is another chair with a man sitting in it.

A mangled sound erupts from me as I pull the sheets up to my chin and roll into a ball.

"Hey there. Sorry. I didn't mean to startle you. It's me, Emmett, from the club."

I shake my head in confusion, unable to recognize him. How much did I have to drink last night?

"Bartender." He lifts his shirt, showing his nipple ring.

My body relaxes a little, even though I'm still confused as fuck.

He holds his hands up. "You're ok. You're safe. This is Callum's room. He slept on the couch. Your phone is beside you on the nightstand charging. Lizzy was worried about you, but Callum texted her and said you were fine and would call her this morning."

Glancing over my shoulder, I see my phone just as he said, with a missed call and several unread text messages.

"I didn't mean to startle you. I was just worried about you, and Callum thought you'd freak out less if you saw a somewhat friendly face." He plasters on a big smile.

"Callum? What happened?"

"I don't know all the details, but while Callum was cleaning you up last night, you passed out."

"I passed out?"

"Sometimes adrenaline spikes can do that."

"How did I end up here?"

His lips pull. "Like I said, I don't know all the details. Callum's waiting for you downstairs. Breakfast is also cooked. I made pancakes, waffles, bacon, sausage, and Eggs Benedict. Along with a tray of fresh fruit. I didn't know what you'd want." He chuckles softly.

"Thank... you?"

He smiles. "I'm glad you're ok. When I saw Knox walking by with that guy, I was worried about you. Then I found out you'd done that. Remind me never to cross you." He chuckles, standing up. "Feel free to use the shower to clean up. Also, Callum bought some clothes he thought would fit you. They're over there." He points to another chair to my left.

How many chairs does one room need?

"We'll be downstairs."

I nod, still too stunned to speak. It's like my ears can hear the words coming out of his mouth, but I can't process them.

He pauses with his hand on the knob. "Would you like coffee or tea?"

"Coffee, please."

"You got it." He tosses me a wink, then closes the door.

Staring at the ceiling, I rub my face and listen for any identifiable sounds, but there's just silence. I roll over and grab my phone to look at the messages.

1:06AM

> **Lizzy:** *Girl, where are you?*

> **Lizzy:** *You better pick up.*

> **Lizzy:** *I just saw douche McDouche being escorted out.*

Lizzy: *I went to the bathroom, but you weren't there.*

Lizzy: *I'm about to use the find a bitch app.*

Everlee: *This is Callum. Everlee is safe. There was an incident, and she's passed out. I'm taking her to my place to monitor her.*

Lizzy: *Callum?*

Everlee: *Tony knows me.*

Lizzy: *SHIT.*

Lizzy: *The owner.*

Lizzy: Sorry for the shit.

Lizzy: *Shit.*

Lizzy: *I'm drunk.*

Lizzy: *What's your address?*

Everlee: *It's late. You should get some rest. But you're welcome to come over tomorrow.*

Everlee: *15087 N Pulgam Rd*

Everlee: *(555) 637-0928*

Everlee: *That's my direct line if you need to contact me.*

Lizzy: *She's ok?*

Lizzy: *Like for real?*

Everlee: *Yes. He definitely got the worst of it. She's safe and will stay safe.*

Lizzy: *Thank you.*

Lizzy: *Tony also says you're legit.*

Lizzy: *He wants me to tell you legit was my word, not his.*

Lizzy: *Oh, sorry. He didn't really want me to tell you that.*

Lizzy: *Ignore me.*

Lizzy: *But thank you.*

Lizzy: *Love what you've done with the place.*

Lizzy: *Shit.*

Lizzy: *Sorry.*

Lizzy: *Bye.*

Everlee: *If you need a ride home, please call me on my personal cell.*

8:53AM

Lizzy: *Are you still alive, hooker?*

Lizzy: *There was no coke off a dick, but it was close.*

Lizzy: *Shit.*

Lizzy: *I assume you have your phone.*

9:42AM

Everlee: *Hey. I'm alive. I didn't pull a Betty.*

Lizzy: *Everlee! Oh my God!*

Everlee: *Sorry. Just got up. Going to take a shower, then go downstairs and get some answers.*

Lizzy: *Are you there?*

Lizzy: *At his house?*

Lizzy: *You are. Duh.*

Lizzy: *Is it nice?*

Everlee: *I'm only in the bedroom. I don't remember the rest.*

Lizzy: *Girlll. Tea time.*

Everlee: *Nothing happened.*

Worried that I lied, I quickly lift the sheets and find I'm wearing a t-shirt over my outfit from last night.

Everlee: *I'll text you in a little.*

Lizzy: *I'm coming over to pick you up.*

Lizzy: *I need a shower and coffee first.*

Lizzy: *See you soon.*

Everlee: *XXOX*

I'm still smiling as I pad across the floor to the waiting oversized standing man-bath. Slipping out of my clothes, I fold them into a neat pile and lay them on the chair nearest the shower and walk in. The shower is so large that I can comfortably move to the side while waiting for the water to warm up. After a minute, the steam fogs up the glass, so I step into the middle, where the water is pouring out of the rainfall showerhead and let it pour over me, washing away last night.

Around the shower are nine other jets, three on each wall. My fingers trace over several buttons on the panel and stop when I get to the one that looks like jets. I've always seen these showers in movies, but never in real life and, of course, I have to try them out. The first one I press looks like an upside-down funnel and the lights change in a rainbow-colored pattern. I push another and music plays. I push a third, and water shoots at me from all sides, causing me to squeal in surprise.

The water hits all over my body, jets angled in certain positions from mid-back to... oh, hello there.

No! I will not get off in his shower.

That's what my mind is saying, but my body is like a raging hormonal teenager who's been waiting for days now to get off.

Herein lies the problem.

I stand there for a moment, letting the water massage me and... my eyes roll into the back of my head. Oh my God. Why have I never done this before? Without thinking, my body moves closer to my new favorite jet, and a moan escapes my lips. I press my hands against the wall, ignoring the buttons as the pressure builds. Another moan escapes. "Fuck."

My legs grow weak as my body climbs, aches, and needs. I step closer and a sound deep inside of me echoes out. My moans are coming closer and closer, my stomach is tightening and then... ahhhh. The angels are singing. My legs give out, and I fall to the floor, while the same jet that just got me off pelts me in the back of the head. But I don't care.

The door bursts open and Callum is standing there, eyes on fire, looking completely feral. He runs into the room, slamming the door shut and grabs a towel, tossing it at me before racing into the shower fully clothed, pressing a series of buttons on the control panel above my head. In an instant, the water, lights, and sounds shut off.

I stare at him in disbelief. "What are you doing?" I lash out when I regain control of my tongue.

He looks down at me, his white shirt now transparent and clinging to his body like shrink wrap. He has muscles, like a lot of them. Fully defined, touch them, feel them, lick them, muscles that I want to run my hands over. Holy fuck, he is gorgeous and a bit of a badass, it seems. His chest and arms are covered with tattoos, his shirt doing little to hide them.

His eyes lock on mine, but we're interrupted by the bulge that's growing in his pants. My teeth scrape across my bottom lip as I contemplate how it would look if I sucked him off in the shower. I still don't know what happened last night and for all I know we fucked, and I don't remember it. And looking at his body this morning... that would be a goddamn tragedy.

"What are you doing?" he snaps.

His words are like a needle popping my vagina balloon, but it's trying to find anything to cover the hole to stop the air from escaping. *Horn dog.*

"What are you doing?" I retort, mustering as much sass as I can.

He takes his shirt off. Not in the overly sexy way one would hope, but the irritated it's clinging to me and I need to be free of these constraints kind of way.

"You..." he throws his shirt down. "Put a towel on."

"I put a towel on?" I'm completely confused, lost in his body.

"No!" he snaps. "Put the towel on." He points to the one I'm holding in my lap, realizing my breast are on full display.

"Shit!" I pull it up, covering my chest.

"You..." he shakes his head.

"What's so hard?" I add, "to say?" When a 'that's what she said' pops into my head, looking at the seam of his pants. I want to put my hands around that happy stick.

God. Lizzy was right. The real thing is better than all my BOBs and dildos. I'm fucking horny for a meaty man stick, a schlonga dong dong. Fuck, call it a cupid's arrow. I'd let it shoot inside of me.

Fuck!

I need to get control.

"You had your hand on the speaker button."

"The speak... er butt- oh fuck."

Balloon popped.

Total mortification.

I'm drier than the Sahara Desert.

"Did you hear..."

"Yes."

"Which is why you..."

"Yes."

My head falls into my hands.

I look up a minute later, words still stuck in my throat.

He runs his hands through his hair, slicking it back, revealing more tattoos on the underside of his arm.

"Fuck," I slip out. He's a goddamn piece of art. A beautiful, sexy, tattooed piece of art.

He extends his hand, offering to help me up.

Yes, please help me up from my post-orgasm collapsed state on your shower floor.

I adjust the towel, so it wraps all the way around me.

"Do you mind if I change really quick?" he asks.

"No... no. Please."

He steps out of the shower and walks over to his dresser and faces the windows. He slips on a shirt, then pulls off his pants.

Just his pants.

He's going commando.

Fuck. Shitballs. Mother ass.

His ass is perfect. Shit. I can't stop staring. It's so tight, and...

He looks over his shoulder. "You're moaning."

My eyes grow wide, and I turn around. I'd say I'm sorry, but I'd be lying, because I'm not. But I am wondering how many times I can embarrass myself in one morning.

The sounds of his feet padding towards the door cause me to look up, finding him fully dressed.

Regrettably.

"Wait."

He pauses with his hand on the knob.

"Did we? You and I? Last night?"

"What?" His brow furrows and his eyes twinkle with a hint of mischief.

Is he playing with me? "You know?"

"I don't know what you're talking about."

"Did we?" I put my finger through the hole in my other hand. Really fucking mature Everlee.

"What is that?"

"Oh my! Did we have success? Shit. Sex. I don't... remember."

He drops the knob from his hand, and the room falls into a heavy silence as he saunters over to stand in front of me, making my breath hitch in anticipation. Like I literally cannot breathe. He's standing so close, I can feel the heat radiating off his chest. He lifts his hand and gently runs his knuckles down my cheek. "One. You passed out. Two, I would never have sex with someone who can't consent. And three..." He licks his lips, then cups my cheeks while his eyes penetrate the depths of my soul. "If we had sex, there'd be no chance you'd forget it."

My head leans into his hand as a breath puffs out, because I'm speechless.

Call the fire department because there is a fire in my panties right now. Well, there would be, if I was wearing any. Holy fuck!

The pad of his thumb traces along my lower lip, and my clit starts to throb.

But then he pulls away and walks to the door.

"Breakfast is ready downstairs."

The door shuts, and I'm left standing in his room, completely immobilized.

He's trouble.

CALLUM - TROUBLE

. . . .

WHEN I GET IN the hall, I close the door and press my back against the wall. My heart is pounding out of my chest. What the fuck am I doing? Barging into her shower?

My brain flashes through images of her crumpled into a pile on the floor. Wet hair, pink cheeks and her body. Her perfect body- curves in all the right places, and her breasts.

Knox would have lost control if he saw them. Her breasts are the perfect size to cup and then suck into our mouth. Her moans...

Exasperated, I look at the ceiling, running my fingers through my hair. I'd make her moan so much she'd lose her voice.

My cock twitches again at the memory. The way she looked at my cock in the shower. I could have had her if I wanted. The hunger was there in her eyes. Fuck!

Get it together, Callum!

When I get downstairs, Jax and Knox are sitting at the island while Emmett is standing between the island and the stove.

"Well?" Knox asks with a boyish excitement dancing in his eyes.

Before I can answer, Jax interrupts, "What the fuck is she doing here, Cal? We talked about this last night."

"That fucker from last night attacked her, and she fought him off. I went to clean her up, and she passed out in my arms. What did you want me to do?"

"I don't know, maybe get her loud mouth friend. It's not like we didn't know who she was or who she was with. No, instead, you found a reason to bring her back here. Not a good idea, bro."

I toss my hand in the air. "Stop. I don't know why you're so worked up."

"Because we don't bring girls here." Knox starts to speak, but Jax cuts him off. "You know what I mean. What if she says something?"

"She doesn't know anything, so there is nothing to say."

"I don't have the fucking patience for this," Jax grumbles.

"No, shit," Knox mumbles, then throws his hands up. He pulls his lips, looking at me, and mouths, "I was just sayin'."

Jax grumbles out something and stabs at the fruit on his plate without bringing it to his mouth.

"She'll grab some breakfast, then be on her way."

Jax drops his fork on the plate. "You mean this large spread E whipped up?" He cuts his eyes at Emmett, who simply winks back at him.

"What? I love to cook."

Jax rolls his eyes with the hint of a smirk playing on his lips. Emmett is the only one of us who can break through Jax's tough exterior and diffuse the situation.

Perfect timing, because Everlee just walked down the stairs, wearing the clothes I picked out for her. Her hair is wet and slicked back and her cheeks carry a tinge of pink on them as her eyes dart around, looking at each of us.

"Your house is beautiful." She nods at the dining room, which is offset to the right of the kitchen.

We just had this space remodeled less than a year ago and knocked down a wall that ran the length of this room, so we could open up the dining room and kitchen. We connected all the rooms through whites, light grays, soft blues, and wooden accents. Emmett got his gourmet kitchen, with a large oversized granite countertop and stainless-steel appliances, and got to design a dining room that is much too large for us.

It's only the four of us that live here and we rarely host parties, so the twenty-seater hand scraped dining room table he picked out is really a bit much, but it's what he wanted. When we were redecorating this space, we carved out a small nook for an in-home office we could use. It matches the rest of the aesthetic, with floor to ceiling glass panels, a wooden desk and modern furniture.

"There's Ali!" Knox says, standing from a stool at the bar.

Her head snaps in surprise, like she wasn't expecting him, which I guess makes sense. Why would she think anyone other than me lived here?

The blush on her cheeks darkens and trickles down her neck as she waves at us, lips pinched in a flat line.

"Pull up a seat, Trouble," Emmett says, scooping some food onto a plate.

Trying to put as much space between us as I can, I lean against the wall opposite of her. But it doesn't help. Looking at her cheeks causes my hands to tingle. Seeing the fabric of the shirt pulled taut between her breasts reminds me of what hides just underneath.

"Ignore him!" Knox bounds over, pulling out a stool for her.

"She seems capable of pulling up her own stool, Knox," Jax grumbles.

"Shut up Jax. I'm just being polite."

She looks at Jax, drinking him up like she has the rest of us. He's attractive. Dark hair, dark eyes and fuck off stamped across his forehead, which seems to be what all the women love. Though some say I have the same look, so I guess he gets it honestly.

Knox still has the seat pulled out, waiting for her. She cautiously walks over and climbs onto the chair, her eyes fixed on Emmett, who is sliding a plate over to her. She completely misses Knox, closing his eyes behind her as he savors her sweet scent.

Tentatively, she picks up the fork and takes a bite of the Eggs Benedict and lets out a moan, then freezes, looking at each of us. Before I can stop myself, my lips curl into a smile because I know she's thinking about what just happened in the shower only twenty minutes ago.

She recovers quickly, her hand flying to cover her mouth in surprise. "It tastes so good."

"That's what she said," Knox chimes in.

"Real mature," Jax mumbles.

"Why are you such a grump this morning? We had an amazing night last night!" Knox retorts.

"Knox." The one word shuts his mouth.

The room grows awkwardly quiet, so Emmett chimes in, "You can moan anytime." He closes his eyes, shaking his head in disbelief. "At my food. At my food is what I meant to say. You can moan anytime you're eating my food. Fuck!"

"Well, as fun as this breakfast is, I'm going to take off to the club." Jax pushes away from the bar. "Everlee." He bows his head before walking out of the room.

She quickly waves at him and watches him leave, with her fork dangling between her fingers. Her phone buzzes, snapping her back to the present, and as she reads her messages, she smiles before a blush tinges her cheeks.

"Everything ok?" I ask, stepping off the wall and taking the seat Jax vacated.

"Yes. Lizzy is on her way to get me. She said she'd be here in ten minutes."

"I could have taken you home, but I figured she'd feel better knowing she could get to you anytime she wanted."

"Thank you." She pauses for a second. "Can you tell me what happened last night?"

I nod. "While I was tending to you, you unexpectedly passed out, and I would prefer if you refrained from doing so in the future." She smiles and takes a bite of her eggs, so I continue, "Once I determined it was more adrenaline related and not alcohol." I give a pointed look at Emmett who holds up his hands. "I brought you here."

"Why not take me back to my friend?"

The same question I've asked myself a dozen times since last night. "You all had been drinking. If by some chance it wasn't adrenaline related, I wanted to watch over you to make sure you were ok. I didn't want to put that responsibility on your friend."

"So you watched over me last night?"

I nod and her eyes grow large. Not with fear, but... embarrassment? "You didn't snore or anything like that."

She shrugs, and relief washes over her as she takes the last bite of eggs benedict.

"Well, thank you. You didn't have to," she says, brushing a fallen piece of hair behind her ear. It's a simple gesture, but captivating.

The doorbell rings, pulling us from our trance.

"I'll get it!" Knox jumps up from his seat like the playful golden retriever he is, darting out of the room. He's back in a minute later, waving his arm in the air. "This is the kitchen."

Lizzy walks into view seconds later with her mouth on the floor. She makes quick eye contact with Everlee and mouths 'OMG'.

Everlee's smile lights up the room as she slides off the chair and walks her plate around to the sink. "If you tell me where your dishwasher is, I can put this in really quick."

Emmett chuckles. "No dishwasher here. Just these hands."

"You wash Callum's dishes?" she asks, confused.

"Well, all the dishes."

"You live here?"

He laughs. "Did you think I came just to cook you breakfast?"

Her cheeks blush as red as the bowl of strawberries on the island. "You know... I really didn't know. This morning has been... a lot."

That's an understatement. Trying to push those thoughts out of my head, I walk over to Lizzy and hold my hand out to shake, enunciating my words slowly in case she's deaf. "Nice to meet you, Lizzy."

"Thanks for taking care of my girl," she says as her knees buckle slightly.

She doesn't seem to have a hearing problem, so then why the ASL? "No problem at all."

"Are you ready to leave?" Everlee chimes, tossing an odd look at me over her shoulder.

"No. I mean yea, sure. You?"

"Thanks again. Emmett. Knox," Everlee says, nodding in their direction.

"No, you don't. I'm a hugger." Knox smiles and holds out his arms. He whispers something to her and a second later, her cheeks are red and she is pushing away from him with a smile on her lips.

Emmett calls out, "See you later, Trouble."

"I'll walk you out." I hold out my arm, leading them out of the room.

"Thanks again for last night,"Everlee says when we get to the door.

Lizzy's head snaps in her direction, but Everlee rolls her eyes, ignoring her.

She stands on her tiptoes and reaches up to give me a hug. My hand brushes across her lower back, just under the lip of her shirt and her skin feels like fire, causing me to suck in a breath. She responds, pressing her chest against mine, and we freeze, each savoring this moment. Taking what we can get.

Before I do something that will piss the guys off, I mumble, "Take care."

She turns, but not far enough away, so my hand stays on her back. When I look at her, I see it there. The want. The need. And fuck me, I want to give it to her.

Her gaze flickers from me to Lizzy and I feel like this game we've been playing with the staring has escalated to physical touch. She wants me to move my hand, but I need her to make me.

She lets out a puff, steps towards Lizzy and doesn't look back.

EVERLEE - WHEN YOU NEED THAT DICK AND ALL YOUR BOYFRIENDS ARE CHARGED UP

ON THE ENTIRE CAR ride back to my apartment, Lizzy rambles about how nice and huge their house is and how it's because Callum's compensating for something. I don't tell her he isn't because that would lead to the embarrassing story of me in the shower and him bursting in. Though I never saw his dreamsicle, I know it's huge because of the bulge in his pants.

The scene replays over in my head and wish I had the balls to have taken him, or at least tried to. No doubt he'd be divine in bed. They'd be divine. They're a group of some of the hottest men I've ever laid eyes on. What would you call a group of hot men? Gaggle pops into my head, but that's for geese. Perhaps a brood of men? It's a stretch, but chickens are a brood, and these men are a bunch of cocks. I'm going with a brood of men.

"You ok?" she asks, pulling to a stop in front of my apartment building.

"Yes." I laugh, remembering her texts. "What was with that text earlier?"

"What are you talking about?"

"The one you sent me. You said, 'I'll be there in ten, unless you're getting boned, then I'll be there in five because I want to watch.'"

"I see nothing confusing or out of place about that text."

"No?"

"No. I'd want to watch because Callum…" she smacks the steering wheel, then grabs it and starts grinding her hips. "I bet that boy knows how to fuuucccck," she sings.

I blush, but can't speak because she's probably right. I thought the same thing.

She stops moving and turns to look at me. "Was there something you didn't tell me? Like how you rode that man-candy's cock-a-doodle-doo?"

"No. I did not have sex with them."

"Them?" She looks at me.

"Him. I mean him."

"You want to have sex with them all, don't you?" She rubs her chin. "I bet they'd be down. Fuck. Imagine your first time getting that donkey dick back in you, and it's with a threesome… shit, a foursome."

"Jax was there earlier, but he left." Why did I add his name to the list? It's not like she needs any more encouragement.

"Four?" Her hands clasp together under her chin. "Please, please, please. If you ever loved me or valued our friendship, you'd jump on that dick train and ride it!" she growls with excitement. "Ride it so fucking hard." She turns in her seat. "And then, of course, you'd come back and tell me everything. Every little detail to the ounces of come you suck down or squeeze out."

"Oh my God. Gross." I smack her arm.

"What? I need to know these things."

"No! No, you don't."

Her eyebrows raise, but she doesn't speak.

"Bye, and thank you for picking me up."

She smiles and stretches her arms out in an exaggerated move. "I'm feeling we should go to the club tonight."

"What? Have you lost your mind?"

"Maybe for that dick!" she says in a deep voice, enunciating every word.

"You have a dick."

"I do and I love that dick very much, but a girl can hope and dream her BFF gets four fabulous dicks as well."

"Bye." I close the door.

"Wait!" she yells. She bends her head down so she can see me outside of the passenger window. "Valentine's is in a couple of days."

"So?"

"Do you want a bouquet of Vixen dicks?"

I can't even dignify her question with a response, so I dismissively wave my hand through the air and head towards my building. As I get to the door, I hear her cackling reverberate through the air, growing fainter and fainter as she drives farther down the street.

Flipping the home app open on my phone, I scan it over the reader. Digital keys are so great. When the door buzzes, I feel a pang, almost like it's the buzzer going off in my life. Like I had a shot to take last night, this morning, and I didn't take it.

The end.

Game over.

When I get up to my apartment, I fall onto my couch, replaying everything that happened between my failed attempts at self pleasurement (yep, a word I just made up), to the Vixen party, to the creep, and lastly to the chaos this morning. What a truly baffling fourteen hours. Dragging myself off the couch sometime later, I walk into my bedroom and find the large red box still lying on my bed.

Shit!

I left my outfit at Callum's house. Well, I assume it's Callum's, but it could be Emmett's... or Knox's... maybe Jax? Shit. I have no clue.

Well, I guess I won't see that again.

But I really liked it and who knows how much Lizzy paid for it. And if she knew I left it, she'd drive me back over there just so I could see them again. She'd probably leave me there to make sure they'd have to drive me home. Because that's the conniving, crafty, sneaky little thing she is. In all the best ways, of course.

Would it be weird to show up at their house and ask for it back? Maybe I should go to Vixen and ask Emmett and schedule another pick up time? No. That seems like a lot of extra work, because he'll probably just tell me to run over to the house to get it. Frustration prickles on my face, so I rub it, but it doesn't do much to help.

Damn it!

What am I going to do? Why am I fighting against this so hard?

Because I want that donkey dick, damn it!

My boyfriends are staring longingly at me from their shelf across the room, begging to be used, wanting to help take this edge away. Or maybe that's just me projecting my feelings onto a bunch of vibrators and dildos. However, they are literally all giving me the green light for go, so I should take it as a sign, right? Especially the big green monster dick. He seems the closest to Callum's size.

Hello friend, I smile and slip out of the clothes Callum bought for me. Which until this very second, I hadn't realized how weird it is he had clothes for me. Like, how? Why did he have clothes that fit me? Is there another woman living there I didn't see? Does he keep an assortment of sizes and styles for women they bring home? What if they're like some kind of weird sex cult and they were trying to initiate me in? Am I upset that they could be, or that they could be, and I didn't get the nod for the invite? Was Jax the leader and when he left, he was signaling a no go?

Why am I thinking about this? My face falls into my hands.

What in the fuck did I drink last night and why am I thinking about these random things?

No. They're not a sex cult, and if they are, Callum would definitely be the leader.

Callum and his big dick energy. My inner goddess is drooling over what could have been.

Yes. That's the thoughts I need to be thinking of.

Padding across the floor, I grab my monster dick off the shelf and fall into bed. I adjust the vibration and let him play on my clit for a minute before I slowly glide him in. He stretches me before he begins to move and rotate around inside of me, hitting on all the delicious spots.

Flashbacks of last night replay in my head. Callum on the balcony. Callum's hands gripping the rail. Callum's chest in the shower. Callum's bare ass.

My orgasm is coming, building higher and higher as the memories play on repeat. My back arches off the bed as my hand travels over my breast and down my body. Rubbing. Imagining it's Callum's.

My breath shudders when I hit my climax as my body pulses and throbs around the green goblin. Pulling him out, I turn him off and lie on the bed for a minute, letting my body relax.

My phone buzzes, and when I roll over to look at it, a sigh escapes. How? I swear to God she has cameras in my house.

Lizzy: *You use the green machine?*

Everlee: *What?*

Lizzy: *Girl, we both know, that I know, you went home and got you some.*

Lizzy: *And that your favorite is the one I bought you.*

Everlee: *OMG.*

Lizzy: *You just finished, didn't you?*

Lizzy: *Still in bed?*

Lizzy: *HAHAHAHAHA*

Everlee: *Your a sick fuck.*

Lizzy: *You're.*

Everlee: *One handed typing. ;)*

Lizzy: *YASSS QUEEN.*

Tossing my phone on the bed, I stare at my ceiling for a moment before I decide to jump into the shower. I'm not a two shower a day kind of girl, but after being interrupted this morning and with all my dirty thoughts, I need something to wash away the night and the morning.

Feeling more relaxed than earlier, I trot into my bathroom and look at my shower tub comboand suddenly miss the luxury of Callum's walk-in. I don't need all the lights or music, but the rainfall was nice. *And the jets...* My subconscious reminds.

While the water heats, I look at myself in the mirror, seeing a minor scrape above my eyebrow and am reminded of the dickface from last night. Why do guys have to be like that? I was having a great time with Lizzy and he had to come over and ruin it, then make me feel like it was my fault because he had self-control issues. But I guess that's the problem today.

I remember going to school and at the beginning of every year, we'd have a kickoff meeting reviewing rules segmented by girls and boy. Boys... two rules. No cleats and no ripped shirts. Girls. Well, pull up a chair and pack a lunch because the list was extensive. No tight pants, no short shorts, no shorts above the knee, no tank tops, no this, no that. It was especially frustrating when going into the stores to buy clothes and almost every piece was something that couldn't be worn at school, so I was stuck having to wear pants every day. Ninety degrees or twenty degrees didn't matter, because it was the girl's job to remove temptation from boys instead of boys learning how to control themselves.

I sigh. This is a pet peeve of mine that pops up far too frequently. Feeling childish, I stick my tongue out in the mirror, then climb into the shower, taking my time since I have nothing else to do today.

After the shower, I dry my hair and put on a light layer of make-up, then sit on my couch and flip through Netflix.

After a Valentine's Day themed romcom, I flip open my work laptop and check my emails. I usually do it later at night, but now seems like a good time since I need to keep my mind busy. No matter how hard I try, Callum's presence continues to haunt my thoughts.

"Shit." I click open the link that reads Valentine's dinner reminder. It's a customer event from one of our biggest clients. They had apparently rented out a ballroom or something and invited my entire firm plus one to dinner on Wednesday. I forgot I'd RSVP'd several weeks ago. I guess part of me hoped I'd be able to find a date before then, but the other part tried not to think about it and completely failed.

My first thought is Lizzy, which is stupid. She used to be my date for these sorts of things, so much so that for a long time my boss thought we were dating. Can I get sick between now and then? I'd have to start building the story tomorrow. Go in fine, because I don't want them thinking I'm just hung over from the weekend, but at around one or two, get a little mopey, a sniffle here or there. Tuesday, go in and talk about the awful night's sleep I had and then leave early. BOOM! Plan locked in place!

My phone dings.

I look at it, expecting a text from Lizzy, but find my restaurant app confirming a reservation at Bo La Vie for tomorrow night at eight for four people.

Confused, I stare at the app, since I hadn't made a reservation, then notice it says Thank you Emmett for making your reservation! In special notes, it reads, *To foods that make you moan*, with a winky face.

I throw my phone down, then pick it up again.

"Asshole!" I laugh.

That wonderful, handsome asshole.

I don't know why he made a reservation for me, but I'm beyond ecstatic. I call Lizzy and tell her the good news and invite her and Tony to come with. She says she'll be there, but Tony won't be able to make it. He has dinner with a customer to talk about some project he's about to start, which probably meant Derek, too. I hesitated a minute before calling her, because naturally Tony would probably expect me to want to invite Derek. I mean, I hope not after last night, but it's still weird ground. Another reason on the list of many, I don't like them setting me up. When things don't work out, it's just awkward for a bit.

I don't know what to do with the extra two seats and debate changing the reservation for only two, but don't know if Emmett would join or wanted to join. Is this his way of asking me out? *In a really weird way*, my subconscious chimes.

Ok. So probably not Emmett asking me out, but who will use the other two seats? Maybe he's just giving me the option? Why am I overthinking this? Bo La Vie!!

Filled with excitement, I run into my closet and flip through all of my clothes, trying to find the perfect outfit for tomorrow night. This will probably be the last time I'll be able to eat there for a while because I definitely will not make a reservation for a month out.

Scratch that. After the sandwiches I tasted last night, I'd probably make it for a year out... I'm just not that patient of a person. Maybe I can get in really tight with Emmett and he will tell me who his friend is that can give me the hook up?

Yes. All the plans are coming together.

EVERLEE - WHEN THEY KISS YOU LIKE THAT

THE CAR DROPS ME off at the front of Lizzy's condo. We decide on her place since it's closer to Bo La Vie.

"Thanks," I say, passing a few extra dollars to the driver, but she's no Betty. Guilt prickles in my stomach for not calling her because even though we've only shared one ride, it felt... different.

The cool wind blows my dress up a little when I step out of the car, so I pull it down before walking up the short flight of stairs to Lizzy's door.

Before I can knock, Lizzy throws the door open. "Hey, girl, hey!"

She always makes me laugh, even if it's just opening the door with a pizazz that only Lizzy seems to possess. When I step inside from the cold, she is there with a warm hug, smelling like vanilla and coconut, her signature smell.

"I'm so excited! I've been looking over their menu all day."

"Me too!" My face pulls. "I didn't realize how much it cost." Adding quickly, "I don't have a problem with the cost, but I have a problem that Emmett probably spent a small fortune on those sandwiches we ate a few nights ago. I feel like I should pay him back."

"Yes, *you* probably should," she laughs.

"I should?"

"Shit. You were volunteering."

"Lizzy," I scold.

She sighs. "Fine. You talk to him and I'll contribute." She hands me a martini when we walk into her kitchen. "A little pre-game action."

"What are you getting?"

"Girl. I have no idea. I've stared at that damn menu all day and everything looks fantastic. I think I'm just going to take whatever the server suggests or the special... I don't know. I saw a sampler, but that's only like three."

"What's a girl to do?"

"Indeed!"

We finish up our drinks and debate on calling a car or walking. We don't mind the walk, and it's only a few blocks away, but the temperatures are dropping. In the end, we decide to walk, in part because of time, but I really think it's because Lizzy wants to go by Vixen. She's always been very clever at catching a man's attention when she's on the prowl. Or in this case, catching the attention of certain men, for me.

Ten minutes later, we're walking down the sidewalk, core shaking, with our hands bundled near our faces. When we looked at the weather, we didn't consider the wind chill factor.

Amateur move.

The wind is whipping, and we're freezing, but we're too far down the road to turn back or admit defeat. Nope. We're both stubborn as shit and would suffer so we can talk about how we defeated the great frost that never was.

We decide to stop in Vixen, only for a minute, so we can regain feeling in our extremities, but when we get there, the doors are locked. "Should have looked at the hours," I mumble through chattering teeth.

"Note to self, Thursday through Sunday only."

The sign for Bo La Vie is just down the road, taunting us with its distance. Close enough to be seen, but still so far to walk in these temperatures.

The sign is beautiful. Simple, yet elegant, sticking off the side of the building with a black background and white block font with round bulbs around the sign. Very classic.

"So close, yet so far away." Tears stream down my face as the icy wind blows.

As we're coming to the road that leads to the back of Vixen, a car pulls to a stop in front of us. After a second, the window rolls down.

"Everlee?"

"Jax."

"Jax?" Lizzy asks.

"Get in the car. Both of you," he commands, sounding less than happy. He jumps out of the driver's side and opens the back door, not waiting for an answer. He's just as handsome as the others, with dark hair and chocolate brown bedroom eyes. There's a small scar on his cheek and another peeking out from the collar of his shirt that tells me he's been in his fair share of fights, but judging by his size, I'd have to bet he easily won. Anyone who would go up against him would have to be mad.

Sliding in, we immediately appreciate the cozy warmth and the luxurious feel of the leather cushion. It feels so soft. He climbs back into the car, turning around with a scowl etched on his face. "What are you both doing? I thought you had reservations at Bo's tonight."

"We did... we do." I quickly correct, nervous under his gaze. It isn't as intense as Callum's, but it's close. "We were walking there."

"In this weather? Are you mad?"

"Apparently," I say, cutting my eyes to Lizzy.

"Hi. I'm Lizzy. BFF of Everlee and apparent bad decision maker."

He smiles. "How about a lift? I was headed there anyway."

"You were?" Lizzy asks, bumping elbows with me.

"Yes. We're having a team meeting there tonight."

"What a kawinky-dink," Lizzy teases.

Jax slowly turns around and pulls down the road. "I can drop you two at the front door, then park."

"No!" Lizzy and I both jump in.

"You don't need to do that," I add in a much calmer and more respectable tone.

"Plus, this way you get to walk in with two beautiful ladies, one on each arm," Lizzy says, pumping her eyebrows.

"That is true." His gaze fixes on me in the rear-view mirror, causing my stomach to stir.

It's only been a day and a half since I'd seen Callum, but he's been on my mind every hour of that day and a half. My poor BOBs are getting the most use they've had since... ever. Callum is a thirst I need to quench and Jax is quickly moving up that list, too.

We're parked at Bo's less than five minutes later.

Jax opens the car door for us, and Lizzy is gushing about him being a gentleman. He offers us each an elbow, making me feel like a million dollars around him. Callum too. Maybe that is what's adding to my thirst. It's been so long since I felt the slightest bit confident, but they... they all make me feel that way with just a look.

A doorman is waiting for us when we arrive. He has salt and pepper hair with olive skin and old, wise eyes. "Good evening Mr. McCall." He looks at each of us with a furrowed brow. "Will they be dining with you?"

"No, I was escorting them in. They have a reservation at eight."

"Yes. Ms. Everlee."

"That's me." I hold my hand up.

"Shall we wait for the others?"

"No. Lizzy jumps in. My boyfriend can't make it and Ever-lee doesn't have one."

That Lizzy. Always looking for an angle. When I shoot her a nasty glance, she just shrugs before winking, knowing good and damn well what she's doing.

The doorman, again confused, this time by Lizzy's random statement about my love life, or lack thereof, directs us to the hostess stand.

"Good evening, Mr. McCall," the woman says when we arrive, nearly melting in her spot. The man knows how to wear a pea coat. That's for sure.

"Good evening, Eliza." He flashes a friendly smile, but offers nothing else.

Such the charmer.

"The rest of your group is here at their table." She directs her arm to the second level.

My eyes travel up, and standing on the edge, hands gripped around the rail, is Callum, wearing a button-down blue shirt, under a black jacket and a pair of faded jeans. Holy fuck. And those eyes... my God. The blue shirt makes them pop even more and right now they're penetrating into the depths of my soul. My lower jaw falls open as my breathing changes.

"Damn," Lizzy moans, looking at him too.

"Your table is this way, Ms. Everlee."

"Enjoy your meal, ladies." Jax waves to us as he starts his ascent up the wide spiral staircase.

Once we're seated, I look around the restaurant. The floors are a beautiful hand-scraped wood, and the colors are very simple, black and white, with large chandeliers. It reminds me a lot of Callum's house. On the far side of the room is a glass panel running the full length of the wall, and behind it is the open kitchen where they're making and preparing the food. There are about twenty large round tables spread throughout the main floor, with several tables on the border for couples. Because we had a reservation for four, they sit us near the center of the room.

Curiosity getting the better of me, I chance a glance at the second balcony to see if there are tables up there, but find those familiar blue eyes resting on me. If I didn't find him so incredibly sexy, it would be creepy, but I don't know if there is anything about him that could be creepy.

Confidence swelling inside of me, I wiggle my fingers at him with a small wave, and he sends back a wink. My legs reflexively clench together. It's just a wink, but fuckin' aye it's the best goddamn wink.

It's a wink filled with a promise of sex. Lots of amazing rock your world sex. Sex that makes you forget your name and where you are. The kind of sex-

"Everlee?" Lizzy asks, concerned.

"Yea?"

"Your cheeks are flush and you're panting."

"Sorry." I blink hard and return to my menu, but not before I see the hint of a smile playing on Callum's lips. It's like he knows the effect he has on me and enjoys watching it.

The head server is over a minute later introducing himself, with two others behind him. Three servers? The younger one, named Sven, begins taking the extra place settings off the table while the second server, named Isla, fills our water glasses. "The owner has prepared a special menu for you both tonight. He called them bite flights to make you..." he looks around uncomfortably and drops his voice, "moan."

My eyes shoot open wide, and I look around the restaurant as realization hits me. Emmett is the owner. He has to be hiding somewhere. The sneaky bastard.

"Ooh, I love a good moan," Lizzy says, clasping her hands together.

When I look up to the second level, I find him standing there with a cheeky grin. So I scowl at him playfully and point my finger. If he's the owner, then why was he bartending at Vixen?

"He also wanted me to tell you, your meal is on the house tonight."

Shocked, I look back up at him, and he blows a kiss, smiling. I mouth the words thank you, and he winks back. What is it with those boys and their winking? It does things to me.

"You will have fifteen total plates, with a drink pairing for each. Each drink has been carefully selected and paired with your bite flight, and will be approximately two ounces. Once complete with the starters and main course, you will have a flight of desserts served with a coffee."

"Wow. I have no words other than I'm so excited to try any and everything."

The servers all smile and dip away.

Lizzy grabs my hand and whispers, "You said you didn't sleep with anyone."

I chuckle, "I didn't."

"Then why... all this? A special menu? Comping our dinner? This would have to be almost a grand for tonight."

"I don't know."

Lizzy lets out a thoughtful hum.

"We need to find out more about these boys." I nod up to the second balcony and see the four of them are deep in conversation, pointing at something on the table. Likely a drawing of some sort. I realize this is the first time I've caught Callum not looking at me. It's intoxicating to watch him. The way the heel of his foot props on the chair leg while his hands grip and rub into his thigh. The way his jaw moves when he speaks or how the light reflects off pieces of his hair.

When the server walks up a minute later with our first tray and printed menu of all the things we'll be trying tonight, an excitement pulses through me. In front of us is a small salad in a glass twice the size of a shot glass, paired with a white wine. I pick up the small fork and carefully stab it into the glass, capturing all the ingredients for the one perfect bite. When I place it in my mouth, I'm overwhelmed by the intense flavor, and my eyes nearly roll into the back of my head. When I open my eyes again, I see Emmett and Callum watching me. Emmett has a huge smile spread across his face and he turns to say something to Callum, who nods, smiling. I have a feeling it's about me and I'm dying to know what it is.

Callum catches me looking, and signs in ASL, *Eat your food and stop watching us.*

How did he know I knew ASL?

I sign back, *Thank Emmett for us,* followed by my command for him to stop watching us.

He smiles, and I watch his lips tell Emmett, who snarls at me when he sits back down, causing me to chuckle. Then Callum signs back, *Maybe I enjoy watching you.*

Maybe I enjoy watching you, too.

With that, I turn away before I can see his response. It feels like I'm in high school passing secret notes to a crush, only now I'm signing in the middle of a very expensive restaurant.

"So he signs too?"

"Apparently."

The servers bring us our second dish. Another salad with a sort of balsamic glaze. I'm pretty sure I'm in heaven right now. How is this my life?

"You have it bad," Lizzy says.

"What? No."

"I'm not faulting you because damn. The only problem is, who do you choose? All four of them seem to be smitten with you and all of them are hot as hell."

"Do I have to choose?" I tease.

Lizzy's eyes grow wide. "I like your style. I always said a man could never hold you down, maybe four can."

Laughing, I continue, "Well, I think we're putting the cart in front of the horse. I'm not dating any of them."

"This sure feels like a date."

"I'm here with you."

"Yea, but no."

"What?"

"You can't keep your eyes off them. We've hardly spoken. Which don't get me wrong, I'm not hating it because I love that you're getting the attention you deserve. Like you said, you're not even dating them and look how they treat you. Imagine if you *were* dating them." She wipes an invisible tear from her eye. "It would be magical."

"I love you. You know that?"

"I love you too, sis."

That's what we are. We're sisters from different misters. When we met in elementary school, we immediately hit it off and were inseparable. During our freshman year of high school, her parents got divorced, and she took it hard. Even harder when her dad started dating again so soon. She lived with me for a while until her parents finally put their foot down and made her go home. But I was always there for her and she was always there for me. My ride or die.

We finish all the starters and several sandwich bites. I've lost count on which tray we're on, but my bladder is about to explode. I've had so much to drink and even though they aren't normal-sized glasses, I feel obligated to drink it all at one time to make sure the pairings all go together. So that being said, I'm feeling a little tipsy.

Emmett seems to have everything planned perfectly except that one detail. When it comes to alcohol, I'm definitely a lightweight. I would tease the guys who took me out, saying I was a cheap date because I was good-to-go after one, maybe two drinks.

"I'll be back."

She nods, tipping back the most recent drink. An Argentinian wine.

When I walk out of the bathroom a few minutes later, Callum is standing there in the dimly lit hall. "We need to stop meeting like this," I say, giving my skirt another tug.

He smiles. "There isn't anyone inside?" He points to the restroom.

"No."

A smile plays on his lips as he steps toward me, and I instinctively take a step backward.

"You aren't going to beat me up if we end up in there, are you?" His words are like velvet.

My heart skips a beat. "No."

He takes another step forward, causing his scent to swirl around me. "Are you having a good time?"

"Mmhmm." It's all I can get out, because my vocal cords have retreated into hiding.

His hand comes up to my face, the pad of his thumb pulling down my bottom lip. "Use your words, Everlee."

"Yes."

He presses his body against mine and I can barely breathe. "Yes, what Everlee?" His words are low and silky, eyes like blue flames.

"Yes, sir."

"Good girl." My stomach is somersaulting on itself as butterflies erupt and my entire body tingles.

All the tension in my jaw releases as it drops to the floor. He called me a good girl, and I liked it. Not liked it, but fucking loved it. Do I have a praise kink I'm unaware of?

He leans in slowly, pressing his cheek against mine. "I haven't been able to get you off my mind," he admits, inhaling my scent, as his fingers lightly dance across my shoulder.

My nipples are hard, and my pussy is purring like a freaking jaguar who's just waking up from a long winter's nap. If they take long naps. Fuck, I don't know, but clearly my brain isn't functioning properly right now. "Same. I..." It's so hard to focus right now, because he's making my head spin. "I haven't stopped thinking about you."

"This is a problem for me, though."

"Why?"

"Because I don't do girlfriends."

"So?" I whisper as his hand moves to the back of my neck.

"You deserve more than what I can give you."

His lips find their place under my jaw and my neck dips to the side, giving him more access as a moan escapes my lips, but I don't care. Not one fucking bit. His lips slide down my throat.

"I love when you moan." His lips brush softly against my skin.

"I'm sorry. I..." His tongue gently licks across my collarbone before his lips kiss it away, robbing me of my breath.

"Don't be sorry. It makes me..."

His hand grabs onto my hip, squeezing roughly like he's fighting with himself.

"Makes you what?" I whisper, turning into him, inhaling his scent.

He chuckles a low laugh. "I can't tell you."

My lips press against his neck. "Please."

"God, you're fucking intoxicating." His kisses climb up my cheek, and I can't wait. This game we've been playing to see which one will give in first. It's going to be me. I need to feel his lips on mine now. I need to feel him inside of me. I need... him. Every part, every inch.

Grabbing a handful of his shirt, I push the bathroom door open with my foot and pull him in, pressing his back against the door. Without hesitation, his lips crash unforgivingly onto mine and his tongue pushes its way in. It's a fucking dream. My panties are soaked as I grind against his body, wanting to feel him on every part of me. The bulge in his pants means he wants me too. Passion swelling inside, I grab his belt, but his hands clamp on my wrists, stopping me.

My head is swimming in confusion. "What's wrong?"

He closes his eyes and runs his fingers through his hair. "I shouldn't have done that."

"Done what? Kiss me? I wanted it."

He shakes his head. "There are rules and I just..." He opens the door and walks out.

Rage erupts inside of me like a volcano exploding in a flurry of confusion. "I don't understand," I snap, following him out of the bathroom.

"You aren't supposed to."

"I thought you wanted..."

He turns on a dime and steps forward, his hand resting on my face. "I do. So fucking much. More than I have ever wanted anyone before. But I can't..."

"I-" I stop myself, staring at him incredulously. "I need to go. Lizzy is waiting for me," I snap, walking around him.

"I'm sorry."

Irritation boils under my skin from embarrassment and my hands clench at my sides as I turn around and walk to stand in front of him. "What did you think was going to happen when you look at me like you do all the time and then follow me to the bathroom?"

"I wasn't trying to fuck in it, if that's what you think. I respect you more than that."

"Are you saying I don't respect myself?"

"No. I'm not saying that at all."

"Then what?"

He shakes his head. "You deserve more than what I can give you."

I roll my eyes, then poke my finger in his chest. "That's fucking bullshit and you know it."

I pivot on my heels and walk back to the table.

Lizzy watches me, and her eyes grow wide, drinking in every detail.

Collapsing into the chair, I take a deep breath. I won't let him ruin this fantastic evening.

"You want to talk about it?" she asks.

"Not yet."

She nods and changes the topic immediately, holding up a sandwich. "This one is probably my favorite. It's so cheesy."

A smile spreads across my face, thankful she knows me so well. She knows when to press and when to just let me be. "It's almost as cheesy as you," I say after taking a bite.

"Everlee's got jokes."

The rest of dinner passes with laughter filling the air as we exchange jokes and discuss Lizzy's upcoming wedding whenever it will be. It's a pleasant distraction from Callum and his... sex appeal. I try to avoid looking at the second balcony for the rest of dinner, but fail. Fortunately, at those times, he wasn't looking at me, but I could tell he was agitated.

We take the last bite of dessert and both slump back in our seats. A moment later, shadows descend on the table and we look up to find Emmett, Jax, Knox and Callum standing around us. Most of the restaurant has cleared out, so it's just us and the remaining staff.

"Well, how was it?" Emmett asks, beaming.

"It was phenomenal. Fantastic," Lizzy sighs.

"It was absolutely outstanding. I didn't know you were the owner."

Emmett smiles. "It's my passion project, and these boys helped me get it off the ground."

"Well, thank God they did, because wow."

Knox steps forward. "He's been talking about it all day. He wouldn't shut up."

"Well, really... it was amazing. Words can't describe. And you really didn't need to do this."

"It was nothing, Trouble," Emmett says. "The look on your face when you eat. If I could frame it and look at it every day," his words fall off. "That's what brings me joy... and-"

"Don't say it," I warn playfully, knowing he's going to say something about my moans.

He smiles. "Is there anything else you want? Need?"

"Gosh no." *Maybe a dick. Anyone's dick at this point*, my subconscious chimes.

"Can I get a picture?" Lizzy blurts. "With all of us?"

"Yea. Of course," Emmett and Knox answer at the same time.

Emmett calls our server over to take the picture. Lizzy puts me in the middle of all the guys while she stands on the outside of Jax. I'm between Emmett and Knox in the front, with Callum behind me to my right and Jax beside him. Emmett and Knox slip their arms around me, with their hands resting on my waist, and a second later, Jax and Callum slip their arms in, resting their hands on my hips. Fire erupts in my core with all of their hands on me.

Lizzy, being Lizzy and having planned this perfectly, gets one picture, then asks for a second with just me and the guys. I roll my eyes when I realize what she's doing.

Their hands are reluctant to drop after the pictures are taken, which does little for the fire stirring inside of me. After a long moment, their hands fall. If not, it would have just been awkward.

Jax steps forward. "If it's ok with you both, I'm going to take you home Lizzy and Callum will take you home, Everlee."

Before I can answer, Lizzy agrees for the both of us.

Glancing at Callum, his face is unreadable. It's hard to tell if this was his idea or not.

"Perfect," Emmett says, clapping his hands together.

There's something about Emmett that just makes you smile. Leaning over, I give him a hug, then kiss him on the cheek. He tickles my side when I pull away, making me giggle.

"What about me?" Knox whines.

"You didn't do anything," Jax reprimands

"I helped with... something. I'm sure."

My cheeks hurt from smiling as I lean over and plant a kiss on his cheek.

"Are we ready now?" Jax asks.

"Yes, we are," Lizzy answers again, looping her arm in Jax's.

We walk to the front, and the doorman gives Jax and Emmett a set of keys.

"See you boys at home," Jax says. "Good night, Everlee." He leans down and gives me a kiss just off the side of my lips that leaves my head spinning. He hasn't been overly affectionate, but that kiss, while it wasn't on the lips, felt... intimate.

The others hop into their cars when the valets pull them up and I wait for them to hand Callum his keys, but they don't.

Once the others leave, he looks hesitantly at me. "Are you ready?"

I nod, and he scowls at me. I will not give him the words he wants.

He huffs, then pushes the door open, holding it for me. A cool gust of wind blows my dress up, and I quickly push it down, trying not to expose myself.

Parked just down the sidewalk is a black Audi Q7 with a man waiting in the cold by the back door. Callum holds his hand out toward the car. "This is us."

He has a driver.

Of course he does.

He lets me climb in first, so I slide across, although the devil on my shoulder is yelling at me to make him walk around.

This is going to be an interesting ride.

EVERLEE - RULES ARE MEANT TO BE BROKEN

Not waiting to find out why the sudden change of plans, I give the driver my address and watch him plug it into the GPS.

Twenty-two minutes with traffic.

Twenty-two minutes of awkward silence in the back of a car with a man I haven't been able to get off my mind for days. A man who drips sex and power.

Twenty-two minutes.

He makes a turn at the stoplight, barely beating the yellow light, causing my hand to brace on the center of the seat and Callum's to do the same.

Our pinkies accidentally touch, and he quickly turns his gaze to meet mine, offering an apology.

"What exactly are you sorry for?" I mumble out.

I feel his gaze land on me, but I refuse to give him the satisfaction of meeting his eyes. I can't if I want to stay mad at him and I don't really even know why I'm mad. Is it because I can't get him off my mind? Because I wanted him to take me in that bathroom even though I usually find that disgusting? Is it because I let myself get attached and dream up some world where I thought he wanted me too? Irritated, I roll my eyes and look out of the window.

"Everlee," he whispers, grabbing my hand.

I yank it out of his grasp and give him a piercing stare. "I know you have your rules, and I don't want you to break them."

"I've gotten permission."

My head snaps back in shock. "Permission?" I nearly shout back. My mind tries to process. From who? A girlfriend? Wife? I didn't see any signs of a woman at his house. Maybe it wasn't his house... Surely he didn't have to ask for permission from the guys. Unless... they were together. No, that's not possible, is it? No. I shake my head. At the bathroom, the way he looked at me...

He sighs. "Everlee." His eyes soften, like he's struggling with something. "Brady. Can you pull over here?"

"What?"

"I need to talk to you. I need you to understand. And I don't need to feel pressured to explain everything in the remaining thirteen minutes I have with you," he says, looking at the map on display at the front.

There's a pain, an ache in his voice, which makes me want to reach up and touch his face and tell him everything is going to be ok, but I have to hold the course.

Brady parks the car and climbs out, standing on the sidewalk.

"He's getting out?" I ask, looking at him standing with his hands clasped in front of him with his black pea coat and beanie on.

"He's giving us privacy."

"What's going on?"

"That's what I'm trying to tell you. I don't... I don't usually have these conversations. This is Jax's department."

"He has conversations with girls for you." What kind of fucked up dynamic did I step into the middle of?

He chuckles and reaches up to cup my cheek, his thumb swiping across my cheekbone.

"Not quite."

"So, then?"

"If I gave you an NDA to sign, would that weird you out?"

"An NDA?"

"Non-Disclosure-"

"I know what an NDA is. I'm just surprised you asked me to sign one. I barely know you."

"That's for good reason."

"Who are you?" My gaze narrows on his face.

"I'm Callum." He smirks.

"No shit. I mean-"

He's chuckling when our eyes meet, and the air changes around us. His gaze becomes intense, sexual, needing. "You are a temptation like nothing I've ever experienced." He whispers, leaning forward. There's something in his voice that causes my stomach to tighten. No man's words have ever turned me on the way his have. Something about the power he commands is like lighter fluid for the sexual flame burning within me. Screw the lighter fluid like a whole container of gasoline.

I tilt my lips up towards his, eager to feel them on me again, but he holds there, an inch away, his eyes watching me.

"The first time was a mistake, and I was weak. I can't do it again."

"Kissing me was a mistake?" I huff, my head swirling.

"God, no. Well, technically yes." He chuckles, "But not in the way you think."

He pulls a small packet of papers from inside his coat and hands them to me. "Please sign these so I don't have to be so guarded with you. So I can kiss you, fuck you, and make you moan all night."

A puff of air escapes my lips, and my clit throbs as moisture pools between my legs. It's like someone turned on the faucet in my panties. Fucking hell.

Words escape me, so I nod repeatedly, looking like a fucking bobble head. "Got a pen?"

He chuckles, reaching into his inside pocket.

"You had me at kiss and sold it with fuck."

"You have a very dirty mouth." He watches me sign my name, then continues, "One that I want to punish." His tongue swipes slowly over his bottom lip as my hands clench onto the seat. Goddamn.

His words set my senses ablaze, and I instinctively close my mouth, not wanting to risk ruining this electrifying moment with any stupid thoughts that escape. His eyes rake over my face and settle on my lips as my resolve wanes. My teeth scrape along my bottom lip, freeing them for any number of words to fall out of my mouth. Fortunately, curiosity gets the better of me. "So, what do you need to tell me?"

He bats the paper onto the ground, swoops over, wraps his hand around the back of my neck, and pulls me towards him. "That can wait," he mumbles before his lips crash onto mine, taking them in an unapologetically hard kiss. The kind of kiss you need on a very basic level. The kind of kiss you need because your life depends on it.

A moan escapes, and I feel him smile before leaning forward more, pushing me back. His hand tightly grips my hip like it's his lifeline, while mine greedily strokes up his chest. I need him. Need to feel him, need to taste him, need everything about him.

"I'm going to make you moan my name," he whispers against my lips.

I look at him, smiling. "I doubt it."

His eyes twinkle with mischief. "Game on." His hands simultaneously lift my dress as he shimmies down my body.

Oh my God. He's going to eat me out in the back of his car with people walking on the sidewalk not even ten feet away. Nervous, but not enough to stop him, I tilt my head up and see the windows are tinted. I don't know how dark, but-

He slides my panties aside before his tongue plunges into my wet depths.

"Fuck me!" I exclaim, pressing the palm of my hand to the window behind me.

"I plan to," he says before diving back in.

Holy shit, he's skilled in the art of cunnilingus. Cunnilingus? Of all the words I could use- shit. So. Fucking. Good.

With the pressure building and the tingles that are racing through my body, I feel like I'm about to explode in his mouth. Holy shit. I think I'm seeing stars.

"Callum," I moan out, which only makes him swirl and pulse his tongue faster.

He slips two fingers in while his tongue plays with my clit, sucking it into his mouth.

"Oh, fuck."

"We're really going to need to work on that mouth," he says before running his tongue up my wet center. "You taste so good. I could live the rest of my life down here."

My body is grinding, moving on its own the closer I get, and his words just put me on a bullet train.

I moan again and again and again.

So much for winning that. He's playing to win and I can appreciate that. Over and over again.

His fingers curl and hit that magic spot, and without warning, my world explodes. Hearts and arrows and little flying Cupids swirl around my head. The groan that escapes my lips is unlike anything I've ever heard. It's deep, from the depths of a well that has never been explored before. My pussy clinches around his fingers as his thrusts slow.

He looks up at me, face still between my legs, his eyes pure sex and fire. What have I gotten myself into? He crawls up my body and finds my lips, pressing his tongue in. Hints of me linger there, but his kiss is soft, passionate.

I'm fucked.

Literally and figuratively.

Eager to repay the favor, I grab for the top of his pants, but he puts his hand on mine. "Not right now. This wasn't for me. Well, not entirely." He winks, sitting us up, then pulls out his phone and sends a text. Moments later, Brady is walking back to the car.

"Do you need to go home right now?" he asks before Brady gets back in.

I shake my head, still unable to form words.

Brady sits behind the wheel and I freak out for a second, wondering if he knows what just happened. There's no way he doesn't know, right? Staring at him through the rearview, I search for clues or signs, but he's unflinching. Not even a questioning brow or a smirk.

"Brady. Can you take us to Rosemary Park?"

My brow furrows, studying his face.

"Can you ice skate?"

I nod slowly, still confused. "But I'm not really in the outfit for it."

"It's ok. They have stuff there we can buy."

"Callum."

He kisses the end of my nose. "Rule One. What I say goes."

I laugh. "Sorry to burst your bubble, but I'm a rule break-er."

"I've gathered as much."

"Rule One. You can tell me what you want to happen and we'll discuss it."

A smile tugs on his lips. "We'll see."

I'll take the small victory for now. He seems to be the type that needs to be in control, and maybe that's what draws me to him. That dominant big dick energy.

We're at the park ten minutes later, and it's packed. I'd seen flyers floating around for it, but dismissed them since it was all Valentine's Day themed. I had no desire to go... before. While I still don't believe in the holiday, I can appreciate its benefits.

Brady drops us off at the main entrance, but before we get out of the car, Callum grabs my hand. "There's still a lot we need to discuss, but for now, we'll enjoy each other's company." He kisses my head and opens his door, not waiting for a response. Brady opens my door a second later, and I step out to Callum's waiting hand.

Damn, he looks fine as sin. That's what he is... a sin. I have a gut feeling I'm going to get hurt because I always do. Guys like this don't fall for girls like me. This is fun right now. I'm a temptation for him. A mystery. And right now, I don't care about any of that. I just want to have fun. *Need* to have fun.

We walk up to the glass-walled building sitting right in front of the rink and when we open the door, a thick hot air hits us right in the face. It's loud from young couples in love to tired parents chasing children around who are putting their hands on everything.

Callum raises on his tippy toes and lifts his arm as a child tears through the shop across the aisle. He's laughing when the child's mother comes racing by to catch him, apologizing.

"It's fine." He smiles before grabbing my hand, looking at me. "Let's get you some appropriate wear." He walks over to a rack which has a limited supply of pants, shirts, and jackets.

He holds up a pair of thick, gray, water resistant pants, a thermal black shirt and a teal, gray, and white jacket. "What are your thoughts on this?"

I glance at the price tag and feel my muscles clench. The markup is atrocious! "I don't really need the jacket. I'm sure I'll be fine without it."

He laughs and leans down so his lips brush against my ear. "I'll not have you freeze to death before I fuck your pretty little pussy."

My head snaps in his direction as I try to figure out how badly I want to be arrested for fucking him in the middle of the store. "When you say things like that, I could strip down right now and still be hot."

His eyes glare playfully. "You wouldn't."

I grab the zipper on the side of my dress and start inching it down, not taking my eyes off his. His lips part as the vein in his neck begins to throb.

He places his hand on mine and spins toward the teenage employee walking by. "Excuse me, she needs a room to try these on."

Half paying attention, she nods to the corner of the building where a makeshift changing room has been created.

"Thank you." He grabs my wrist and nearly pulls me across the store, weaving through all the shelves and scattered hats, gloves, light-up wands, and bouncy balls that are strewn all over the floor. He knocks on the door and when no one answers, he pushes it open, glances behind him, then pushes us both into the room.

A squeal of laughter erupts from my body, but he quickly puts his hand over my mouth. "Don't make a peep." He locks the door and looks at me with a wicked grin.

I grab his hand and start to speak, but it one motion he's on his knees with my panties around my ankles. How is he so fast?

"Callum," I whisper.

"Not a sound... or a moan." His eyes twinkle.

"You know I can-"

I can't finish speaking as he lifts one leg, tossing it over his shoulder, and buries his face in my still glistening pussy. It hasn't even been thirty minutes.

He slowly licks from back to front before slipping his tongue in. His eyes dart up to meet mine and my God. I bite my bottom lip, trying to hold back the moan that's begging to escape. It's not like anyone can hear me anyway since it's so loud in here, but something inside of me wants to obey him.

He slips two fingers in and swirls them around in a circle as my stomach clenches. I'm pretty sure all this stomach clenching counts as exercise. Six-pack here I come! My fingers snake through his hair before grabbing tightly, holding him in place while I rock on his face. He slips another finger in, stretching me, and my knees buckle.

"Callum," I moan out quietly, emotion getting the better of me.

He stops. Pulls out his fingers, then looks at me. It takes a second before my eyes focus on his. "Rule one."

I shake my head back and forth. He can't be serious.

He pulls my panties back up. "You better get changed quickly."

"You. Are you?" Completely flabbergasted and still needy, I try hard to form a sentence, but it doesn't work.

He wipes his fingers across his lips before kissing me on the forehead. He unlocks the door, pokes his head out, and walks out.

I'm standing like a high diver on the edge of the platform and he just walks away.

Fuck rule one.

I make my own rules.

Slipping out of my dress, I try to ignore the light brushing of my panties across my throbbing clit, then get an idea. Before putting on my new outfit, I slide my panties off and put them to the side. After getting dressed, I put them in my pocket and save them for later. Folding my dress over my arm and straightening my back, I walk out of the dressing room to a waiting Callum, who is bent over in a seat, I'm sure working on getting his erection down.

Casting a cool glance at him, I walk past him to the register with tags in hand. He chuckles behind me, obviously amused by my current bratty behavior, then slips his hand around my hips. There's another teenager working the register who seems to have smoked weed prior to his shift, because he could give two shits about the chaos happening around him on top of the fact his eyes are red and his fingertips are orange with Cheetos dust on them.

He looks up from the register a second or two after the total appears and drags out the total of three hundred and twelve dollars. Before I can pull out my card, Callum is handing over his black card.

"I can get it," I say, tilting my head to the side.

"I know, but I wanted you to *come*. So my treat."

My eyes nearly pop out of my head. Did he really just say that? The weight of his carefully chosen words was palpable, heightened by the deliberate pause on the word "come."A new game seems to be afoot, so I adjust my imaginary top hat and pipe and nod. "Thank you. I wanted to *come*, too."

His lips pull to the side and the guy at the register says in a monotone deadpan, "Yay. You both wanted to come."

Callum and I both look at each other and snicker.

"You can get your skates around the corner," the doped teen mumbles, pointing at a wall before handing me the receipt.

"Can I get a bag?"

The guy's brows pinch into the most dramatic v, so I hold up my dress.

"We don't sell those here."

I shake my head and huff, "I know. This is what I was wearing."

"Why did you bring it with you?" he asks, his head tilting back, seemingly too heavy for him because he's struggling to maintain his balance.

I close my eyes, trying to maintain my patience. "I just bought these clothes and changed."

"Oh, right." He nods emphatically, staring at us.

"So, can I get a bag?" I press.

"Right..." He hands me a bag, and we walk around the corner to wait in line for a pair of skates.

Spotting the perfect time to exact my revenge for the dressing room, I wait until Callum is talking to the attendant pulling skates and slip my panties into his pocket. "Here's the receipt for your purchase."

He nods, completely unaware of my extra gift. "What size?"

"Eight," I tell the kid behind the counter.

He hands us our skates, then points to a screen. "We limit the number of people on the rink. When it's your turn, your number will be called. It's not too bad of a wait right now. Here's your ticket."

I peek over Callum's arm to see what number we are and how long we'll have to wait and snort when I see we're number sixty-nine. "My favorite," I mumble.

"Nice," the kid behind the counter drones.

"Eww!" I retort before we step away. The screen above the door that leads to the rink is flashing sixty-seven. "Shame we don't have more time."

"We could leave," he suggests. His eyes catch mine and my stomach clenches. Goddamn, he's all fire and ice and everything nice.

"Nooo," I coo playfully. "I really, really wanted to come." Ignoring the sexy as hell quirk in his lips, I bend over and put my skates on.

"You should have followed rule number one," he whispers, bending over and tightening his laces.

"I told you... I'm a rule breaker," I answer back, pulling my laces tight. Can't have any loose laces or wobbly ankles. I'm clumsy enough as it is and definitely don't need to crash and fall out there.

"That's fine, but there will be consequences, and that's probably the easiest rule."

"How many rules are there?"

He smiles. "Sixty-nine."

I snarl my upper lip at him.

SIXTY-NINE, the computer voice calls out.

When he stands up, he sticks his hand in his pocket and his eyes grow wide as his gaze slowly travels over to my face and I'm waiting ever so patiently until our eyes lock. "You will pay for this."

"I hope so." Without waiting for a response, I turn and walk through the door and he slaps my ass.

CALLUM - LOSING CONTROL

THIS WOMAN.

She tosses a glance over her shoulder at me as she pushes along the ice. I don't know what it is about her that has me... enraptured. But damn it. We had a meeting tonight, like we do every Monday, but I could not focus. Not when she was so close and just out of my peripheral. I watched her for most of her dinner, laughing and smiling. The woman tonight is so different from the woman I saw at the club. This one is relaxed, carefree... happy. But there is something there, hiding behind her eyes.

My hand slides back into my pocket to grab her panties and my cock twitches as I watch after her, knowing there is nothing between those pants and her pussy. She does a half spin with ease and skates backwards, looking at me.

Yea, she can skate.

We make several laps as I skate just behind her, watching her hips move from side to side. She does another twirl, but her feet get twisted. Her arms fly out to the side and her eyes get wide in shock.

Laughing, I push forward with ease until I grab her hands and spin her around. She wobbles at the speed of the turn, but I don't let her fall. Once she rebalances herself, she looks at me, eyes dancing.

"So you can skate."

"I never said I couldn't." She smirks.

A scream from a child right behind us pulls my attention and a young girl is speeding past us, out of control. She's about to fall, so I reach out for her and grab her arm to help balance her just as her dad skates up beside us. "Sorry. I didn't want her to fall," I say, handing her wrist to her dad. He laughs. "I appreciate it. She sometimes forgets she's just learning how to skate. No fear in this one." He waves at us and falls back with the rest of his family.

"Such the hero," Everlee teases, shifting her weight into me.

She pushes quickly in front of me and does two quick spins, raising her arms in the air above her head, showing the smallest bit of skin around her hips. A flashback to her in my shower hits me like a ton of bricks and I don't want to skate anymore. I want to take her home and press my cock inside of her until I'm swallowing her orgasms.

With my mind made up, I press forward, grab her hand and pull her towards the door. "We're done here." I wait a beat, letting her tell me no, but her eyes pulse wide with want.

I started something in the car and continued it in the dressing room. Frustrated with my lack of self-control, I let out a growl of annoyance. Not a complete loss, I remind myself, since I was able to barely escape the dressing room. If not, I would have fucked her and the men did not approve of that. I was simply allowed to take her out and talk to her about us- gauge her interest in a group fuck.

Ten minutes later, we're sliding into the backseat of the car. I ignore the smirk on Brady's face as he shuts the door and walks around to the driver's side.

He starts the car and looks in the rearview, eyes flickering between the two of us. "Was the ice skating enjoyable?"

"Very." Everlee smiles.

His eyes shift in the rearview to look at me. "Where to, sir?"

"Home."

"I have to work tomorrow," Everlee whines. She's picking at the zipper of her jacket like she wants to say something else, but isn't sure if she should. She looks at her watch and her eyes pop open wide.

It's almost eleven, a relatively early hour for us, considering our typical nights stretch until three in the morning. But maybe, for her, it's late.

"Me too." I toss her a casual wink.

She tilts her head to the side, staring at me.

"I can have Brady take you home now, later, or first thing tomorrow morning."

"Tomorrow morning? Awfully presumptuous of you, isn't it?"

"You say presumptuous, I say hopeful." I squeeze her leg playfully and when her jaw falls slack, I look down and notice my hand is further up her leg than intended. She's not shocked, rather turned on. The veins in her neck are thumping hard and fast, causing my cock to twitch.

Her eyes dart back and forth between Brady and me, revealing the inner battle she's waging on whether to choose familiarity and go home or take a chance and come home with me to see what the night holds. She blinks slowly and in that second, I know what her decision is, which causes a jolt of excitement to pulse through me.

"Your house is fine and he can take me home tomorrow morning."

Brady nods without speaking and turns out of the pickup lane.

She looks out of the window for a second, and I can't help but wonder what she's thinking. Does she know what she could walk into? We share, and not all women are ok with that. Will she be?

My worried gaze falls onto the paper tossed on the floor with her signature. She didn't even read what was on it and had I been in more control of my feelings, then I would have stopped her. Made her read what she was signing. But no. I was not in control and that bothers me most of all. I didn't care if she read it. Hell, I barely cared if she signed it. I needed the box checked because I needed to taste her- to feel her. To make her moan.

This is not me. I do not lose control. Loss of control is for the weak and I am not weak.

I'm Callum fucking McCall.

Almost as if sensing my concern, she bends down and picks up the NDA and reads it. Out of the corner of my eye, I watch her eyes read line for line, waiting for any look of disappointment or concern. I keep waiting, but don't see it. Instead, I see... realization? Confirmation? Almost like she suspected something, and this document is what she needed to read.

She slides over to sit next to me and runs her hand up my leg.

Relief pours through me as I tilt my head, looking at her. "I'm glad you finally read it."

"Yea, probably not the best decision I made."

It feels as if a sharp blow has landed squarely on my chest.

Sensing it, she quickly adds, "Signing without reading first."

Feeling only a little better, I rest my hand on her leg and look out of the window. She didn't ask questions about the group clause, which is usually the first question that women ask when they read the NDA. Why didn't she? Did she not read it? See it? Is she trying to ignore it, hoping if she doesn't talk about it, then it won't exist?

The landscape is changing from buildings to trees, the closer we get to home. The usual calm feeling I get when I get closer to home is not there. Instead, it's replaced by worry. What if I screwed up? I pressed the men, really Jax, into presenting her with the paperwork. I was greedy and wanted her, even though we had all agreed to give it some time before we had another woman.

She leans her head against my shoulder and wraps her hands around my arm.

We pull in a few minutes later and when Brady moves to open her door; I stop him, wanting to do it myself.

She slips her hand in mine and I guide her up the back stairs.

"Are you ok?" she asks quietly.

I study her face intently, trying to decipher the emotions behind her eyes. "I'm uncertain."

"Uncertain?"

I sigh. "I can't seem to control myself around you, and it's putting me in a weird spot."

"A weird spot?"

Before I say too much, I open the door and a voice yells out from the kitchen.

Knox.

"How did it go? Did she say-" He slides into the room with his bountiful energy, but stops talking when he sees her.

"Oh. Hello there." A smile stretches across his face as his tone changes to mock innocence. "How was your evening?" he asks, grabbing her hand and planting a kiss on the top of it.

She's nearly radiating with a soft glow under his affection. "Good. Yours?"

"I've been waiting here on pins and needles to see what you'd say."

"Say?"

Face contorted, he looks at me just as Jax and Emmett walk into the room. "I haven't talked to her yet."

She looks between all of us, and the uneasy feeling that has been twisting in my stomach is back again. Why do I care so much if she walks away from us? I barely know her, so it wouldn't be that big of a deal if she said no and left.

That's a lie.

I don't know, but there is something about her. Something... I just can't put my finger on.

She looks like she's getting lost in her thoughts. "Everlee?"

"What? Huh?"

"Do you want something to drink?"

"Old Fashioned?"

Knox squeals. "Can we keep her?"

Jax glances at him disapprovingly. "She's not a pet."

With a swift movement, Knox grabs her hand and twirls her around, their faces inches apart as he dips her backwards. "I know, but one can hope."

Her lips part and her eyes darken as she stares at him, entranced by his wild smile and golden locks, no doubt. Her cheeks flush, just as he stands her back up, head in a daze.

Her furtive glances in my direction suggest a mix of curiosity and apprehension. She's still uncertain about our family dynamic and that's ok. She hasn't left yet, so there's still a chance.

For now.

Jax leads Emmett and the rest of us into the kitchen and she follows, taking the same seat at the bar she sat in only days ago.

Emmett sets five glasses onto the bar and begins prepping our drinks.

"Is everyone getting the same thing?" she asks, breaking the awkward tension in the room.

"It's our house drink," Knox beams.

Emmett gives her the first one, and we all watch her slowly tilt it back. I'm closest to her and watching her lips hit the edge of the glass... It's stupid the way my body reacts, so I look away and find Jax glaring at me.

"This is magical," she hums.

Emmett beams. "It's the cherries. Luxardo all the way."

She scoops it out with her finger and sucks it into her mouth. Her eyes nearly roll into the back of her head and so do ours, watching her and listening to her moans. Even

Jax is nibbling on his bottom lip. When he sees me watching him, he rolls his eyes.

"It was a really good cherry." She stifles a laugh.

"Get her another!" Knox cheers and Emmett jokingly slides the whole jar towards her.

She laughs and her eyes twinkle before she catches us all off guard. "So lay it on me."

I look at Jax, preparing to speak, but Everlee cuts me off. "From Jax. Doesn't he usually handle this sort of thing for you?"

Everyone's eyes are on me with a mixture of shock and awe. They- I'm- not used to being cut off. My words come out clipped. "Yes. Jax handles the terms of the arrangement."

EVERLEE - I PREFER PENII NOT PENISES

ARRANGEMENT? CURIOSITY IS KILLING me. I'm a cat walking la-ti-da into a den of lions. I just hope it doesn't get me killed.

Fucked to death, I'm ok with. It's been a while since I've felt an actual dick in me and Lizzy would be ecstatic to hear it's four. What will she say when I tell her about this? She'd lose her mind.

I feel a pang of... what? It's not guilt, or remorse, but I just remembered I signed an NDA. I can't tell her about this. How am I going to keep this from her? There's no way. She's my best friend. She'll know something is up. We share everything. I chuckle at my current predicament and realize we don't share *everything*.

"Let's finish our drinks and then we'll talk," Jax directs.

Callum appears to be the alpha of the group, which would make sense. He seems the one in control over everything with his rules, coupled with the way everyone looks at him to make decisions. He also naturally takes the seat at the end of the bar, and I realize now he was also sitting at the head of the table at Bo's tonight discussing whatever it was they were looking at. At least part of their night was talking about me, since he had to get permission from them to take me out. Although I'm getting the feeling that having him go down on me twice was not part of the agreement.

Jax would be his beta. The one the others look to when Callum isn't around, the one who handles the negotiations. Negotiations? I get the feeling the arrangement I'll be presented is a take it or leave it sort of thing, but a girl can try.

I don't know where Emmett and Knox rank, if they rank at all. Emmett sort of has his own thing with Bo's, and I'm not quite sure what Knox does. He seems to be the faithful, obedient server, but I have a feeling he's much more complex than that. He dealt with dickhead from the club without question. I get the impression he's efficient with that sort of thing, perhaps ex-military. Was his fun-going personality a facade?

He catches me looking at him and winks, then blows a kiss.

There's no way it's pretend. It doesn't mean he can't be both, just uncommon, I guess. I have no experience with any of this stuff, but I know everyone serves a role in the relationship. Is that what this is? A relationship?

I laugh since I'm basing all of this off the books I've read. In most cases, I wouldn't call myself sexually vanilla. I'm not experienced in group play or whatever you call it. It isn't an orgy, is it? Maybe I'd have to get my books and do some research if this is happening. Googling is not an option, because I'd end up on some site, get horny, masturbate and forget to do actual research. Although isn't that what happens when reading my books, too? The good ol' one handed read. Should be a hashtag created. Maybe there already is. I need to get back to the conversation with the boys and out of my head. I could be going down an unnecessary rabbit hole for no reason.

I finish the last of my drink and my stomach tightens into a ball of nerves as everyone looks at me with a mixture of glances. Emmett's is weary, Knox's is hopeful and Callum's... his is guarded. Is he angry with me?

This is not at all how I expected this night to go...

Jax calls my name. "Are you ready?"

I look around the room one more time. "Yes."

"I'll be in my room," Callum states without emotion. He reaches into his pocket and pulls out the NDA and another document, and hands them to Jax. He then reaches into his other pocket and pulls out my panties, and the room looks between us.

"You can keep those." I wink and I'm happy to see a smile tugging at his lips. He isn't mad at me, but uncertain. His word replays in my mind. He's nervous I can't handle the arrangement, but little does he know I've already talked myself into it while we were sitting around the bar silently. I want all these men, if that's what it ends up being. I know it's what I'm hoping at this point. Four men that are probably the hottest I've ever seen. Muscles, tattoos, and those eyes.

Callum tucks my panties back into his pocket and turns to leave the room, followed by Emmett and Knox.

"We'll go into the office." Jax points at the large glass paneled room off the kitchen.

I nod, too nervous to speak.

The office is as impressive as the rest of the house. Two of the walls are floor to ceiling glass panels and on the far side of the room are dark wood shelves with a mixture of books and other modern decor on it. In the center of the room is a large desk with a single chair behind it and, in front of it, four dark brown leather chairs.

"Please take a seat," he offers, then takes the seat beside me. I expected him to sit behind the desk, a show of authority and control, but Jax knows I'm no threat and feels I know my place. He's making it more intimate, making me feel more comfortable, and I appreciate that.

He flips the NDA open and looks at it, confirming my signature before we talk. Trust but verify, I suppose.

"Why the NDA?"

"I'm going to assume you've put some things together about us. We have certain kinks that not all people understand or accept, so we need to protect ourself and you as well. We don't kiss and tell, and want to make sure others don't as well."

I nod without speaking.

"Do you have other questions? I usually have a whole discussion planned, but you seem to have mixed things up a bit."

"Sorry." I fidget with my hands.

"Don't be sorry. It's nice to see Callum let down his guard, even though it bothers him."

"Why?"

"He needs structure. Control."

"I got that impression, based on some things he's said and done."

"I have to ask... only because it will change the tone of the conversation. Have you had sex?"

"I'm not a virgin." My head recoils in shock, not expecting that question.

He chuckles. "Sorry. I meant with Callum."

"Oh." Embarrassment flushes my cheeks as I wipe my hands down my face. "No. Not yet."

A smile flickers on his face, but then he shakes his head. I presume, trying to focus himself. "Let's get this over with, then. I don't want to be the one standing in the way of what Callum wants."

I suck in a breath.

"What theories have you drawn so far?"

I hesitate because if I'm wrong, I'll feel super embarrassed.

"Don't be shy. You can't say anything I haven't heard."

I swallow the lump in my throat. "That you all... share?"

A smile flickers across his face. "Anything else?"

"Callum seems to be in charge, followed by you. I haven't figured out Emmett and Knox's role yet."

He nods, not adding any other information. "Anything else?"

My eyes bulge out of my head. Is there something else? I'm sure there is, but I can't think of it right now, so I shake my head.

His hands reach across the space and grab mine, flipping it over and rubbing my palm. It's affectionate, but also sexy. I didn't think he was interested, but the way he's acted tonight before dinner and then now... his thumbs brush across my wrist and he pauses. "We're a group, a unit. Call it what you want. We share."

His thumb swiping across my wrist turns me on. Is the wrist an erogenous zone, because it's making my heartbeat quicken... or maybe it's the idea of having all four men to myself. Four cocks in this aching pussy.

"How does that make you feel?"

Excited. Scared. Like a little horn toad ready to get her freak on. Is this why Callum felt uncertain? Because he didn't think I'd be ready for this? How could I not be? These men are fucking gorgeous and they want me. Me!

I must look like a deer in headlights, because he chuckles. "You don't have to answer right now."

"I..." I start, then stop. "What else aren't you telling me?"

He nods and drops my hands.

This is it. The awkward elephant in the room. The one in the corner, sipping on her tea with a lace umbrella over her head, legs crossed, waiting with bated breath.

"This isn't a long-term relationship sort of deal. We have found it's better to only do it a few times at most. That way, no one gets too emotionally attached."

It feels like a gut punch. Did Callum think I'd turn it down because I'd want more than a bang? A *world changing, mind-altering bang*. One that would likely break me for all future sexual encounters. One that would be the epitome of all sexual relations for the rest of my life and one I could never talk about? I'd bang them then have to be let out into the world, searching for the same feeling, the same height of satisfaction. It would turn me mad with lust, cycling through guy after guy, looking for what I can't have. Send me into shady sex clubs. *Not all sex clubs are shady.* I agreed with myself, but how would a non-shady sex club benefit my internal monologue about me turning into a sex crazed spinster who'd be broken after my encounters with them? Encounters, because I will try to push it to the very max. He said a few. Not one or two, but a few. Few meant a small number of, but it was not an exact number and left open for interpretation of the word small. Small could be three... it could also mean three hundred. *If you were comparing it to three thousand.* Relative.

I have to bring myself back from the brink of the cliff I'm racing towards. I heard his unspoken words. Instead of stating the obvious, he tried to smooth it over, but what he really means is so the females don't get attached. Why wouldn't they? Having four desirable men to sexually ravage your body. Hell, I'm attached right now and have only had Callum tongue fuck me in the back of a car and in a makeshift changing room. Imagine what he could do if given enough space. Add in the others and actual dicks...

The elephant is now swiping hundred-dollar bills in the air with a gold chain around her neck.

"And if I want more than that?"

His lips pinch in a hard line.

"I see." Nothing.

He leans in close, his leg brushing the inside of mine. His hand rests on the space between my neck and my cheek. "I'd love to fuck those pretty little lips of yours," he says as his thumb pad traces over my bottom lip, pulling it down. He leans in closer. "I, too, want to make you moan around my cock."

My breath hitches at his words, but then he pulls back.

"Here's a document you can review. If you agree to this arrangement, you will need to sign this and also mark the things you'd like to do, not like to do, and maybe like to do."

I look over the document, and random things catch my attention like anal, edging, and double penetration. I fight the urge to look down. It's not like I have x-ray vision and can see my v-hole, to actually visualize two penii entering me. I call it penii even though I know it's not a word because I feel like it should be a word. Penises sounds too sussy.

He stands up. "Take a day or so to think about it." He chuckles. "Actually, take until the fourteenth. If you say yes, I can promise it will be a Valentine's Day you'll never forget."

Feeling a mixture of emotions, I stand and walk out of the room, looking over my shoulder briefly to see him staring at my ass. As I turn the corner, my eye contact never breaks from his. He's standing there in taut perfection. Goddamn, he, too, is hot as fuck. I'm going to hell.

EVERLEE - JUST SAY SIR AND I'LL GIVE YOU THE GODDAMN WORLD ON A PLATTER

I ONLY GLANCE AT the contract one time before I get to Callum's room. I knock, but the door is cracked, so I gingerly push it open and peek inside.

Mother Shitballs!

He's in the shower, music on, head up to the rainfall, hands pressed against his face and his... I have to lean against the door frame to help hold me up. His beautiful, beautiful cock. Hanging there begging to be touched. To make it come alive. And his tattoos. They're all over his torso, running down his hips, wrapping around his back. I forgot about them, because the business owner the world sees is always dressed in collared shirts and suits, but beneath his impeccable exterior lies a tattooed, enigmatic, and undeniably sexy man beast.

His dick is like a siren song calling me. It feels like my body is operating independently, and I'm merely a spectator to its actions, pulling me across the floor. Tossing the contract on the floor, I slip out of my clothes. I know this is most definitely breaking the rules, but fuck them. It will be up to him to stop me and I pray to all the Gods and Goddesses he doesn't, because I need to feel that thing inside of me. I need to get fucked. Maybe then it will take away whatever madness is making me want to agree to these terms. I know I'll want more. That's the only thing holding me back. I'm going to love it and want more. But I won't be able to have it. That is the part I have to come to terms with.

I slip into the shower behind him and reach my hands around his hips, then run them down his legs. He tenses for a moment, then relaxes. He turns, towering over me, his bright blue eyes staring at me as water drips off the tip of his nose over his pouty, parted lips.

"I didn't think you'd come."

"I haven't yet."

A deep, throaty laugh bounces around the walls.

I can't stand it any longer. Needing to feel him, I slowly drop to my knees, his cock already standing at attention. My goodness, it's huge. My hand wraps around his base as my eyes flit up to meet his. With the water pouring down on him, running from his hair, down his chest, he looks impossibly sexy right now, all muscles and tattoos. His hair is even darker and his eyes bluer.

A puff of air escapes from my lungs just before I press my lips to the tip of his cock.

"Everlee," he groans through set teeth.

"Hmm?" I ask, running my tongue along the underside and taking just his head in my mouth, swirling my tongue around it.

"I know we don't have the green light. You didn't sign the contract."

Is that why he looked the way he did when I walked in? I take him in my mouth, letting him hit the back of my throat, then drag him out slowly.

"Is that a problem?" I take him in my mouth again.

His words shudder in the slightest. "It's not following... the rules," he struggles to breathe out.

"We've already talked about this," I whisper against the head of his cock. A bead of arousal seeps out, so I swirl my tongue, lapping it up before I swallow him in again, letting him hit the back of my throat. My hand twists and runs down the length of his shaft each time I pull him out. "I can stop..."

He lines up his cock ready to slide into my mouth, but this time when he presses in, his hands tangle in my hair and satisfaction radiates through me.

He thrusts three times, hitting the back of my throat, making my eyes water. I try to relax so I can take him further, but then he pulls out. He swoops down and lifts me to standing and forces me back against the shower wall. The cold of the glass stings my hot skin, but only for a second. His mouth takes mine, his tongue forcing its way in while his hands grab my breasts. "Fucking perfect."

His lips trail down my jaw to my neck, where he bites and sucks, causing my knees to buckle briefly and a moan to escape my lips.

"I'm going to make you moan so much you won't be able to speak tomorrow and I'm going to fuck you so hard you won't be able to walk."

His words pulse through me and make my entire body feel like a live wire ready to explode, causing my arousal to gush out of me like freaking Niagara Falls running down my leg.

"Good girl," he mumbles against my neck, before his tongue swipes the water away before sucking the skin into his mouth again.

"Fuck me," I pant instead of plea.

"I plan to."

Need consumes me as I lift his chin and take his mouth with mine, hooking my legs around him. His hard cock presses right at my entrance, causing my hips to tilt forward. "No, no, no. We won't rush this. I shouldn't even be doing this, but you're like a drug I can't say no to. The boys will be pissed they aren't here, so I'm going to enjoy this as much as I can to help with the aftermath."

My body rocks against his, feeling the length of his cock sliding up and down between my wet pussy, brushing against my clit. I grab his shoulders and rock my hips harder and faster.

"You don't listen, do you?" He pulls away, leaving me panting. "Do you have any hard no's?"

"What?" I shake my head. "I don't know."

He tilts his head to the side. "Give me a safe word."

"Safe word?"

"Oh, baby." He brushes a kiss on my nose. "A safe word-"

"Shit. I know what a safe word is. You... this... my head is just discombobulated."

"Discombobulated?" He smiles, brushing his thumb across my cheek.

In a pulse of frustration and embarrassment, I push against his rock-hard chest, but he grabs my wrist, pinning me to him. "Safe word."

My head is spinning, so I spit out the first word that pops into my head. "Cupid."

He chuckles. "Cupid?"

"Sorry. It's that time of year."

"Don't apologize," he says, leaning down to take my mouth in his. This time, he's softer and more passionate. His kiss causes my head to spin and I whimper into his mouth. His body presses against mine as his cock rocks against my needy little clit.

"Your moaning is going to be the death of us all."

"Do you think..."

He pulls away and looks at me.

"Do you think they want to watch? Would you get in less trouble?" A tightness starts in my chest and pulses down my body. I can't believe I just asked that.

"Are you ok with that?"

"I'm not against... the sharing." Is this the wrong time to be having this conversation?

"But?"

"My problem is..." A smile tugs on my lips to hide the embarrassment ravaging its way through me. "The time limit set in place." Feeling more confident, the words rush out, "I haven't even had you all yet, but I know once I do, I'll want more."

His lips meet mine in a harsh, but brief, kiss. "You're mine tonight, but they can watch if it's what you want."

"How?"

"How do you want them to watch?" His brow furrows, confused by my question.

Chuckling, I shake my head. "What are my options?"

He smiles, the kind of smile that tells you, you're in over your head, but you know no matter what is said you won't care.

"We have the shower camera and intercom here. They can come into the room, or..." He pauses, studying my face.

"I've already signed the NDA and will sign the other contract tomorrow once I change a few things."

His laughter booms. "Of course you'll change something." He steps towards me, running his hand down my torso, rubbing his finger over my clit. "You're so wet."

I moan again. I've never realized how much I do that. If someone asked me before if I moan a lot, I'd have said no, but knowing how it affects these men, I'm acutely aware of it every time I do. Perhaps, it's simply that I haven't had a man's hands on me in months and they just stored themselves up in a little moan bank.

"The other option is a voyeur room." He reads the confusion on my face and continues, "It's like a regular bedroom, but there's two-way glass on the wall they can look through. We set the lights low so you can't see them, but they can see us. Unless you want to see them."

My eyes light up.

"You like that?"

Should I be so excited about that? My teeth scrape along my bottom lip. He presses his fingers into me, nearly lifting me off the ground, pulsing them in and out a few times. Knees getting weak, I wrap my arms around his neck for support the closer I get to climax.

"You aren't coming yet. Have you ever been edged?"

"I don't think so."

"I told you I was going to punish you for breaking the rules and now even worse for making *me* break the rules. You won't come until I let you come. I'm going to get you close and then stop. Over and over again until you can't fucking stand it. Then I'm going to fuck you so hard until you come around my cock that you're going to see stars, and then I'll fuck you some more."

I stare at him in shock. Needy, lustful shock and I can't wait.

He walks over to the intercom on the wall and presses a button. "Voyeur room. Now."

Jax chimes back a second later with a modicum of concern. "Did she sign?"

"Not yet. She wants to negotiate timing."

"Callum," he warns.

"We'll discuss later. If you want to watch me edge her, then fuck her, and listen to her moan, then meet me there in two minutes."

He flicks the shower off and scoops me up in his arms, not waiting for an answer.

My pulse is racing with excitement. Who am I right now? And fuck! I can't tell Lizzy about any of this. She'd be proud of me right now, my little cheerleader in the corner thrusting her fist into the air.

"How many rooms do you have?" I ask, tracing my finger around the tattoos on his chest.

He smiles, but doesn't answer.

The cool bite of the air outside of the hot steamy shower causes goosebumps to spread over my skin. He swings the bedroom door open, and I freak out, clutching to him.

He looks down at me with a quizzical brow. "You're concerned about someone in this house seeing me carry your naked ass into a room where they are about to see me kiss, lick, and fuck you?"

My head falls back dramatically, then pops back up quickly. "What are you going to do to me again?" I smile, letting my finger glide between his pecs.

"You have no idea, love. Just remember your safe word. You say it and I will stop immediately."

My body feels electrified right now. Every hair is standing on end, every nerve responsive and waiting. My heart is nearly pounding out of my chest. We pass several closed doors, then he stops in front of a door on the left.

He bends down to grab the handle with his hand that's supporting my ass, and a moment later, we're walking into a dimly lit room. It's huge, probably the size of two rooms in one, and in the middle is a large circular bed with red satin sheets. Three of the walls are draped with decorative black curtains, with several dressers placed around the room.

He tosses me on the center of the bed and my eyes immediately settle on the wall to my left, which is made of large glass panels. The fear and hesitation I felt coming up here is quickly replaced with excitement. I've never done anything like this before, nor had I ever thought I would, but right now... I have to pinch myself to make sure I'm awake because this doesn't feel real.

"Are you ok?" Callum asks, walking over to me. Damn, he looks delicious, like a sexy Greek god, muscles cut, sharp jaw line with his dark hair slicked back like a mafia king. Ok Greek God, mafia king... I don't know. So many thoughts bombarding me right now! I want to lick and suck every tattoo on his body, then climb on top of his cock and ride him until I come and then come again. *While his friends watch*, my subconscious adds.

"Yes. Just waiting for you."

His quiet laugh hides the deep growl from within his chest. But I heard it. I felt it.

He slowly crawls onto the bed, mounting me, with his cock laying on my stomach. He grabs my wrists and lifts them above my head, pinning them to the pillow behind me as he leans down and whispers, "Remember your safe word."

I decide to the test the waters because I'm liking the way it feels to see the fire in his eyes when I say the two magic words. "Yes, Sir."

His eyes catch mine and they don't disappoint.

"Say it," he commands softly.

"Cupid," I whisper.

"Good girl." He grabs something above my head and a second later, I feel it being clasped around my wrists. Curious, I tilt my head back and confirm... pink fuzzy handcuffs.

He slides down my body, taking my left breast in his mouth, while his other hand teases and squeezes the right, rubbing the sensitive bud between his fingers. A heat shoots through my core, straight to my clit, making my body light up like fireworks. My back arches off the bed, pressing my breast further into his mouth. "Moan for us," he softly commands.

The word *us* throws me for a loop then I remember. They're watching me. My head falls to the side, looking at the darkened glass, wondering if they see me, because I can't see them.

"Do you want to see them?" Callum asks, almost reading my mind.

I look back at him, asking myself how far I'm willing to go down this rabbit hole when the word escapes my lips. "Yes."

A second later, their faces are there.

My guys.

Well, my future guys, because looking at them all sitting there with their cocks in their hand watching me causes the flurry of butterflies in my stomach to go wild.

"Everlee," Jax says, slowly stroking himself.

"Hey Ali," Knox says, hand paused.

"Trouble," Emmett says, and I can't help but smile.

Callum takes two fingers and guides my chin back to him. "Shall we?"

"Please."

He smirks and quickly turns me on the bed, the satin making me slide around like water. He aims my pussy right at the men. I can't see much, but I can tell their posture has changed. Changed for me. I can feel their eyes raking across my body, lusting after it, and the nerves I thought I would feel are replaced by something else entirely. I feel... powerful. Sexy.

Callum backs off the bed, pulling me with him so my ass is on the edge and his knees are on the ground. "Shall I make her come this way, boys?"

"No," they all say in unison.

I pop my head up and stick my tongue out at them, eliciting a laugh from the group. I'm still watching them as Callum's tongue swipes up from the bottom. Oh, fuck me. Pretty sure my eyes just rolled into the back of my head.

"She tastes so fucking good." He hooks my legs over his shoulders and his arms around my legs, holding me to his face. He licks and swirls his tongue around my needy little cunt like it's his last meal. The moans continue as I'm inching closer and closer to release. Needing to feel a modicum of control, I rotate my shoulders so my handcuffed hands latch onto his hair, holding him in place while I fuck his face.

I hear someone say, "She's getting close," but I'm not sure who it is.

Callum pulls back, my body still thrusting like a dog without balls humping the air. My body and my mind finally catch up to the fact Callum has pulled away just enough so that I can't even feel his breath on me, because that's where I was.

Am.

One breath and I'm coming so fucking hard. This has been hours in the making, ever since he left me wanting in that changing room. My hands eagerly try to find my clit to finish what he started, but it takes a second too long to figure it out with the handcuffs and Callum is throwing them over my head again.

"You will learn to follow the rules," he growls.

"Rules are meant to be broken!" I snap back.

"And so are you," he threatens. "If you try to come again without my permission, the punishment will be a lot worse than the edging."

Eyes glaring at him, I suck on my bottom lip, causing him to let out a heady groan.

"I want to feel that pretty little mouth around my cock again. I want to feel it hit the back of your throat and I want you to choke on it."

He stands up, helping me off the bed, and I drop to my knees faster than I ever have before. Something about his words sends me over the edge and makes me feel things I've never felt. "That's it, good girl." He strokes my hair and I nearly melt into a puddle on the floor.

It takes me a minute to position my hands around his cock because of the cuffs, but I make it work. I run my tongue along the length of his shaft before swirling it around his head, sucking it in like a lollipop. He lets out a gasp at the same time his hands tangle in my hair.

The sounds he makes and the way his body moves for me, because of me, makes me want more. I repeat the same steps over and over again, teasing him. If he wants to edge me, I can edge him right back.

"Shit, Everlee."

I can't take any more. I take his full cock in my mouth, relaxing my throat so he can get as deep as possible. His legs give the lightest shudder as I hear a groan escape his lips. The boys moving out of the corner of my eye grab my attention for a second, and they give me fire. I bob on Callum harder and faster and watch their hands move faster. I have the power of sucking four dicks at once and I can make them all come together.

Need consumes me, and I whine out.

"Not yet!" Callum pulls himself out of my mouth and tosses me back on the bed.

He climbs down my body like a man on a mission and thrusts his tongue into me. "Fuck!" I scream out, my legs clutching to his ears like a pair of earmuffs. My ass lifts off the ground and with it, Callum. I sit up and realize I'm vertically fucking his face. The boys, right in front of me, their eyes wide in amazement. I want to lean back, but if I do, I know we'll topple back to the bed. "I'm about to come," I cry out.

We crash back to the bed and I think he's going to pull away again, but he commands me to come and that's all I need. He sucks my clit as he inserts two fingers. My body is moving, writhing in pain and lust. I'm so close I feel like I'm going to explode, like I'm going to burst at the seams. He adds a third finger, and the pressure is almost too much. His moves are precise, but quick. He pulls out a finger, curves the two remaining, finding that magical spot, and a deep guttural sound emerges from deep inside of me. I struggle to find anything to grab, my toes and my fingers curling, the muscles in my body tight. "Oh, God!"

"I'm your God right now."

My eyes lock with his, my chest still heaving as my body is riding the wave, lost in a state of euphoria. Seconds turn to hours turn to days. I'm lost. When my body comes down from the biggest and best orgasm I've ever had, I feel a tingly in my toes and fingers and a throbbing in my core.

I can't even catch my breath before I hear the click of the locks on the handcuffs. With my hands free, I roll to my side and find him sheathing his cock in a rubber. "I'm going to fuck you now." He crawls onto the bed and over me, murmuring against my neck. "I'm going to make you come so hard again that you'll be seeing stars."

Even though I've just had the absolute best orgasm of my life, I need more. I want more. I need to feel his cock seated deep inside of me. My body is already moving again on its own like a sex crazed animal in heat. *This is what six months without a dick will do to you.*

If I can't get them to agree to give me more time, then this is it, and I need to make it count.

"I need your dick in me now." I sit up, looking at him.

"Ask nicely," he toys.

"Please put your dick in me and fuck me like there's no tomorrow, so I may cream all over it. I want my arousal running down your cock to your balls. I want your thick, delicious cock so far inside of me I can taste it in my mouth. I want-"

"Fuck Everlee. Just say sir and I'll give you the goddamn world on a platter."

"Sir."

The blunt end of his cock presses against my soaking wet pussy and I shift, but I don't have to wait. He plunges inside of me so hard and so fast that the sound which passes through my lips is unlike anything I've ever heard. My body is alive. I want to sing out in jubilation as every fiber of my being is electrified.

He stills for a second, letting my body adjust to the size of his girth. He's much larger than monster BOB, which is my biggest. The pressure is intense, but he's my God right now. My body is shuddering with delight. He pulls out slowly, then slams in again, holding himself there. Watching his cock move inside of me, he moves in rhythm, harder and faster.

"I've missed dick," I mumble out by accident.

Fortunately, I don't think he heard through the sounds of his own grunts and groans. In one swift motion, he flips us over, his cock still pressed into me. Straddling him now, I sink further onto him, our chests heaving. I take this moment to appreciate the sight of him laying underneath me, my palms pressed into his chest, his eyes sparkling.

"You're so fucking beautiful," he says, grabbing my legs.

I slowly rock, gyrating my hips back and forth, savoring every delicious inch of him. "Oh, my..."

His hands clamp to my thighs. "You're so tight. You feel so good wrapped around me."

I slowly pop my body off and slide back onto him, causing him to let out a low moan. "Now who's moaning?" I tease.

A second later, the bed is rotating, catching me off guard.

"We want to see your face while you fuck him," Jax says through the intercom. His hand is pressed against the wall, which I assume is the control for the bed.

I feel like a queen right now. I sit back on Callum's cock and run my hands over my breasts as I rock my hips back and forth, putting on a show for the others.

"Touch yourself," Knox chimes.

I look at him through the glass and watch him stroke himself.

Obeying his wish, my hands slide down, finding my clit, and begin to rub. It's still hypersensitive from my last orgasm, but I don't care. My body needs it. I need it. They need it.

Tingles prickling through me, I circle faster and faster as my hips move with the same speed. My free hand grabs my breast, pinching my nipple as I bounce on Callum. His hips thrust up, causing me to crash back on him. My hands press to his chest for support, raising off him just enough so he can fuck me from underneath. A mixture of sounds tumble from my lips again and again. He leans up, taking my breast in his mouth, swirling his tongue over my nipple.

"Oh... my..." My body is getting close again. It's like that deep wave you know is going to take you over the edge of the fucking world. "I'm about to... come... again."

He flips us over and rams into me harder and faster than before. The look on his face is pure fire.

Lust.

Need.

I cry out as he picks up even more speed, the sound of sex bouncing off the walls as his balls slap hard against my ass.

My arms latch around his neck as I hook my ankles around his back. I watch the way his eyes flicker and notice the wrinkle that appears on his forehead. I listen to the sounds he makes, the grunts and groans, the feel of his biceps in my hands. If this is all I have, I need to remember it. I will remember it.

My legs inch up higher, giving him more access. His finger finds my clit, and he works it, but it only takes two circles and I'm screaming out his name. The pressure inside of me builds and then he comes. There's a low groan that rips through him, vibrating my very core. I lean up, pressing my lips to his in the most passionate post coital kiss I've ever experienced. His chest presses against mine, and I can feel his heartbeat pounding as our breathing slows.

"Everlee. You're worth every rule I've broken tonight."

All I can do is smile, since my tongue refuses to make words. I feel like one of those air blown things at car dealerships, their arms and legs just a bunch of mush being blown around. After a few moments, I look over at the window and see the boys sitting there, not moving. Part of me feels guilty they aren't here with me, but the other part knows my body literally cannot function with four of them right now. It would be too much coming off a six-month hiatus.

Callum kisses my forehead, bringing me back to him.

"Let's get you washed up."

I don't know how much time passes. My body is spent and my head is woozy from that in-between state of awake and asleep. The place where you feel like you're on a merry-go-round that's descending further and further into the dark abyss. That's where I am.

I'm still vaguely aware of what's going on around me, but I'm happy. Satisfied. I can't remember the last time I felt this satiated. I feel like a limp noodle. A happy limp noodle that's just been thrown against the wall to see if it's done and yes, I'm done.

My body is rocking back and forth, as the opening and closing of doors sound around me, but I don't open my eyes until I feel myself being submerged in warm water.

I open my eyes and see Callum standing there in all his naked glory, smiling down at me. "You rest. We're going to take care of you."

We're...

The smell of lavender and lemon grass waft up as I continue to sink further into the tub. A pair of hands rub on my feet, another on my shoulders, and a third lathering up a washcloth. I wonder where the fourth person is, but my question is answered when I feel him slide into the tub behind me, holding me against his chest, so I don't sink under the water.

He gives soft commands to wash and rub and then I'm gone.

EVERLEE - I'M VANILLA AS FUCK

THE SMELL OF COFFEE and bacon wafting through the air wakes me up. Confused, I open my eyes and quickly remember I'm at Callum's house. Or their house? I don't know what to call it.

It's early because the sun is barely beginning to peek out from behind the veil of darkness. Feeling a prickly feeling on my back, I roll over and find Callum sitting up in the bed, tattooed chest exposed, with his e-reader in hand, wearing a pair of glasses. Just behind his ear is a hint of silver weaved through his dark locks. How is it possible he could get any hotter? I lift the covers just enough to see he's wearing a pair of tight black boxers that fit low on his hips, exposing the forkalicious v that is like an arrow, directing needy cunts like mine to the man candy below.

Am I salivating?

"Good morning." He smiles.

"Yes," I mumble, still drowsy, before realizing it was a statement, not a question. "Good morning," I correct, rolling onto my stomach, looking at him.

"How do you feel?" He places his e-reader on the nightstand beside him, along with his glasses.

"Good." I want to scream fucking great, but I feel that would be too much energy for this early in the morning. "Did you all wash me last night?"

He chuckles. "I hope that wasn't a problem. They wanted to take care of you."

"It's ok." I smile, closing my eyes for a second.

"There's coffee on the table beside you, and Emmett is fixing some breakfast downstairs."

"How does it feel?" I mumble into the pillow before rolling to sit up.

"How does what feel?" There is a sense of reservation and caution in his voice.

"To have a fantastic cock." My eyes bulge out of my head as I swallow the mortification boiling inside of me. "Shit. I mean cook. To have a fantastic cook at your beck and call?"

He smiles as he rolls on his side, letting his finger lazily stroke across my collarbone. "The cock... pretty fantastic and the cook isn't so bad either."

His breath smells minty fresh, which reminds me that mine does not. Needing to put space between us stat, I roll out of bed, because if not, I'll be crawling on top of him and sinking onto that delicious cock in about six point nine seconds. His last thoughts of me can't be stinky breath McGee. "You're dangerous," I mumble.

He pumps his eyes at me as they rake over my body. "You look good," he says, rolling out of bed.

Looking down, I notice I'm wearing a pair of his boxers and one of his t-shirts. When I look back up to say something, he's stretching his long, tattooed torso towards the sky.

Heaven help me.

He looks over his shoulder with a wicked gleam in his eye and I hurriedly turn away.

Devil!

He's the devil in a beautiful man's body. I can already feel myself getting moist at just the sight of him. "Where are my clothes from last night?" I ask, voice wavering as I look around the room, needing to change the conversation.

"I had Brady pick you up some this morning." He points to the bench at the end of the bed.

"This morning?" Grabbing my phone and ignoring the three missed text messages and one missed call from Lizzy, I retort, "It's just past six in the morning."

"We know a place." He offers nothing else as he walks across the room to his dresser, slipping on a pair of black joggers and a gray shirt that fits more like a schmedium the way it hugs his biceps and pecs.

Glory be. I'm screwed.

I slip on the very cute black leggings and gray sweater dress with a pair of black flats. The seamless fit of everything should be a cause for concern, but it seems to match Callum's meticulous nature perfectly.

"I'll meet you downstairs when you're ready." He nods. "Also, there's an extra toothbrush and brush in the bathroom if you need it."

"Do you do this for all the women that stay the night?" I tease.

"We rarely allow that." He closes the door behind him and I'm stuck in the middle of the room with my jaw on the ground. What does it mean that I've stayed the night twice, and we aren't anything official?

I'm getting ahead of myself. Needing to freshen up, I pad across to the bathroom and brush my teeth and comb my hair. The girl staring back at me in the mirror looks happy. Satiated. Almost glowing. With a small pinch, I give my cheeks a rosy color, then make my way downstairs to a full kitchen. All the men are sitting around the oversized bar sipping their coffee and tea, reading the paper, and doodling.

"Good morning," they all say in near unison.

A blush creeps onto my face. Why am I being so shy around them now? Especially after what happened last night?

"Do you like pancakes, egg, sausage and cheese?" Emmett asks, both of his palms pressed onto the counter, causing his biceps to flex. His hair is still wet from a morning shower and slicked back with the hint of a five o'clock shadow on his face. He reminds me of a sexy lumberjack only he cooks instead of chops wood.

I nod, unable to form words with my mouth or tear my gaze away.

"Good. I made you the Emmett special."

"It's so good," Knox exaggerates.

"It's ok," Jax teases, tossing a side eye at Emmett.

"It's like heaven in your mouth," Callum notes.

My eyes shoot over at him. He's watching me with his usual intense gaze. "Heaven in my mouth was last night." Someone blows out a low breath, chuckling. I have to assume it's Knox, but I don't look away from Callum to find out. "Sounds delicious." I sit on an empty stool at the bar and Emmett slides a plate over to me.

"It's like a sausage, egg and cheese biscuit, only it's on pancakes."

When I take a bite, all the flavors hit me at once and it's really like heaven in my mouth and a fucking whimper escapes. This is not me. I rarely do that, but my God he is a fantastic chef. Have you ever had something so good your body just sings and rejoices? There's a gospel choir in my mouth singing the praises of this damn delicious concoction.

Realizing the mood in the room has shifted, I look up and see the men's hungry gazes on me. I want them. This. I just want it for longer than they want to give it to me and I have to be ok with that.

Can I?

A few nights of damn near guaranteed mind-blowing sex only to walk away from it and never experience it again? I have to talk to Lizzy about it, but need to figure out a way that doesn't violate the NDA.

Stupid NDA.

"I have a question."

"Yes, buttercup?" Knox says with his devilishly charming grin.

"Why the safe word last night?"

"Yes, Callum, why the safe word?" Knox turns his entire body to look at him.

Callum shoots a glance at Knox, who turns back to face me, pulling his lips.

I can't help but smile before I look at Callum, who isn't speaking.

Jax enters the conversation. "Because he had plans for other things, but he lost control."

"I didn't!" Callum interjects.

Jax looks at him coolly over his shoulder, clearly not as nervous speaking his mind as Knox is. "It's ok to lose control every once in a while."

Callum rolls his eyes.

"What else were you planning on doing?"

All the boys look at one another before Jax answers for the group. "We'll save it for when you sign the papers. We don't want to ruin the surprise."

The kitchen falls into silence as we all think about what that means. After last night and some comments made, I'm beginning to think I'm in fact sexually vanilla, and they are some sort of delicious dark chocolate. While nervous, I definitely want a taste.

It's like that moment in my smut groups where I thought I read spicy books because there was a sex scene and they said cock and pussy two times, so I asked for smut books and then HOLY FUCK. My subconscious is rolling on the floor laughing at me because I had no idea what smut was until I knew. It's like hello cliff. Let's take a free dive off of you. Fortunately, my smutty social media groups were on point and enlightened me. They said 'Here. Hold my vibrator.'

Then.

Then I knew what smut was.

I feel like I'm reliving that situation now, thinking I was maybe a sexual milk chocolate, maybe like a white chocolate with a swirl, but now these guys... yea. I'm vanilla as fuck.

When I finish my sandwich, and before I leave, I pull Jax aside. In the craziness of last night, I misplaced the form I need to mark and sign, but I also wanted to clarify what I can and cannot say about last night. While he's met Lizzy, he doesn't fully grasp the connection she has with my sex life and she'll be able to see right through any lie I try to tell her. She'll know I had sex, then put two and two together and come up with Callum and if I try to deny it, she'll only become a dog with a bone and not let go until she gets to the bottom of it.

Jax allows me to tell her- if *she* brings it up- that Callum and I had sex, but gives me strict guidelines on everything else. No mention of group play, the room, the rest of them, the contract, or the fact there's even an NDA to begin with.

I understand why they have an NDA. They have a kink that few people understand and they don't want it getting out and staining their reputation in the business world. Which speaking of, I'm curious how many pots they have their hands in. I know of at least Vixen and Bo's, but I feel like there are more. All upscale, with a certain class to it, and they're planning on something else.

CALLUM - LYING TO MYSELF

As soon as the front door clicks, all the guys look at me, but no one speaks for a moment. If we had a clock on the wall, the tick tick tick of the seconds passing would echo loudly through this room, but we don't.

"What are you doing?" Jax asks point blank, holding nothing back.

"I don't know."

"You fucked her last night, and she didn't sign."

"So." Knox twirls his cup in his hand. "We watched, and I didn't hear you complaining about it."

"Shut the fuck up," Jax bats his hand in Knox's direction. It's more a statement of frustrated friendship than anger. Knox and Jax have a bond that has been forged over the years that goes deeper than any of us, but nevertheless, Knox loves to annoy the shit out of Jax, and he makes it easy.

"I'm just speaking the truth," he says, throwing his hands into the air and walking over to stand next to Emmett.

"Do you think she's going to sign?"

"Yes. But she wants more. That's the only reason she didn't sign last night."

"More?" Jax drops his head.

"I'll give you the goddamn world on a platter..." Knox says in a deep voice, mocking me.

Jax cuts his eyes at me, like Knox is my responsibility.

"I nearly came when you said that," Knox continues, squeezing Emmett's shoulders from behind, like Emmett's his bodyguard.

"Seriously. Shut the fuck up," Jax says, pushing away from the counter, causing Knox to duck behind Emmett. "I'm not coming after you. I'm just going for a run."

"Built up sexual frustration? I get it, bro. I'll come with," Knox offers.

"Hard pass."

"What the hell, man?"

"I need space from you," Jax chuckles, shaking his head.

"Fine. I'm going for a run too. You can't stop me from doing that. And if we accidentally, not on purpose, happen to be running the same direction, then that will be a surprise to me."

"You're an idiot."

Knox just shrugs and runs up the stairs, cutting Jax off.

"Remind me why we keep him around?" Jax asks.

"Because you need my bubbly personality to add a small glimmer to your rusted soul," he calls from upstairs.

Jax mumbles something as he walks up the stairs while Emmett and I both chuckle.

"I'm surprised Jax hasn't killed him yet," Emmett says, drying the last plate and putting it in the cabinet.

"For all his grumbly talk, he would miss Knox too much if Knox was anything different than the pain in the ass he is."

"It's too early for all of those words." Emmett walks around and sits beside me at the bar.

"What's up?"

"Just checking on you, brother. Trouble seems to be mixing things up around here."

A breath blows out of my nose.

He claps his hand on my shoulder. "I haven't seen you like this. It's a good thing."

"I don't know what it is about her. I mean..." I shake my head. "I've heard of instant love and I'm not saying that's what this is, but... it's definitely instant something. I saw her on the cameras when she got to the Cupid party, and there was something about her. She seemed broken and sad... but not in a bad way. I mean, I know that sounds bad, but... I don't know." A sigh blows from between my lips. "I can't explain it, but I just want to fight her battles for her. She seems like she's been through it, but she's a fighter."

Emmett laughs.

"It's like I want to hold her and comfort her, while at the same time, fuck her and break her."

"Yea. She seems different from the other girls we've had. They were eager to be pleased, but Everlee... she definitely wants to be pleased, but she also seems to enjoy pleasing."

My hand latches on Emmett's arm. "She sucks cock like a fucking pro. E, I swear. She sucked my cock into her mouth and I about fucking came. In like two seconds."

"We saw. We had bets."

"Fuckers."

He laughs. "I will say it seems very natural with her here. We haven't ever let anyone stay the night and she has twice already and... I love it. It's just... natural."

"We can't let ourselves get attached. This is a temporary thing. It always is. We have rules so we don't get hurt again."

"I know."

We stare at each other without speaking. I don't know what he's thinking, but I know what's on my mind...

I hope I'm not lying.

EVERLEE – I WILL NOT MASTURBATE AT WORK

WHEN I GET HOME, I toy with the idea of taking a shower, but part of me doesn't want to wash off the remaining lavender scent on my skin. A reminder of last night that I want to hold on to for as long as possible. When I get to work, I text Lizzy, letting her know I'm safe, which results in an immediate call.

I'm chuckling when I answer the phone. "Hello?"

"Where the hell have you been?"

"Good morning to you, too."

"No. No. Nope. Spill."

"What are you talking about?" I try to play coy as best I can.

"Hooker, please. I know you were hoeing it up last night with Mr. Fancy Pants."

"How would you know something like that?"

"The looks you two were casting. How you came back all hot and bothered from the bathroom. How he demanded he was taking you home."

The longer I'm quiet on the phone trying to figure out how to tell her, the more excited she gets. I can nearly feel her bouncing through the phone. "Can you do lunch today?"

"Hell to the fuckin' yea, I can! Where are you taking me?"

"Meet you at the salad place at the corner of Third street, say noon?"

"Yasss Queen! I'm so happy your pussy got pummeled last night. Ciao Chica!" She hangs up before I can say anything else. I'm still smiling when I open my laptop and flip through a few emails trying to read them, but failing miserably.

After the fifth time I've read the same email, I reach into my bag and pull out the contract. Maybe if I just go through and check the boxes, then I'll be able to focus on my work.

My subconscious takes her spot on the floor to laugh at me.

Reading down the list, I check the boxes for yes, no, and maybe. Even though I've been trying to tell myself I'm not sure I'm going to do this, the other part of me is yelling to do the damn thing.

What if I can make it so good for them, they change the rules for me? This would no longer be a few times thing, but a more long-term kind of thing. What would it be like? A sex movie reel flickers through my mind. Sex in the kitchen. Sex in the voyeur room. Sex in the shower, bathtub, balcony- I'm sure they have a balcony. Sex in Vixen. We would just be having lots of sex all the time everywhere.

What would it be like to date club owners?

They'd be gone every Thursday through Sunday night with half-dressed women throwing themselves at them, because come on, who wouldn't? Would they eventually find one they wanted more than me? What would my future look like? I'd always planned on getting married and having kids. With them, that doesn't seem to be an option because I can't marry four of them, and kids. I laugh. How would you explain that? Whose would it be? Could you imagine little Sammy or Juliette going into school and telling everyone they have four daddies and one mommy? During parent-teacher conferences, five of us show up? On emergency contacts, only the mother and father can be listed. Whose name would go there?

My head collapses onto my desk.

"Are you ok?"my assistant asks, walking into the room.

"Yes." I look up and realize what's on my desk and quickly shift papers on top of it and act like I'm cleaning up my desk. "What's up?"

"A group of us are going out to lunch. You haven't left your office all morning, so I wanted to see if I needed to pick you up something."

"What?" I look at the time on the corner of my computer and it's almost lunchtime. Holy cow! "Sorry. No. All good. I have lunch plans."

"With a special someone?" Her eyebrows pump up and down.

"No." I chuckle.

"Oh. You seem..." she struggles with the words to say, then just spits them out. "You're glowing, so I thought that..."

She thought I got laid! Well, I did. But freakin' aye! Do I have a billboard attached to my chest that says ask me about my pussy?

She starts to walk out, then taps on the door frame. "Oh. Angelica from Meyers wants to know who to put as your plus one for tomorrow's dinner."

Shit. I completely forgot about the customer's dinner. "Let me get back to you?"

"Sure. She just requested it by four this afternoon."

Shit! Shit! Shit! I had the perfect plan to flake out on dinner, which started yesterday and I completely forgot. There's no way they'd buy I'm sick now... especially after my new sex glow. I grumble as I pull the contract out from under the stack of papers.

"It's all your fault." I point accusatorially at the paper.

Then an idea hits me. Maybe Callum will go with me. Taking a few deep breaths, I flip my phone back over and dial him up. Thankfully, he dropped his number to me this morning in case I had questions about the contract. He answers on the third ring. "Everlee? Are you ok?" His voice is tense.

"Yes. Yes. I'm fine, but need a favor." I bite the inside of my cheek as nerves get the better of me.

"Anything."

"I need you to be my date at a dinner tomorrow."

"On Valentine's Day?" his words are hesitant.

"Yeaaa... for a customer meeting at work."

"Oh."

His voice drops an octave, like when you have to deliver bad news, but you're trying to think of a way to spin it. I'm sure there are rules or something about dates. They don't date, they just have really great sex.

"Listen, I know the rules and everything. I just committed a while ago to attend this event because it's one of our biggest customers. I thought by the time V- day rolled around, I'd be in a relationship, but I'm not. With no prospects. I can't bring Lizzy, because she's been my plus one so many times, they think I'm an 'in the closet lesbian', which who knows maybe I am which is why I haven't found a man and I had this plan to fake an illness yesterday, but I completely forgot because I was so excited about dinner at Bo's and now this morning they see my new just been fucked glow, so there's no way I can pull off being sick." I take a deep breath once the word vomit stops.

"That's a lot to unpack."

"Sorry."

"Do you think you're a lesbian? I mean, this could really change things?" Humor dances in his voice.

"Callum," I scold.

"I'm kidding. I knew you weren't after the way you sucked my cock last night."

A puff of air escapes my lips.

"You like that, do you? Do you want me to tell you I'm sitting at my desk at Vixen with my pants pulled down and my hard cock in my hand, pumping it, thinking of your perfect little pussy?"

My thighs clench together. "Callum," I warn.

"How I can't wait until you're sliding onto it again? How I can't wait to watch the others with you? Taking you in every hole you have at the same time."

"Callum," I breathe out, pinching my eyelids together and gripping the edge of my desk. I *will not masturbate at work*. I *will not masturbate at work*.

"How-"

"Jesus Fuck Callum. When I see you, I'm going to-"

"Come all over me?"

Unable to take anymore, I disconnect the call and avoid throwing my phone across the room like a hot potato. My skin is on fire, my heart is racing and I'm fairly certain I look like I pissed myself with the probable moisture that has leaked through my skirt. My fault for not wearing underwear today, but this skirt is one of those kinds you can't wear underwear with.

My phone chimes with a dick pic and my knees buckle.

Fucking hell.

> **Everlee:** *What the fuck are you trying to do to me, Callum?*

> **Callum:** [wink face emoji] *That's my way of saying I'd go with you tomorrow night. I just need to figure out how to break it to the boys.*

> **Everlee:** *Would it help if I signed the contract?*

Three dots appear, then disappear. Then appear again. I stare at my phone, waiting for a response, but the dots keep coming, then going, coming, then going. Curiosity and anticipation are killing me.

My phone dings, and I look at it, only to find Lizzy asking where I am. Shit!

Everlee: *Leaving now. Be there in three!*

I grab the list off my desk and stuff it into my purse because the last thing I need is to leave it lying around and have someone accidentally pick it up.

No, thank you!

A few minutes later, I'm walking into the salad shop and find Lizzy in the corner by the front door with her arms crossed. "You better have a good reason you left me waiting."

"It was five minutes," I say, looking at my phone. Callum still hasn't responded, causing disappointment to weave its way through my body, to my stomach where it tightens into a knot. Why am I letting myself get worked up over this? I shove my phone in my pocket and give Lizzy a hug.

She grabs me by the shoulders, looks me up and down, pinches my cheeks and smells my hair. I'm sure people in the salad shop are wondering what in the hell is going on.

She points her finger at my chest, just above my breast and says, "You've been laid."

"What?" I grab her arm. "Do you want to yell that a little louder so everyone else can hear?"

She takes in a deep breath.

"Don't you dare."

"Or what?" she teases, her eyebrows raising to her forehead. "Everyone should know you got a piece of ass." She grabs my wrists, pulling them down, bringing our faces to an inch apart. "How was he? Oh my God. I bet he was amazing. He looks like he would be."

"I never said we did."

"Hooker, please. You and I both know you got your little kitty kitty taken care of last night. So spill."

Thank God Jax allowed me this one thing, because she'd be impossible. I'd have to avoid her for a week or more for her not to pick up on it. "It was amazing."

"Yes!" she yells, thrusting her fist into the air, garnering several curious glances. She chuckles meekly. "My favorite author just released her book a week early! Yesss." She pumps her fist in the air again.

People turn back to what they were doing and her gaze lands on me. "Can you believe them? Authors releasing books early is exciting!"

"But yours didn't. Your feelings are hurt over something you just made up." I laugh at her. She's complete chaos, and I love it. She always has been. We were and still are inseparable. In school, we were known as the dynamic duo and teachers knew we could never be in class together. One year in tenth grade, they accidentally put us in the same chemistry class and so, of course, we partnered up. Almost set the school on fire. To be fair, the gas line was faulty. At least that's the story we're sticking to.

We order our salads and find a table in the corner. "So?" she asks.

I roll my eyes, both excited and not excited to tell her. I don't want her getting her hopes up about this relationship since it won't last very long. Maybe it's just what I need, though. The hump I need to get over to help me get back out there. Literal and figurative hump.

But this hump is going to break me for all future humps. Gahh!

She clears her throat, bringing me back.

"So after we left, he was planning on taking me back to my house, but then we got to talking, then he..."

Lizzy has a fork of salad in her mouth, frozen, but she motions for me to continue with her other hand.

My eyes get big and my head bobbles from side to side.

And then her eyes get big with understanding. "In the back seat of his car? Where was the driver? You didn't do it in front of him, did you?"

Her question about the driver told me there's no way I could ever tell her about the situation with the other three guys... even if I could. She joked about it before, but that's when it was only a joke and not for real. "He was standing outside on the sidewalk." My mouth pulls to the side as my stomach tightens, remembering the start of my wild night.

"Callum was just like yo dude park right here while I have my dessert? Go wait outside in the frigid cold?"

"Not quite like that, but kind of."

"So you." She props her arm on the table, leans across and whispers, "Got your little boom boom yum yummed, parked on the side of the street with the driver just chilling outside waiting, and people walking by?"

I nod, taking a bite of food, knowing it won't hide the blush from my cheeks.

"Kinky."

She plops back in her seat and takes another bite of food. "Continue," she says in a very diplomatic voice, waving her hand like the Queen would.

I'm smiling so much my cheeks are hurting. "So then he surprised me and took me ice skating."

My phone dings.

Callum.

Callum: *Where are you?*

Everlee: *Salad Shop eating lunch.*

I answer without thinking, then put my phone back on my lap. I wasn't mad at him, but I was a little irritated about the whole bubble incident earlier.

"But you weren't in the clothes for that."

I shake my head so I can focus on Lizzy. "I know... so he bought me some and then..." My head face plants into my palm.

"No," Lizzy says, grabbing her salad bowl up under her chin and stuffing her mouth full like a kid would do with a bowl of popcorn at a movie.

I nod. "Again, in the changing room."

Her fork drops in her bowl and she stares at me wide-eyed.

"But he didn't let me finish."

"That bastard."

"Right." I laugh. "So I took my panties off and, when he wasn't paying attention, I stuffed them in his pocket."

"Oh my God. Who are you Queen and what have you done with my shyish Everlee?"

"I'm not shy."

"Well, you also did more exhibitionistic things last night than you ever have before."

If she only knew. But she can't. A flashback of me riding Callum's cock on the bed with the others watching as I played with my clit has me blushing again.

"Girl, do we need to get you a fan, because damn?" She flaps her hands wildly at me.

"Stop."

"So then. Please tell me you got to tickle the pickle after all that. You needed it, after all."

"What's that supposed to mean?"

She bats her hand. "Girl, you know. Now stop procrastinating and get to the good part."

"After skating, he took me home where we... you know..."

"That's it? That's all I get?"

"Fine. He had another snack in the shower."

Lizzy smacks the table loudly. "Three..." She lowers her voice. "Three times? I'm going to call him the Cookie Monster... shit. Nom, nom, nom is the name of the game with him. Shit!" she repeats.

"Well, we went back and forth and then we went to the bedroom." Where three other guys watched, I want to say, but don't.

"Let me guess? Nom Nom?"

"Yes, and then bang bang." I shake my head again. It always sounds stupid when I try to come up with cutesy little names for things.

"Big?"

"Huge. I'm so sore today."

"Wow," she breathes, looking into the air.

"But then after, he ran us a bath and washed me."

Lizzy's head hits the table dramatically. I'm sure from all the outbursts and movements she's been making, fellow patrons are likely concerned for my safety.

"Everything ok over here?" A voice booms behind me at the same time I feel a hand brush across my shoulder and a tingle shoot up my spine.

Lizzy tilts her head up, so her chin is resting on the table and once she sees who it is, curses out a string of expletives and then sits up.

Callum is standing just behind me, with his gaze set on me.

"What are you doing here?"

"Everlee? Don't ask the man that. Offer to pull up a chair for him."

Poor Lizzy. She's already invested in my relationship with a man I'd only be with for a few more days, likely. The pain at that realization stings pretty badly.

His brow furrows as he studies my face. "Are you ok?" His knuckles brush across my cheek.

Lizzy lets out a loud sigh and looks like she's been love struck with Cupid's arrow.

"I'm good." My lips flatten. We both knew I wasn't doing a good job of hiding anything and he can probably make two guesses to figure out what's wrong.

"I didn't mean to interrupt your lunch. I just wanted to say hello."

I stare at him, causing him to wink back at me.

"You aren't interrupting. We're just getting caught up on girl chat."

"I'm sure that's what you're doing." His eyes twinkle knowingly.

I just pump my eyebrows with an 'I told you so' glance.

"I'm going to grab a bite to eat, but I'd like to talk to you for a minute before you go back to work."

"I'm sure you would... nom nom..." Lizzy mumbles.

My eyes shoot daggers at her. She shrugs her shoulders defiantly and mouths, "What? I'm sorry. Not really."

I don't know if Callum heard her, but if he did, he doesn't react. I'm sure I'd hear some snarky comment later, and the thought of that fills me with more excitement and trepidation than I want.

"Man can wear a suit. Who would have thought a businessman like him would have a little freak to him?" Lizzy says when he walks away.

I want to tell her about all the tattoos and everything else, but I can't. Tattoos may not be an issue, but I want to keep that to myself. He's worked hard on maintaining his image outside of the house, and I don't want to spoil it. If he reveals that to her, then so be it.

CALLUM - SHOWING HER WHO'S THE DOM

NOM NOM? I DON'T know if I want to know what that means, so I act like I didn't hear it. I order my salad and find a seat in a booth near the back corner. From where I'm sitting, I can see part of Everlee and I can't help but watch her. She's smiling and her eyes... they seem... happy.

Lizzy seems to be a big personality, easy to swallow those up around her, but Everlee seems to hold her own, laughing every two seconds.

I'm halfway done with my salad when a shadow descends on my table.

Standing there with a face full of sass and cheeks tinged a little pink is Everlee. I toss her a quick wink and a smile.

"May I sit, sir?" she asks, quiet enough so only I can hear her.

My eyes flash and she smiles, obviously satisfied by my reaction.

"You may." I pat the seat beside me and slide over. When she sits, I grab her hand and whisper, "You don't need to do that in public."

"Maybe I want to," she says before she mouths sir.

I lean over, so my lips are brushing against her ear. "Careful or I'll bend you across this table and fuck you in front of everyone."

"Maybe that's what I want."

Her eyes flicker up to meet mine, with a hint of uncertainty dancing behind them. It seems like she is trying to be more adventurous than what she's used to. Maybe because she thinks I want it, or maybe she realized how much she liked it last night. When she was riding my cock, she was performing. Not just for me, but for them. I saw a change in her. She liked the others watching her. It turned her on. I don't think she's ever done that before and that's what's dangerous. I want to be her first for all of these new things I want to show her. I want to pleasure her and watch her be pleasured. Fuck me. Just the idea of watching the others fuck her... I've always enjoyed watching, but there is something about her. It's like I get to experience it all again for the first time, through her eyes.

She's staring at me... waiting.

This woman.

"Oh, really?" My voice drops to a flirtatious tone.

Is she trying to dom me in a salad shop? Let's see how much fun we can have. "Turn your body towards me some," I command, stepping into this role with ease.

She hesitates for a second, glancing around. I can't figure out if the hesitation is for fear of getting caught, or fear of liking it too much. If I had to guess, I would say the latter.

My fingers direct her chin towards me. "Use your words, Everlee." My tone is low, commanding.

"Yes, Sir."

"Good girl." Turning away from her, I take a bite of my salad. "Now stay still."

She nods, but I tilt my chin down at her in expectation. "Yes, sir." She's nearly panting, her skin is hot to the touch with a hint of pink, and her pulse is jumping in her neck.

My left hand falls on her leg by her knee, and I squeeze gently. She likes this. Her teeth run across her bottom lip, I'm sure to stop the sound that's begging to float past them.

My fingers start to slide up her leg and her eyes flicker to mine with a hint of something I can't place. Humor? Mischievousness? Curious, my hand continues to slide up her leg, the blood pumping through my fingers like a steady drum until I slip them under her skirt. I take another bite of salad and keep pushing my hand up until...

My eyes shoot to hers at the same time my fork clamors to the table.

Fucking hell.

My lips part and I'm nearly robbed of breath.

The look on her face is pure fucking gold, like I just found the end of the rainbow. She knew. She knew what I'd find, and she was waiting. Watching.

"Everlee," I hiss through set teeth.

"Yes?"

"Why the fuck aren't you wearing any panties?"

She bites her bottom lip and I grab just under her jaw and hold her there for a second, trying to talk myself out of bending her over this table and fucking her right here. My heart is beating out of my chest and this woman. That look in her eyes.

The humor.

The defiance.

I want to fuck it out of her and show her who is in control. Not her. Never her. Me.

I am in control.

Though someone could argue right now that I am very much not in control.

"Goddamn you." My mouth crashes to hers, my tongue pushing its way in, not waiting for permission. Taking what I want. What I fucking need. This kiss is fire. Blue flame, hot as fuck fire. Burn you to your core, so you're nothing but a pile of ash when it's done.

I pull away, captivated by the bewildered look in her eyes.

"We're going. Now," I command, nearly pushing her out of the seat.

"Where are we going?" She stands there dazed, looking at me, trying to process what's happening.

I grab her hand and pull her outside, aware that my movements are frantic and hurried. Very fucking much aware that I'm losing control. *She* makes me lose control.

Brady looks up at me as we approach the car and I ignore the smirk smirking across his smirking smirked face. I'm hot. With lust, fire, and anger. Anger that I'm allowing her to do this to me.

Swooping into the car, I nearly drag her in behind me and Brady closes the door and stands back on the sidewalk, waiting.

"Take your shirt off now before I rip it off." My voice is rough, husky.

Without hesitation, she pulls it over her head at the same time I pull down my pants, freeing my already hard cock. I reach into my pocket and curse.

"I'm clean and on birth control," she says, not giving me time to change my mind. At least I can take some solace in knowing she needs me as much as I need her.

"Me too. Clean." Unable to wait any longer, I lift her up and slide her onto my cock as her skirt rides up to her hips. Goddamn. "You feel so fucking good," I groan out, unhooking her bra with one flick of my fingers. The clasp is in the front, so all I have to do is push the bra and it slides down her arms behind her back.

Before she can shake it off her wrists, I take her breasts and squeeze them before taking one in my mouth. Control is gone. I need her like a fire needs oxygen. I suck her breast in my mouth and let my teeth scrape over her perfectly pebbled nipple.

"Callum," she pants as she grinds her pussy on my cock, arms still pinned behind her in makeshift handcuffs.

"I'm going to get into so much fucking trouble for this."

"Then let's make sure it's worth it," she murmurs against my neck before she bites.

My cock twitches inside of her like I've been shot with adrenaline.

"Fuck Everlee." My palms run down her back, pressing her towards me before I grab her hips and lift her before slamming her onto me. Damn it, I want to get deep inside of her. Deeper than I've ever wanted to be. It's like I can't get enough right now. "Where's your contract?"

"Now?"

"Yes. Now."

She wiggles her arms free and digs into her purse and grabs it out while I continue to grind my cock into her. "It's not signed yet."

"Show it to me."

She flicks it open with one hand and holds it up.

Looking over it, I find what I'm looking for and a devious smile plays on my lips. "Of course you'd be perfect." I nod, indicating she can toss it on the ground. "Do you remember your safe word?"

She nods.

"Words Everlee," I say just before I nip at her neck, sucking her skin until her back is arching.

"Cupid."

My mouth closes on hers again, mimicking the soft rocking of our bodies.

"You feel so good," she whimpers, pressing her forehead to mine as she watches my cock disappear inside of her.

"So do you, baby."

Needing to taste her, I rub my finger over her clit, and she leans back, giving me access. "You're so wet." I suck her arousal off my fingers and watch her eyes pulse wide. Pressing my finger back to her clit, I get it as wet with her arousal as I can, then slide it around her and press it against her forbidden hole.

Her eyes lock on mine as realization sets in. I give her a moment to stop me, but pray she doesn't. When she doesn't speak, I press my lips to hers in a softer kiss. When my tongue presses into her mouth, my finger presses softly against her entrance. She lets out a moan as her body continues to ride my cock and I swallow it down. Moving slowly, savoring every feeling between our bodies, I press in again until she lets out a squeak.

"That's new." I chuckle.

"Shut up and fuck me." She rocks her hips forward.

"Yes, Ma'am."

Her head falls back in pure bliss as my finger in her ass helps to guide us, rock us. With my free hand, I rub on her clit until she is making the noises I want to hear.

We're rocking, moving faster and faster, as wet slaps, grunts and groans fill the small space of the car.

"If you're not quieter, the cops are going to get called."

"Let them come. They'll bring the handcuffs."

Her eyes flash with excitement and I can't help myself. I press my lips to hers and punch my cock into her harder and harder. The car has to be rocking, and we're parked on a busy downtown street in the middle of the afternoon, but I don't care. The only thing that exists right now is her pussy and claiming it.

"I'm..." she stutters, as her pussy quivers around my cock.

"Come with me," I command, hands pressing tighter to her back as I send my cock deeper into her.

Two thrusts later, with my mouth on hers, she unleashes another groan from deep within as her orgasm tears through her and her pussy clamps around my cock. Hot damn. Seconds later, I'm exploding inside of her as our thrusts slow, each of us riding every delicious wave. Releasing from her kiss, I slide my head down and take each breast in my mouth, giving them a quick suck and a nibble before I reach down inside the door and pull out some wet wipes.

"Just in case you need a good anal sesh in the back of your car?"

Her comment catches me off guard, as does the light in her eyes. She's happy... and so am I. Playfully, I toss the wipe in her face, causing her to giggle before she climbs off my cock.

"You know. This would have been a great time to have a condom. I don't have panties, so now I get to walk around the rest of the afternoon with your come leaking out of me."

"Maybe I wanted to mark you as mine." The words are out of my mouth before I know what I'm saying.

The light in her eyes flashes dim, like I've struck her with a hot lance across her skin. "Yours for a few group fucks." There's a certain bite to her words that causes a pit to form in my stomach.

"It's supposed to be only two fucks, period. So you're capped out." I was trying to tease her, but the look on her face tells me it didn't come across that way. "But I don't think the boys would allow that, which is why I'm going to get in a lot of trouble."

"Was it worth it?" she asks, voice holding a slight tremble. Her eyes won't meet mine and I'm filled with rage. Not at her, but at the prick who took away her confidence. There are glimmers of it while we're fucking, but then in moments like this, it's like her emotions get the better of her and fear creeps in. Fear like she's not good enough or some bullshit like that.

This.

This is the look I saw in her eyes when she showed up at Vixen on the night of the party. It's tearing me apart inside to know she is so beautiful, but has these doubts. Damn it! Why do I care? I'm not supposed to get attached.

I don't get attached.

My hands cup her cheeks, and it takes a second for her eyes to meet mine, as fear and self-doubt flicker behind them. "It was worth every goddamned second." I look out of the window and see people walking by. "I'd do it again if I didn't think we'd get in trouble."

It takes a minute, but like water rushes over the sand, changing it slowly, I can see my words washing over her. Her eyes change and then she slowly starts unbuttoning my shirt.

"What are you doing?"

"Don't worry." She leans over and kisses my chest. "I missed seeing this." Her hands run softly over my chest like she's trying to remember everything about me, this moment. "And these."

Her fingers trace over several of my tattoos. Tattoos that I keep hidden from the world. They are pieces of me that are my story. A story I don't talk about with most.

"Such a man of mystery. So guarded. Hidden from the world." Her hands fall to my stomach as she stares at me—my chest, my face, like she's looking at a piece of art.

Leaning forward, I kiss her forehead before disposing of our wet wipes in the trashcan in the back. I grab her bra off the floor and hand it to her so she can get dressed and after she does, she just sits there, hands on her lap.

"Do you want these?" I ask, holding up her panties from last night. "I washed them for you."

"You washed them or had someone else wash them?"

My head snaps back in defense. "I washed them. In the sink with lavender soap."

"You hand washed my panties?"

I playfully tap her nose. "I'm not completely helpless."

"Hmmpf."

"Hmmpf?" I mock, tickling her side, causing her to squeal.

"Thank you." She grabs them and stuffs them in her bag.

"You aren't going to put them on?"

"Doesn't really go with my outfit."

My fingers stroke my chin as I figure out a way to fuck her again without us getting in trouble.

She takes a deep breath, then leans over and picks up the contract off the floor, then digs through her purse.

"Use mine." I hold my pen in front of her face after retrieving it from the storage on the door.

She signs the paper and lets out a puff of air, like she's signing away her heart.

I hope not.

She looks up at me, with a playful smirk on her face. "I'm keeping this pen. It's a good fucking pen."

"I can't wait until tomorrow night."

"For the dinner?"

"That, but mostly because we'll get to punish your filthy mouth."

EVERLEE -
CLITERATI FOR
THE WIN

THE REST OF THE workday is a bust. I can't get my thoughts off what happened after lunch and the threat? No. Promise? Callum made. Tomorrow is the night I get my world rocked by four hotter than hell men. I feel like I should jump on my smutty social media book groups and look for recs on fivesomes. Those smutty fuckers always deliver. Give me a rec on monster love. Boom. Boom. Boom. Need a rec on mermaid love, a three headed Cyclops, a God, or a book where one character has tentacles, and the other has feathers? You'll get twenty recommendations in less than five minutes.

They. Are. Fantastic!

They are my Cliterati. An elite group of highly read females (and males) who can give you your true heart's desire. They're like a Rolodex of sex. A Sexodex. A Rolosex. I'm getting too excited. Although my chair would argue I've been in this state all day.

Not wanting to waste any time, I grab my phone and flip through several groups, copying and pasting the same request.

Book Recs Needed: Fivesome. FMMMM. Quick reads, less than 250 pages. Must be spicy! Research needed stat!

Shit! What if I didn't have all the F's and M's in the right spot? Placement is very important.

Before panic sets in, I notice I already have six notifications across the three different groups.

See.

Amazing.

My phone buzzes.

Lizzy: *How was it after I left?*

I start typing, then stop. Erase it, then start over. Erase it again. I don't know what to tell her because I want to tell her everything and nothing.

My phone rings, and I laugh when I see it's a video call.

Reluctantly, I press the green button and before I can get to my office door to close it, she yells, "You had sex with him again! At lunch?"

"Geez Lizzy." I prop my hand on my door and shake my head at my assistant, who I'm fairly certain heard every word. "No," I say, for added measure, before shutting the door.

Slinking back to my desk, full of embarrassment, I prop the phone on the stand.

"You lie like a rug. Spill."

"You know it's a freakish gift you have."

She smells the air. "I can smell sex on you a mile and a half away."

"Weirdo."

"So you boinked again?"

"Yes, we boinked," I repeat her childish term back to her, shaking my head. Sometimes it's like talking to a teenager, but she keeps us young and keeps me laughing.

"Tea, girl."

"Well, I just went over to talk to him. A friendly conversation." *About a sex contract for him and his buddies.* "And I must have had a look in my eye or something. Because he told me to sit beside him. He started running his hand up my leg and found out I wasn't wearing any panties."

"You hussy."

"The skirt..."

"Both are valid."

"Anyway, when I say his eyes lit up... it was like fire. Pure, unadulterated lust. He nearly pushed me out of the seat and said we're leaving. He pulls me into his car. Feral. Wild. It was erotic."

"So you ba-doinka-doinked in the back of his car. Poor driver man. I hope he gets paid well."

"It was amazing."

"Told you... you needed the dicky dick up in you."

"You were right."

"I know."

"I have to go, though. I'm at work."

She mocks my words back to me. "Real quick. I meant to ask earlier. Are we still going dress shopping tonight?"

"We didn't have plans to go shopping."

"I know. But I figured if I phrased it that way, you couldn't say no, because the guilt of forgetting a date with your BFF would be too much to handle." She throws the back of her palm across her forehead and sighs dramatically.

"You're too much."

"But seriously. You're going to a gala tomorrow night with McStudmuffin. You know your man is going to look fine as hell. He can wear the newspaper and..." she whimpers out. "You have nothing in your wardrobe close to the level he's going to bring tomorrow."

Eesh. Her words weigh on me for a moment, before I come to terms with the fact she's right, but part of me also wants to get something nice and sexy. Like a present wrapped up for the guys delivered by Cupid himself.

"You know I'm right."

"Yes. We can go." I add quickly, "But it can't be a late night. I have to get some work done because I've been absolutely useless today." It's a lie. I had to get home and read my smut to prepare for tomorrow night.

"What time do you want to meet?"

"I have a meeting at four, but I can leave after that. Hopefully forty-five after."

"Or fifteen til? You crack me up. I'll do some research. Is it themed?"

"Likely. I don't know."

"Find out."

"Love you, boo."

"Ditto and text me back. You're going to look fireeeee," she sings the word fire as the call disconnects. A lot of energy, that one. Big coochie energy. That's what she has.

Guilt creeps in as I stare at the now black screen on my phone. She's so happy for me because she thinks I've potentially found someone to fill the hole Dick left. He always went by Rich, short for Richard, but times have changed and I've decided to go the other route. Obviously the more mature route.

Taking another moment to push the negativity aside, I pop my head out of the office and give my assistant the name of my plus one and inquire about the dress code. Black tie. Simple. General.

When I get back to my desk, I quickly text Lizzy and Callum, then check my recs and am happy to see I have fifty notifications and a few repeated recs. Tonight is going to be a good night. Bottle of wine, my e-reader and some takeout sushi.

Resolved to get some amount of work done today, I flip my phone face down so it won't tempt me anymore.

Finally.

It's only seven after two. Not my best day, admittedly.

The next two hours breeze by as I knock out several reports, put together a bid for another client, answer twenty-seven emails and delete over sixty as I prepare for my meeting. Maybe I should have sex in the back of a car on my lunch break more often.

At forty-three after, I'm riding the elevator down.

Crushing it!

Lizzy is downstairs waiting for me with her car parked out front. "I know this will be the first time in a while you've been in a car without having an orgasm, but let me remind you how us common unsexed folk have to live. I'm also not opening your door for you." She cackles, running around the front of her car.

"It's so hard to find good help these days."

"Don't I know it?"

"So where to?" I ask, sliding in.

"There's one shop I want to hit first. I'm fairly certain they'll have what you need and we can be done."

"Is it La Belle?"

"Oui."

"Their dresses are so expensive."

"But totally gorge!"

I can't argue with that.

"Can't you write it off as a work expense?"

A sound somewhere between a snort and a laugh tumbles out of my mouth. "No. I can't. Are you mad?"

She shrugs. "A girl had to ask."

We're at La Belle, forty-five minutes later. Traffic getting out of downtown was a nightmare, but we kept busy talking about her and Tony. Lately, I feel like most of our conversations have been centered on me and I want to share the love. We talk about Lizzy's infatuation with a Valentine's Day proposal. She said Tony was acting cagey, and they were going to a very nice restaurant, even though he wouldn't tell her where. Lizzy said she was only joking about the proposal since it's only been a couple of months, even though he's been dropping hints over the last week or so. I told her I didn't think it was a good idea, but she reassured me that if he did, she'd have a super long engagement, which we both know is a lie.

Her goal in life since middle school has been to find a man, settle down, get married, and have a dozen kids. I thought that was my goal too until Vixen happened. Now, I don't know what I want.

"Welcome ladies," an older woman chimes when we walk in. She's wearing a knitted green pencil skirt with a white top and a green chunky necklace. Her short silver hair is curled and rests just above her shoulders and she smells like a floral perfume.

"We had an appointment at five- thirty. Apologies for being a couple minutes late. Traffic."

"No worries at all. You're the last appointment of the night, so there's no need to rush." She laughs. "Well, we close at six thirty... so only rush enough for that. Champagne?" she asks at the same time a light brown-skinned male with a shaved head wearing some sort of block pattern suit walks around the corner carrying a tray.

"Yes, please."

We each take a glass.

The man sits the tray down, pulls down his jacket and holds out his hand. "I'm Andre. What can I help you with this evening?"

"My friend here needs a dazzling drop-dead gorgeous dress for a gala tomorrow night."

"My friend here loves spending someone else's money." I shoot her a nasty side glance.

He nods, "Yes. We've had several people stopping in here over the last several months getting fitted," he says, looking me up and down, causing me to retreat inside of my shell a bit.

"We don't want any of those dresses. She needs to stand out," Lizzy says, her hands flying away from her body like stars... or jazz hands.

"You have a nice figure, so we may get lucky with the sizing and won't have to do any alterations."

"Thank you."

"Do you have a color in mind?"

"She wants red."

Andre looks at me, and I nod. "Sure, let's start there."

"Fire," Lizzy whispers, this time with definite jazz hands.

We go to the red section of the store and on the end of one aisle is a display of dresses that are absolutely stunning. It's a red sequin dress with an ombre to black at the bottom, a daring neckline plunge, and a mermaid train.

Lizzy smacks my arm repeatedly. "Could you imagine?"

"It's beautiful."

"These just came in, so no one at your gala will be wearing this."

Lizzy snatches my champagne. "Go try it on."

Andre flips through, finding my size, and walks me to a dressing room.

"Let me know if you need help!" Lizzy shouts from outside the cloth curtain.

Nerves are pulsing through me as I look in the mirror. The dress is stunning and the girl looking back at me looks uncertain. Can she pull off this dress? Will she look like a fish out of water? Sighing, I step out of my clothes and slide the dress on, pulling the zipper up the side. Taking a deep breath and thinking encouraging thoughts, I turn around and see myself. Like me. The me I used to be before dickface fucked with my head. She is beautiful and confident and *fuck*. She is wearing the hell out of this dress. A tear prickles on the rim of my eye, but I quickly blink it away and stare at the ceiling for a second to regain control of my emotions.

The back is a low scoop, resting just above my hips, accentuating my back beautifully.

"What's taking so long?" Lizzy whines.

Rolling my eyes, I shift my girls around in this dress and love the way they look. I could get those little sticky cup things and push them up a bit more, but I like this natural look and I think the guys will too. Plus, after the party, the cups may impede my sexual escapades.

Priorities.

"I'm coming out. I wanted to look at it first."

When I pull the curtain back, Lizzy's mouth drops. "Fire!" she nearly screams. Thank God we're the only customers in the store. If not, she may start a slight panic. Andre comes over to inspect the fitting. "Honey, you in this dress may just turn me straight."

"It may turn me into a lesbian!" Lizzy adds.

"Stop." I blush, looking in the mirror again, rubbing my hands down the dress. It's stunning.

"She'll take it!"

"Lizzy!"

"What? You know you want it. I know you want it. I'm just moving the process along so you can't come up with some BS reason not to say yes to the dress."

Andre grabs her arm. "Love you! Do you need a job here?"

They both look at me, waiting.

"Fine. We'll take it."

Andre's brows rise in shock. "You have been my easiest fitting of the year." He chuckles. "But if you know, you know, and honey, you should know. Whoever you're going with tomorrow night better appreciate you because you are... completely gorge."

We get in the car fifteen minutes later and Lizzy turns her full body and grabs my arm with a smile plastered across her face. "I can't believe you spent that much on a dress."

"You brought me there!" I defend. "Plus, it was probably going to be one of the cheapest."

"Keep telling yourself that," she teases. "But seriously, you should have spent a mill on it. It looks amazeballs on you and he's going to looosseee his mindddd. Maybe he'll propose to you too, because why wouldn't he?"

I laugh. "He's not proposing to me. I don't know if he's the settling down kind. I think he's just going to be fun for a while."

"What? No. He's smitten with you."

"No. I think I'm just new."

She rolls her eyes. "There is new, and then there is what you two have. I'm pretty sure my hair stands on end when he comes around you."

Laying the groundwork for this fun short-term thing appears to be a harder sell than I initially thought. She has to be misreading things because it's not just the two of us. Sure, it is right now, but it also isn't. The others are there, and I want them too. I want to experience all of them and I will tomorrow night. Ideas flitter through my mind at all the things I'm going to experience. I'd had a threesome once in college, but a fivesome. A wave of excitement travels from my chest, past my stomach, to my clit, which is now throbbing.

Divert! Divert! Divert! I yell at myself like a submarine blast echoing through the tight metal chambers. Tonight is going to be research and planning and tomorrow I'll implement said plan into action.

Bring on the magic sticks! Nope. Beef whistles? Crevice crawlers? One eyed yogurt slingers? I cringe. I tried to channel my inner Lizzy, but it's clearly a *her* thing and not a *me* thing.

She drops me out in front of my apartment building, giving me a quick hug and a hopeful smile. I grab my bag and the dress, throw it over my arm and hike up the stairs. There's not a great spot in my apartment to hang my dress, so I find a place in the living room that is tucked out of the way. Excited to see what the night has in store for me, I race into my bedroom, kick my shoes off, slip into my jam jams, grab my e-reader and wait for my sushi to be delivered.

EVERLEE - TOMATO TOMATO

THEY CLOSE THE OFFICE at lunch so we can all go home and get ready for this evening. Usually, these big events are on the weekend, but our client wanted to make it a Valentine's Day gala. There were rumors around the office that Meyers is flying in a chef from France, apparently one of the most sought after in the world.

Last night, I skimmed through several books and found the key smut sections very enlightening, so I have a good idea of what I need to do, so I don't embarrass myself. And! And! I didn't masturbate while reading. Goodness knows I wanted to because dammmnnn, but I'm letting it all build up for tonight. I'm pretty sure I'm going to be ruined sexually anyway, but I was proud of myself. Small victories.

Dinner starts at six, but we're expected to show up at five for hors d'oeuvre and champagne. My goal for this evening is to not mispronounce hors d'oeuvre, but ever since that Christmas movie where this wealthy couple had to go home and visit their less than wealthy family and were offered 'whores do veray' which ended up being spray cheese on crackers, I can't say it any other way.

Callum texts, letting me know he'll pick me up at four fifteen. He wants to make sure we don't get stuck in traffic and doesn't want to be late. I can appreciate that, but it means we'll likely get there thirty minutes early, and thirty minutes stuck in the car with a man-God is going to be trouble for me.

Tonight, I opted for light makeup with a hint of shimmer and a simple updo with hanging curls. I wanted to get the hair off my neck, but not make it overly complicated for the post-party shindig tonight.

Nerves are taking a grip the longer I have to wait. Glancing at my phone causes my heart to race. Three minutes.

My phone buzzes.

> **Lizzy:** *Girl. You better be getting ready to send me a pic!*

> **Everlee:** *Yep! You caught me.*

> **Lizzy:** *You weren't going to? After the countless hours I spent with you shopping?*

> **Everlee:** *You mean the fifteen minutes?*

> **Lizzy:** *Tomato Tomato.*

Reading her text makes me laugh because I read it the same way and was confused for half a second until I read it again the way she would have said it.

Glancing at the clock again, I have one minute, so I place my phone on the table, set the timer, and give her a few model poses. I quickly check the photos, then send them to her and wait patiently-not-so-patiently for her texts.

> **Lizzy:** *Did you wax? Shave? You aren't on your period, are you? Oh, that would be horrible.*

Everlee: *No. Yes. No. And the worst.*

Lizzy: *Get you some thundersword, girl.*

Everlee: *Thundersword?*

Lizzy: *Yes. Sexcaliber, Yankee Doodle.*

Everlee: *Where do you even come up with these names?*

Lizzy: *Fine. Cock. Boring. Go get you some cock.*

Everlee: *I plan on it.*

Lizzy: *Yea girl!*

Everlee: *I won't have my phone, but I will text you tomorrow when I get home.*

Lizzy: *I'll do a drive by tonight of his place, pretend to be a pizza girl or something to check on you.*

Everlee: *No, you won't. Plus, they'd recognize you.*

Lizzy: *Right. And they probably order some high-end fancy schmancy pizza. Get it flown in from Italy or wherever.*

There's a knock on my door.

> **Everlee:** *He's here. Gotta go. Love you, boo.*

> **Lizzy:** *Love you too. Have fun and use lots and lots of protection and lube.*

> **Everlee:** *Geez.*

> **Lizzy:** *Bye, love.*

I put my phone on the charger, then make my way to the door and check through the peephole. Fuck me. He's standing there looking... words have vacated my mind. My stomach tightens and my pussy starts pulsing and that's just off a quick glance. I'm going to have an entire car ride with him and the rest of the night. But more importantly, how am I going to walk away from this?

When I open the door, his eyes rake over me as his lips part. "Fuck me... you're... shit... Do we have to go to this dinner?"

His words make me blush. I've never made a man speechless before, but man do I feel his words. I know I look good in this dress, but his reaction is enough to drive me wild with desire.

Maybe I should have used the ol' one handed read last night, because I'm going to have to walk around most of the night with my legs clenched together whimpering like a newborn puppy looking for its mom's teat.

"You look very handsome as well. And yes. We have to." Handsome is an understatement, but if I told him what I really thought, we'd never make it to the party, and we have to. At least for a bit. He's all six-foot something God in a white button down, with a deep red vest that matches my dress perfectly, and a black jacket with black pants. Very basic, but at the same time, not basic at all. His hair is slicked back, his beard is shaved to the perfect five o'clock shadow, and his blue eyes are like fiery crystals.

"Let me send a pic to the boys. They were really upset they couldn't come tonight, but," he bobbles his head from side to side. "It would be kind of hard if you asked for a plus four."

"That's why you don't date or have this arrangement long term?"

His face falls. "It just gets complicated. We try to avoid that."

"By sexually ruining girls for any other men. You're effectively creating spinsters, you know?"

He laughs and holds out his hand. "Let's go. We don't want to be late."

My hand fits in his perfectly. Of course it does. Everything about him- us -is perfect. He follows me down the stairs, cursing under his breath most of the way. "Are you trying to send me to an early grave woman? Your back," he huffs.

I look over my shoulder and wink.

He grabs my wrist and pins me against the wall and leans in, taking my lips in a passionate kiss. I moan into his mouth just before he pulls away. "I can't wait until you're moaning around my cock tonight, while Emmett and Knox fuck you at the same time."

My cheeks turn the color of my dress, but then I lean in, brushing my lips against his ear. "What about Jax?" Hearing myself causes me to cringe internally, but I try not to show Callum. I'm horrible at dirty talk and what's sad is that wasn't even dirty. I was trying to be sexy, but I'm fairly certain it just came out as a question with my voice in an awkwardly low octave. But his dirty talk... there's something about it that's so raw, so filthy, so perfect.

"Don't you worry, Red, he'll be there too." He smirks, glancing at his watch. "What's the minimum time we have to stay?"

I smile before continuing down the stairs.

Brady is waiting with his hand on the car handle, ready for us. When he sees me walk through the door, his eyes grow wide in surprise, only further making me feel like a queen. He helps me into the car and whispers, "You look amazing, Ms. Everlee."

"Thank you, Brady."

By the time Callum gets in the car, his phone is dinging over and over again.

"Is everything ok?"

He pulls out his phone, with a worried brow on his face, but it quickly changes to humor."All good. Let's just say the boys are both eagerly awaiting the end of this dinner and want to kill me."

Trying my hand at being sexy again, I suck my bottom lip into my mouth. "Me too. The after dinner piece... not wanting to kill you."

Awkward.

I sigh at myself before running my hand up his leg and over his crotch.

Yep. Super awkward now.

Jesus, fuck Everlee! Get out of your head!

"You really are trouble."

"Yea. Not the first time I heard that." The last time was... you guessed it. High school chemistry class. Seeexxy.

We pull up to the convention center twenty minutes later. A red carpet is rolled out from the roundabout drop off to the front door, making me feel like a movie star at a big premiere.

Most of the car ride was quiet, with Callum running his fingers along the inside of my palm while he looked absentmindedly out of the window. I'd pay all the money in the world to know what's going on inside of his head. Part of me hopes he's trying to figure out how he can live the rest of his life without me in it. That tonight and possibly some other night wouldn't be the end of us. Of this.

This is wrong. I shouldn't have asked him to come. Why did he say yes? He said they don't do dates. Everyone's going to think we're a couple, and he's my boyfriend. Did I really want to go through the entire night correcting them?

Did I want to even correct them? What would I say? No, this hot ass man isn't my boyfriend. We're just friends with benefits for the rest of the week?

We step out of the car and his hand slips around my back, causing a tingle to shoot up my spine. "What's wrong Everlee?"

Shit. Even the way my name rolls off his tongue. "Nothing," I lie.

He grabs my hand and pulls me off to the side, away from the red carpet. "Red."

"It's nothing, really. I don't want to talk about it."

The back of his hand brushes along my cheek. "I'll let it go for now."

I try to smile, but know I don't succeed. I'm going to ruin this night before it even starts. *Get your shit together, Everlee.* That's what Lizzy would say. She'd be jumping up and down in front of me, hyping me up. She'd tell me to get that donkey dick or some other crazy name she'd blurt out and tell me to just have fun.

Filled with courage and the hype from invisible Lizzy, I grab his hand and pull him back onto the red carpet and continue our walk. There are only a few couples in front of us, so we don't have to wait outside for long. A few of the dresses are from La Belle, which makes me love mine even more. Theirs looks nice on them, but I truly love this one.

We get up to the huge heart-shaped balloon arch at the front and have to take a picture. I was going to decline, but Callum pulls me over, insisting.

When we walk in, we stand for a second at the doorway, admiring all the exquisite decorations. They really went all out for this.

"What did you say this was for again?"

I laugh. "I guess I didn't say. This is one of our largest customers. They are hosting this gala to raise funds for one of their charities, so our company bought several tables as a show of support. They did it on Valentine's Day, because it's a special day for the charity owner."

"Is that it over there?" Callum asks, pointing to a table tucked off to the side under a large balloon archway.

"Yes."

"Can we go over?"

"Of course," I say, leading him over, hand still in mine.

"Good evening. Don't you make a handsome couple." The older lady, behind the table, beams. She's wearing a draping black sequin dress with a pearl necklace and matching earrings.

"Thank you," Callum chimes, reaching his arm around me. "I think so, too."

"Thank you so much for coming tonight and supporting us. It really means the world to us and these children."

Callum smiles. "Can we still make donations?"

"Yes, of course." The lady perks up.

Callum reaches into his pocket and pulls out his checkbook. I start to make fun of him in my mind for carrying a checkbook, then nearly choke on the air I'm breathing when I see how much he's donating.

Ten thousand dollars.

Holy shit. Who is he?

He hands the check to the woman, who also nearly chokes. She blinks quickly, looking from the check up to Callum, then back at the check as a tear forms in the corner of her eye. "Thank you so much, Mr. McCall."

McCall. Him and Jax are brothers? That makes sense and I can see it. Tall, dark, and handsome. Alpha, beta. I'd have to guess Jax is a little younger, but not much.

"Can I give you a hug?" the woman asks, already walking around the table.

"Of course." He drops his arm from around my back and opens his arms. The woman walks right in and looks so tiny compared to him.

She pats his chest. "I don't want to get make-up on your suit." She grabs his hands, then looks at me. "If I was younger, I'd give you a run for your money."

"Any man would be lucky to have a good-looking woman like you," Callum coos.

The woman blushes, then walks behind the table and scribbles something down. "Here's a receipt for your records. What name would you like to be added to the scroll of donations at the end of the event?"

"Anonymous is fine."

She reaches forward and grabs my hand. "You're a lucky woman."

"Don't I know it." I grab Callum's hand, and we head to the bar.

"Do you want an old-fashioned?" he asks, bringing my hand to his lips and placing a gentle kiss on my knuckles.

"Will it be as good as Emmett's?"

"I doubt it. He's truly perfected it."

"I'll try it and switch if needed."

While Callum orders our drinks, I look around at the people filtering into the building and still don't recognize anyone.

He hands me the drink, then places his hand on my lower back, his pinky dipping just below the edge of my dress, grazing the top of my ass. He leans over and whispers, "I can't wait until my cock is buried-"

"Everlee?"

We turn around, and Mr. Randall is walking over with Annalise, my assistant, a step behind him. She sees Callum and her eyes grow wide as she leans back, clutching her chest, mouthing damn. I chuckle briefly, then turn my attention to Mr. Randall. "Hello, sir."

Callum's fingers dig gently into my back. Is he jealous? Obviously, he knows it's a different kind of sir.

"So glad you could make it and bring a date." He motions towards Callum. "I really thought you were going to call out sick." He chuckles.

I chuckle.

We all chuckle. But if he only knew the truth. That's why I'm chuckling.

"Callum, this is Mr. Randall, CEO of McClintock Enterprise."

"Very nice to meet you. I'm glad I made the invite list," he says, removing his hand from my back to shake Mr. Randall's. The cool air hits my skin where his hand had been, and I miss our connection. Seconds later, it's back, and I breathe a sigh of... not relief, but of comfort?

"We'll see you in a little. Going to walk around and find more people, then head towards our table. The chef is going to walk around soon to introduce herself before everything starts. She's going to do a cooking demonstration on the stage of what we're eating tonight."

"That sounds exciting."

Callum nods, but doesn't speak.

Mr. Randall and Annalise walk away, then Callum looks at me. "Who's the chef tonight?"

I shrug. "Someone from France. I'm not sure. I wasn't paying attention to anything related to this, because truth be told..." I lean in close. "I *was* planning on calling out sick, but you sort of put a wrench in those plans."

"Glad I could oblige," he smirks.

CALLUM - PAST MEETS PRESENT

As we walk into the grand ballroom, I walk a few steps behind Everlee, which is a problem. That dress. Damn. The way it hugs all of her curves. The way the back swoops down and sits just above her ass. She is hands down the most beautiful woman here tonight and what's wild to me is she doesn't know it. I think that's one of the things I find so attractive.

We pause at the seating chart at the entrance to locate our number, then weave through the tables until we find it. Most people still aren't here yet or are out front getting drinks or taking pictures, so it's fairly empty in here. A few are trickling in or sitting at the tables, but for the most part, it's just us.

The room looks amazing. The ceiling has large pieces of pink and white fabric drooped between golden rods nestled in between enormous chandeliers. There are twenty or thirty large round tables which seat ten people, covered in white tablecloths with a pink or red accent stripe down the middle. The centerpieces are large glass cylinders filled with white, red, and pink pebbled hearts coupled with golden arrows sticking up the middle, and the place settings are brushed gold chargers underneath white porcelain plates with a golden rim. They've really done up the Valentine's theme, but it's elegant, not gaudy.

Sitting down, I twirl the half empty glass in a circle on the table. Everlee is quiet, like something is weighing on her, and while I want to ask her what it is... I feel like I already know. In some ways, I feel the same. Even though we haven't been on an official date, we have done a lot of date like things and she has stayed the night twice. Nothing about her is like the times we've spent with the other women. She's been different from the start and I don't know if I want this to end at the end of our contract, but I don't know how it can continue. We tried that once already, and it didn't work out. I thought we were going to lose Knox and I don't want to go through that again.

I *will* protect my family.

"You know," Everlee starts, then stops. "That was really nice what you did earlier. The donation. It's not why I invited you."

Is this what has been bothering her? Did she think I thought she was using me? I smile. "I know why you invited me."

"Because I seem to have a problem attracting decent men who want to stick around?"

I tilt my head to the side disapprovingly.

She pulls her face, then smiles. "And your cock, of course."

"With a filthy mouth like yours." My thumb pads over her chin, "I don't see how you don't have guys lining up."

"Callum?" a woman's voice with a soft accent chimes behind us.

My stomach drops for a moment as my eyes lock on Everlee's. When my muscles remember how to move, I slowly turn in my seat and my eyes nearly pop out of my head.

"Callum. It is you." Sophie's gaze quickly flits to Everlee, then back to me.

"Sophie." I'm in complete shock as I stand to give her a hug. "Everlee mentioned a highly sought after French chef was being brought in and I wondered if it was you."

Everlee's head tilts in my peripheral.

She holds her hands out, smiling, the same warm smile she's always had with the dimple on her left cheek more pronounced than on her right. "I guess I shouldn't be surprised you'd be at an event supporting children. I know how much these organizations mean to you."

Everlee shifts uneasily in her chair and I want so badly to reach across the way and take her in my arms and tell her not to worry. Sophie is my past, and Everlee is what? My future? I don't know what she is, but I know she is my right now.

"Yes, they do." I turn to look at Everlee. "Sophie, this is Everlee."

"Your date, I presume?" Her eyes catch mine and I know what she's thinking. She knows our rules, because she is the reason we have them.

Nodding my head slightly, I look at Sophie and she pumps her brows once before she looks at Everlee.

Sophie's eyes widen in awe as she gazes at Everlee. "You look absolutely stunning," she whispers, her voice filled with sincere admiration. She takes hold of Everlee's hands and plants a delicate kiss on each side of her cheek. She looks back at me, hands still holding Everlee's. "How is Emmett? I miss him. All of you, really."

"Emmett's doing good. He recently just opened up his own restaurant here in town. Bo La Vie."

She chuckles, clasping her hands together. "Good life. Yes. I suppose you all live the good life, don't you?" Her words fall off.

"You should come by. The guys would love to see you."

"I'm only in town for a few days."

"Perfect! You can come by our club one of those nights."

"A club with you and the boys?" She smiles. "Could be trouble."

"So that's a yes?"

"Oui. Now I have to get backstage and get ready to wow you all with my expert culinary skills. Enjoy your dinner!" She leans over and gives me a kiss on the cheek. "Ta- Ta. And nice to meet you, Everlee!"

I watch her walk away, nerves preventing me from looking at Everlee immediately. She's going to have questions, and I don't know how to answer them. Honesty is the obvious choice because I won't lie to her, but I don't know how I can get her to believe that Sophie is a friend and in the past. I don't know much about Everlee's past, but I know that whatever it was, it seems to have destroyed her confidence, which makes me feel things it shouldn't. Namely, destroying the piece of shit that made her feel like that.

When I look at her, my hand rests on the side of her cheek. "Everlee." My words are soft as I read every emotion flitting across her face.

"She was one of your..."

"Yes. But it was a long time ago. She has since moved on and has a wonderful husband and three beautiful children. We get a Christmas card every year from them."

"It's fine," she says, and I know she's not fine and this feeling I'm not used to creeps in, moving under skin like a snake in the grass. Damn it. I want to console her, give her confidence, give her that fire in her eyes that I've grown accustomed to seeing.

Stepping forward, so my elbow brushes along her chest while my hand still cups her cheek, I gaze down at her. "Your pussy is the only pussy I want my tongue in, my fingers in, and my cock in. No one else's."

"Until when? This week and then I'm gone? Time to move on to the next woman?" She holds her hand up. "I'm sorry. I shouldn't have said that. I knew what I was getting into when I signed the contract."

Taking a deep breath, I grab her hand and bring it to my lips. "I don't know what our future holds. But I don't want the could be, to get in the way of the now. If you've changed your mind and don't want to come over tonight, I'll understand. No hard feelings." Lies. I've been looking forward to tonight and the feel of her pussy and the need that ravages like a fire within, wanting to see the guys fuck her. I've not been much of a voyeur, but something about wanting to watch them with her turns me on.

"No. I want to come over."

"Let's have fun here, and then we'll see what happens. Ok?"

She nods. "If you'll excuse me, I'm going to run to the ladies' room."

"I can walk you."

"No. I'm ok." She gives me a half smile and starts walking towards the main hall.

I sit down and watch her, fighting with myself to run after her and whisk her away into a hall and make her see how much I want her, or staying here and giving her space to process.

I pull out my phone and shoot a quick text to the boys.

Damn it!

EVERLEE - HASHTAG WENDY DICK

I KNOW I'M BEING immature right now, and I'm really trying not to let my emotions get the best of me, but it's tough. Since I'd left Dick, my self-confidence has been completely shot, and it wasn't until these guys that I started to get that back, but seeing Sophie and... her status... I can't help but wonder what they see in me.

When I get into the main hallway, I look around for the small alcove the restrooms will be tucked in. Get your head in the game, Everlee. This is why I hate this holiday. It's some ploy to make people express how much they mean to one another. Why not do it all the time? Why wait for one single day in a year?

Frustration and jealousy getting the better of me, I walk into the bathroom and stand in front of the mirror with my hands on the sink and stare at myself. I'm really regretting not bringing my phone with me because I could use a Lizzy pep talk right about now.Have her tell me to ignore the insanely talented chef that made all of this amazing food and focus on the fact he's here with me. On a date. Even Sophie took notice of that, something perhaps she never had? Lizzy would say that Sophie is jealous of me because she knows I'm getting all those cocks tonight and she's not. Only Lizzy wouldn't say that because she can't know about the quadcocks just the unicock.

Feeling moderately better about myself, I wash my hands and pat them dry with the warm towel that is rolled up on the sink.

Focus on the quadcock and the fine ass man sitting beside you tonight.

With a renewed feeling, I open the door and walk right into dickface, waiting outside in the hall.

"Everlee?"

"Di... Richard?" I should have called him Dick, but I'm trying to be mature - at least to his face.

"Wow. You look amazing." His eyes are bugging out of his head, which gives me a modicum of satisfaction. If only he looked at me this way when we were together.

"What are you doing here?" we both ask in unison.

"I'm here for work," I blurt.

His brow furrows. "Wendy, too."

Wendy. Wendy and Dick. Hashtag WendyDick.

"I saw your company listed as a sponsor, but didn't think you'd be here."

"Why?" I ask accusatorially.

"Well, you hate this holiday."

"I wonder why?" I hold up my hands. "Nevermind. I'm not getting into this with you. Have a pleasant night."

"Richard? Who is this?"

Fuckballs on a wall. Could this night get any more awkward?

My body is turning around before I can stop myself and in front of me is a petite woman walking out of the bathroom, wearing a bubblegum pink a-line dress I've seen two others wearing so far and I laugh inside. I don't hate her because she's with my ex. I hate both of them because she knew

about me and didn't give two shits when she fucked him...
for months.

"Oh. Everlee."

"Hi. Let me guess. La Belle?" I ask, pointing at her dress.
She looks down and frowns. "Yes."

"Must be a popular style." Zing. From what little I know
about her- yes, I post breakup snooped because I was
lonely, pissed, and bored- she prided herself on fashion,
and the fact she's wearing the same dress as at least two
other people means she's beyond angry. She was probably
in the bathroom crying.

Well, that flips her bitch switch on because her eyes narrow and she's shooting arrows at me. Little cupid's arrows.
Pew! Pew! Pew! "I didn't think you were dating anyone. Did
you come alone?"

"One. The fact you're snooping to see if I'm dating anyone
is weird and, frankly, not healthy. And two-"

"And two. She came with me. Rather, I came with her," a
deep voice booms behind me. The hairs on my arm stand
on end as my stomach tightens and my titties tingle. Callum
approaches the group and slips his arm around me and rubs
my back. The final countdown song plays in my head and
I'm pumping my fist in my mind.

"I... uh... uh... ok."

"Richard," Dick says, sticking his hand out.

"Callum." He grabs his hand and shakes.

"So you two?" Wendy asks, pointing between Callum and
me.

"Yes, Wendy. Would you like to fuck him too?"

"Baby, you can't just pimp me out to people. Plus, I only
have eyes for you." He kisses the top of my head.

"Welp. Guess he's not interested, but this one still is for
now." I point at Dickface. "Unless that's why you've been
stalking me, because you thought he and I hooked back up.
Don't worry, we haven't, nor will we ever. Once a cheat,
always a cheat. Good luck with that. Hope it works out for
you." I turn and walk away, with Callum right by my side.

Holy forking shirtballs, that felt good. My heart is racing, and I feel like jumping up and down like a boxer in the ring. Ahh! Whew! I definitely feel like Ali right now, but like if he was words. Wham bam thank you ma'am!

Callum grabs my hand and pulls me into the stairwell.

"What are you doing?" I squeal.

He pushes me back against the wall and takes my mouth in his. His kiss is needy. Hungry. I don't know if he's trying to prove something to me, but I'm here for it. His hand slips down the back of my dress, dips inside, then he pauses, looking at me.

"Fuck Everlee. No panties again?"

"They don't fit with the dress."

"Do your clothes ever work with panties?" He takes my mouth with his again and continues moving his hand over my ass and finds my clit with the tip of his finger. "You're so fucking wet."

My back arches and I rotate my hips so he has easier access, causing a whimper to escape my lips. He slides his hand out, sucking me off his fingers, then kisses me once more. "Dinner can't come soon enough, because I can't wait to get my dessert."

A hint of my lipstick stains his bottom lip, so I wipe it away with the pad of my thumb. It was supposed to be smudge proof, but perhaps they don't test for playing aggressive tonsil hockey.

Dinner comes and goes, and it's better than fantastic. There was some sort of lemon butter dill salmon and wagyu beef filet with scalloped potatoes, asparagus, mushrooms, and salad. It was really way too much, but when it's that good...

When desserts come out, Callum leans over and whispers not to fill up, because we'll be having ours at home, which sends a tingle up my spine. They bring out a band and people file onto the dance floor, so we take that as our sign to leave, but Mr. Randall grabs everyone's attention and requests a picture. As we're about to leave, Callum grabs my hand and pulls me back onto the dance floor. When I follow his eyes, I find WendyDick is out there, too. He grabs my right hand with his and places his other hand on my lower back, pulling me into him with a very authoritative yank.

"I love this dress on you, but I think I'm going to like it more when it's off." His thigh finds its place between my legs, rubbing on my sensitive spot.

"Callum," I pant.

He lightly brushes his knuckles along my cheekbone. "I don't know how I'm going to quit you." His lips press to mine softly as his tongue slips in and gently dances with mine. A flush moves around my body, and it's like everything around us has faded out. The sounds, the music, the people, it's only just the two of us.

When he stops kissing me, the world comes crashing back around me. My head is in a daze and when I look around, several people are looking at us, one of them being WendyDick. Yea, they're a unit now. Dick's eyes are narrow and angry and Wendy's are in awe. Bitch is jealous, and I'm ecstatic.

"Want to get out of here?" he murmurs, his lips gently brushing against my ear.

"Yes."

He grabs my hand and whisks me off the dance floor like you see in those ads for perfumes.

It's time. My stomach fills with knots and butterflies at the same time my heart gets a fine crack etched into it, ready to break.

EVERLEE - WHIPPED CREAM NOT JUST FOR EATING

THE CAR RIDE IS quiet as the anticipation and nerves build. Brady pulls up to their house, and Callum steps out first, then moves around to open my door with his hand outstretched. "My lady."

My fingers slide in between his and squeeze tightly like they are a lifeline. As the nerves build and twist inside me, my stomach tightens with each passing moment.

"Are you ok?"

"Yea, just a little nervous. Mostly excited."

"If it's ever too much, then just tell us."

The door swings open silently, revealing a scene straight out of a romance novel - rose petals on the floor and a tray with champagne and two glasses waiting on a little table.

"Oh, geez." Callum rolls his eyes.

"What?" I chuckle, nervously.

"I may have texted them about Sophie."

"Oh."

"So they may have gone a little overboard on decorations. Knox loves any reason to decorate."

Looking down the hall, I'm overwhelmed by the amount of streamers strewn from ceiling to wall separating us from the kitchen.

"So they don't always do this?"

"Not at all. You seem to have changed everything up."

So he's saying there's a chance.

Eager to see the boys, I bend down to take my shoes off, but Callum places his hand on my arm and stops me. "Let's let the boys get a glimpse of you in your outfit before we take anything off."

Excitement pulses through me and robs me of words, so I nod, then watch him pour us each a glass of champagne. When he hands me the glass, I immediately tilt it up to take a drink, trying to calm my racing heart. Bubbles. Focus on the bubbles.

After he places the bottle back on the tray, he grabs my hand and leads me down the hall to the kitchen, where the guys are standing completely nude with whipped cream sprayed on their chests and down around their cocks. A heat rushes through my body, pushing all the nerves out as my eyes drink up these men. My men.

My pulse is still racing, but for a completely different reason.

Suck it, Wendy!

"Fuck, you look divine!" Knox mumbles, swiping a bit of whipped cream off his chest.

"Hot... so, so hot!" Emmett continues.

"Beautiful," Jax says. Always simple, but effective.

Knox walks over, circling me like a shark circles its prey. His hand runs down my spine slowly as he trails kisses from my shoulder up to my neck. "I've been waiting all night to taste you." My eyes find Callum standing beside the counter watching us, his gaze hooded and his bulge growing.

Knox's hand skims up to my shoulder and gently pushes the strap off to the side. My eyes move to Jax, then to Emmett. They are so hot, standing there with nothing on but some whipped cream.

"Emmett. Join Knox," Callum commands.

Emmett slowly walks over. "Hey Trouble," he says as his hand cups my cheek, then leans in for a kiss. His lips press against mine, soft, tender, but full of... promise. The kiss deepens, as I close the gap between us, reaching my hand up to his cheek and he lets out a groan, then pulses his tongue in. I'm pretty sure my eyes just rolled in the back of my head with the way he's kissing me. I could kiss him forever. And Callum. Fuck! It'd be hard to choose. Emmett's kiss differs from Callum's. Soft and passionate, versus Callum's sexy and provocative.

Emmett pulls off my lips and begins working his way down my neck to my collarbone as he gently eases the strap off the other shoulder. The only thing holding this dress up at this point is the curve of my breasts.

"This has to go," Emmett says quietly, giving the dress an extra tug, so it slides down my body, falling into a puddle of sequin red fabric at my feet. I'm standing in front of them, completely nude. Well, except for my shoes- those are still on.

"Fuck, you look so good," Jax sighs, running his teeth over his bottom lip as he stands with his hand pressed on the counter, watching me. My stomach is twisting with anticipation.

God, I hope it's anticipation and not something else, like a massive gas bubble from dinner tonight. How mortifying would that be? With every thrust, a fart escapes. Gives another meaning to the soundtrack of sex.

Focus Everlee.

"Jax," Callum calls. "Go taste her."

Doing as commanded, Jax stalks over, his dark eyes focused on mine, then drops to his knees.

The simple gesture of falling to his knees in front of me has me feeling like I'm about to come and he hasn't even touched me yet.

His tongue gently runs up my wet pussy, from back to front, landing on my clit.

"So sweet," he mumbles against my skin.

Knox and Emmett continue to kiss my neck and shoulders when Callum gives another order. "Take her breasts."

They each take a breast in their mouth, their tongues swirling around each nipple before taking it between their teeth gently. My hands are having a hard time finding their place between Knox and Emmett's heads or Jax's.

My gaze shifts back to Callum, who is still by the counter watching us. A puff of air blows out, followed by stuttered oh's as Jax continues his gentle assault on my pussy. His mouth is heaven, the way his tongue moves and slides along my clit. He sucks as he presses a finger in, causing my knees to buckle.

"Oh, fuck," I cry out, still trying to figure out where to put my hands. Of all the things I was worried about and thinking through before tonight, hand placement wasn't even on the list, but I'm now realizing that it should have been near the top. I feel like I am doing some jacked up version of the robot.

"So perfect," Emmett coos, bringing me back from the edge.

Callum walks over to stand behind me, pressing his hard cock against my back. He snakes his hand around my throat, then turns my chin to look at him. My lips part as Jax moves me closer and closer to climax, but Callum takes it as an invitation. His tongue swipes across my bottom lip before taking my entire mouth in his. His kiss is passionate. Hungry. Consuming.

My hand reaches around the back of his neck, holding him to me. I'm in heaven. All their mouths are on me, licking, sucking, and fucking. My hips thrust as Jax's tongue pulses in and out, while Knox's finger slides down and begins working on my clit. "Oh... oh my." My legs are getting weaker by the second as my orgasm inches closer and closer and I climb orgasm mountain. I see the summit when Jax pulls away, as well as the others. I'm left panting and wanting, standing in the middle of their kitchen.

Bunch of assholes.

"Let me taste," Emmett says to Jax. They watch me as their lips touch.

Damn. I did not see that coming, but it was so hot. Emmett pulls back a second later. "Yes. She does taste divine."

"Let's get you to the table," Jax offers.

With everything going on, I hadn't noticed the table had a variety of fruits, whipped cream, and chocolates on it.

"What's this?" I ask, chuckling.

"Once you climb up there, it will be our dessert," Emmett says, running his finger through the whipped cream on his chest and feeding it to me.

Jax guides me over with his hips and cock pressed into my backside while his teeth graze along the edge of my throat. "I can't wait to sink my cock into your tight little pussy," he says before nibbling at my neck.

"Samesies," I whisper back in a low voice and regret it almost immediately.

Stupid. Fucking stupid. Samesies. What the hell? I need to work on my bedroom talk because that... that was an epic fail.

His hands grip my hips, as he lifts me up like I'm nothing but a feather, and places me on the table. He bites my ass just before I sit down. There's a red satin pillow at one end, so I lay my head down while Callum slowly unbuckles my shoes, letting his finger lightly rub along all the sensitive parts of my foot, causing my entire body to buzz.

Knox and Emmett walk to the back side of the table and each grab a can of whipped cream and begin spraying it on my body. Emmett over my left breast and Knox around my hips, to the apex of my legs. After Callum sits my shoes out of the way, he comes back and begins rubbing my feet.

I don't know what I had in mind about tonight, but this is definitely not it. The amount of attention and care... I feel like a goddess.

Jax grabs a can of whipped cream and mirrors what Emmett is doing, circling it around my other breast. Once they're done, they begin decorating my body with various kinds of chocolate and strawberries. Curiosity killing me, I peek down at one point and between the white whipped cream and chocolate, I feel like the Valentine's Day version of a snowman.

"This may be our best creation," Emmett brags.

"She looks delicious," Jax says.

"I can't wait to taste her," Knox agrees, swiping his tongue at a piece of whipped cream on my stomach.

A ding echoes and Emmett excitedly walks into the kitchen. A moment later, he's back with two bowls. "Hot chocolate."

With a mischievous grin, he sticks his finger in the bowl and savors the taste as he licks it clean.

He gives a bowl to Knox, who gently pours it down the center of my makeshift bra, then swirls it around each breast. The heat contrasting with the cool whipped cream causes my back to arch off the table. It feels like fire against my skin, if fire was erotic and sensual. Emmett takes the bowl in his hands and pours it on my stomach and swirls it around the mound of white above my pussy, then down each leg.

I'm a mess.

Whipped cream, chocolate sauce, strawberries, and chocolate morsels cover my entire body.

"Who wants dessert, guys?" Callum asks.

They all raise their hands and move towards me like animals diving onto their prey. Knox sprays the remaining whipped cream on my nose and my lips. A second later, his tongue is lapping up the sweet cream and oh, his kiss. He's fast and wet, his tongue skillfully moving with ease.

Distracted by the kiss, I hadn't noticed someone had crawled onto the table and landed between my legs, but a second later, their tongue is licking through all the creamy sweetness, causing goosebumps to raise all over my body.

"So perfect," Emmett mumbles, licking the chocolate up my body to my breast.

With all this attention on me, I feel like I should give something back, so I reach to grab Jax's hard cock and hear him let out a sigh. My hand slides down his shaft with ease, slicked up from the whipped cream, but I pump slowly. "I want to taste."

His eyes, meeting mine, flutter with excitement.

My heels dig into the table as I push and slide my body up and hang my head off the edge. The tip of his cock presses against my lips, so I swirl my tongue around it, lapping up all the whipped cream before sucking him into my mouth. He hits the back of my throat and triggers my gag reflex, but I adjust slightly and try to relax my jaw.

"Shit Everlee," Jax hums in a deep and gravelly sound of appreciation. "Your mouth is a fucking dream."

"Isn't it though, brother?" Callum asks, lifting his head from my pussy.

He thrusts into my mouth again and again, getting faster and faster.

"I say we move this party into a bedroom," Emmett suggests, eating the last strawberry off me.

They all stop thrusting, licking, and sucking and look at me. Their eyes are so intense with hunger, all I can do is nod.

Emmett scoops me up in his arms, garnering a squeal from me. He runs up the stairs and down the hall, and it takes me a moment, but I realize where we're going.

The voyeur room. Only this time we'll all be in there.

Emmett throws me onto the bed and crawls over top of me. "My turn for a taste, Trouble." He slides his body down mine, lifts my legs over his shoulders with authority, and buries his face. He's hungry like a man who hasn't seen food in days and I'm a plate of all his favorites.

"Oh." My body does a wave on the bed. "Shit, Emmett."

"He has a mouth of the Gods," Knox mentions.

"I'm about..." Waves of pleasure wash over me as my orgasm hits me fast and hard. "Too late."

Jax brushes his hand across my cheek as my insides still clench. "We're all clean and get tested frequently. Do you want condoms or no condoms?" he asks breathlessly.

"I want you all to fill me with your come," I pant between waves of bliss.

He smiles a devilish, wicked smile. "We're going to fill every hole of yours with our come. You are ours. Now open that dirty little mouth and suck my cock."

He barely waits for it to be fully open before he thrusts it in. Remnants of the sweet cream linger on his cock, making me want to devour it all the more. "That's right, Everlee."

Callum climbs on the bed and watches me suck his brother's cock as he slowly strokes his own, his teeth scraping over his bottom lip.

"I think it's time we give our girl what she wants," Callum says, and everyone freezes, tossing the towels to the side after they finish wiping away the rest of the whipped cream.

Knox steps forward and lowers himself on top of me. "Are you ready, Ali?"

I nod.

"Words, baby," Callum reminds, using his fingers to guide my chin towards him.

"Yes. I'm ready."

Knox lines up the head of his cock, teasing me. I look up at him as his head lowers to mine, taking me into a kiss. "I'm going to love fucking you."

"Samesies," I hear whispered and catch Jax out of the corner of my eye with a grin spread across his face.

I cast a nasty glare at him, causing him to chuckle the same time Knox presses in. Pleasure unfurls inside of me, causing a whimper to escape.

"You feel so fucking good," Knox growls, pressing into me again.

"More!" I cry out with a guttural moan. In a quick swoop, Knox rolls us over so I'm sitting on top of him. My eyes dart around and find all the men watching me with their hands on their cock, eyes hungry as they stroke themselves. I feel so wanted, so alive. My body is already buzzing, preparing for another orgasm as I continue to grind onto him harder.

"I need more," I call out again.

Knox leans back, so I'm lying on top of him. A pair of hands clamp on my hips as something wet slides over my forbidden area, robbing me of breath. Emmett is kissing my shoulder a second later.

"Are you ok?" Knox asks, looking up at me.

"Mmhmm." I smile back, eyes focused on him. I didn't want to tell him I was nervous, but also excited. It's been a while since I've had anyone back there, and I've never had someone in my vagina at the same time. The pressure... is it going to be too much?

Emmett presses a lubed finger in slowly, working the area and prepping it.

Knox lets out a small chuckle.

"What?" I huff.

"Your eyes, they just got so big. Like they do in cartoons. Sorry. I shouldn't be laughing, but it was so cute."

"I'm glad I can amuse you."

Emmett continues to work, and as I grow more accustom to him being there, I slowly start rocking back on both Knox, and Emmett's fingers.

"Are you ready?" Emmett asks.

"Yes."

Knox stops moving, so I rest my head on his chest. I'm so ready. Nervous still, but also ready. I've read this in my smut books and I'm finally getting to live it. Just relax, Everlee.

The lube cap clicks closed again, just before Emmett's cock presses at my entrance. Ooh buddy. That's definitely bigger than a finger. I quickly try to flip through all the images in my mind to picture what's about to go in my ass, then freeze. He's got a nicely sized cock. I'm not sure he's going to fit back there, especially with Knox. Holy spirit, activate! Holy spirit, activate! My stomach feels like it's being turned upside down as he pushes in and pauses at the tight ring of muscle, allowing me to stretch around his girth.

He continues to slide in further, stretching me, and Knox lets out a quiet sigh. I forgot Knox can feel him, too.

"Your ass takes cock so well. It's like it was molded for my dick," Emmett says, pulling out slowly before he pushes in again, hands rubbing along my back, trying to keep me relaxed.

This time, Knox moves below, both in rhythm. I feel so incredibly full that it's hard to describe. It's one of the most intense feelings I've ever experienced. It's like my body is singing.

"I can feel your cock inside of her," Knox moans, pressing in again, picking up speed.

After several thrusts of them both inside of me, I ask for more, rocking back and pressing onto Emmett. His hands glide down my back and around my side to find my clit. "Oh, shit."

I hear Jax say something over my shoulder and see Emmett nod. Everyone slows for a second just as I'm about to have another orgasm. Are they edging me?

Looking over my shoulder, Jax is lining up behind Emmett. Oh, fuck me, is he taking Emmett? I'm not prepared for this. After a minute of prep, Jax slides into Emmett, causing his cock to twitch inside of me and for a second. Emmett's eyes roll into the back of his head before they settle on me with a smile. He likes that... a lot. My gaze turns back to Jax, who also seems to enjoy it, standing there with both hands on Emmett's hips, taking him. My pussy pulses in waves. Can I have an orgasm like this... just watching them? Jax is pure sex. All muscles and tattoos.

"You like that, Ali?" Knox asks from below. "I can feel you dripping down my cock."

Emmett thrusts in again and now it's like I'm being fucked by the three of them. His thrusts feel different, deeper. Knox lines up his thrusts with Emmett's and we continue. Oh goddamn. My orgasm. So close. Oh fuck. It's going to be big and painful, but in such a good way. I don't know if my body can handle it.

Callum steps in front of me, his cock in hand. "Do you want some?"

"Yes, please!" I blurt out. Not sexy at all. But this orgasm...

"Yes, what?" His blue eyes narrow.

"Yes, Sir."

"That's a good girl." He rubs his fingers over my swollen lips, then grabs the back of my head and guides me to his cock. "Now take this cock and suck it like a good girl." He presses it in and my insides quiver with excitement.

How could something that should be so wrong feel so right? I'm theirs and they are mine. My orgasm is like a deep wave building within my body and when it crashes, it's going to be like a fucking tsunami taking everything with it.

Need consumes me and I press back onto Emmett and Knox while Callum fucks my mouth. The sound of wet smacking fills the room as everyone moves in perfect rhythm, opposing sides, but meeting inside of me. It's beautiful. Poetic. I understand why they limit this, because it's fucking magical and I never want it to end.

Emmett continues to work my clit until I feel it. The wave of the tsunami cresting, then crashing.

"Fuck, Everlee," Knox pants, just before he comes. It's like a chain reaction. Emmett whimpers, followed by Jax.

My eyes look up at Callum, head of this sex train, and house. I feast on the beauty of his body, marked with all his tattoos, scars, and muscles that are flexing with each thrust. Confident the boys will hold me up if I fall, I wrap my fingers around the base of his cock and suck him in deeper. He rewards me with an appreciative groan as he continues to thrust faster, his fingers getting wrapped in my hair, holding me in place.

"Get ready to swallow me down, baby," he warns.

He explodes into my mouth and I swallow him down as fast as I can. I've never been the type of girl who enjoys the taste of semen, but right now, in this moment. My God, I can't get enough. My hands move from his shaft to his balls, where I rub and squeeze, trying to get every drop out.

"Fuck baby," Callum heaves, before pulling out and gazing down at me with fire in his eyes.

The arm that had been holding me up buckles and I collapse on top of Knox. A second later, Emmett gently pulls out, then Knox. Jax and Emmett move to the set of dressers on one side of the room and grab wipes or something, because it looks like they're cleaning themselves up.

"I'll be back," Jax says, still stroking his cock as he walks into the adjoining room.

The bathroom. The enormous bathtub. I vaguely remember it from the night Callum and I were in this room. He carried me in there to clean me up and take care of me. They all did.

A few minutes later, Jax walks back in. "It's ready."

Fully satiated, I lift my head off Knox's chest, and immediately miss the soothing beat of his heart.

"Come on, Trouble," Emmett says, scooping me off Knox's chest.

Knox cries out, "Hey, you're taking my blanket."

I reach out to him as Emmett carries me further away. "Don't worry. He'll come."

"He already did," I mumble, taking Emmett's nipple ring in my mouth and twirling my tongue around it.

He looks down at me with a smirk on his lips. "Yes, he did." He kisses the top of my forehead.

When we get into the bathroom a moment later, I realize how much I don't remember of the space. It's like an indoor spa. Massive. And what I thought was a bathtub before looks to be the size of a hot tub. It's a huge porcelain square tub in the middle of the floor. It doesn't seem to have the bubbles like traditional hot tubs, but it could be because they're turned off. On the far wall behind the tub is a row of rainfall shower heads spread over ten or more feet with jets on the walls. On the right side of the space is a smaller room, encased in wood, perhaps a sauna?

Emmett drops me off at the bathtub... er, hot tub? I'm still not sure what to call it. I climb in, and a moment later, the boys are joining me. Jax flicks something on the switch and music plays throughout the room and the lights dim as another set of lights turn on in the hot tub. They are changing from purple to pink, green to blue. He must have poured some sort of scent packet into the water because lavender and lemongrass stir through the air.

My back presses against the wall as the warm water soothes me, with Emmett sitting on one side of me and Jax on the other. Callum and Knox are both across from me. The water feels amazing, and a second later, the jets turn on, blowing hot water down my back with one on the seat, blowing through my legs. It's not as forceful as the others, but positioned in a way that makes me not want to clean up. If my time with them is limited, I'm going to make it count.

Callum and Knox grab a foot and begin rubbing. I moan out, tilting my head backward onto the side of the tub.

"Oh baby, don't do that or we won't make it out of here," Jax warns.

Damn, he is handsome. All dark and mysterious. He doesn't have the same blue eyes that his brother has, but my goodness. He, too, looks like some sort of mafia king. Dark hair slicked back, dark eyes, chiseled jawline with tan skin and tattoos. Callum hits another spot on my foot and I reflexively let out another moan.

Jax's hooded gaze rakes across my face, to my neck, to my breast that are playing peekaboo with the colorful waves of water. Taking that as an invitation, I inch my hand towards his cock and feel it getting hard again. He looks at the rest of the boys, then looks back at me.

"Do you want my cock?" His head tilts to the side playfully.

Trying to be sexy, I bite my bottom lip and nod.

He slips his arm around me and pulls me over to sit on his lap, facing him.

"No," I huff. "I want to watch them, watch you fuck me."

"Jesus." His lips crash onto mine for just a second before he turns me around and sits me on his cock. Full of confidence, I rub my hands over my breasts, putting on a show for the others. The way their eyes lock on me, like I'm the hottest thing they've ever seen, gives me.... Confidence. Life. I've never felt more desired, more attractive, than I feel right now. While Jax guides me up and down on his cock, I move my other hand under the water and find my clit.

A puff of breath escapes as I rock my hips back and forth on Jax. Callum's hand slips from the edge of the tub under the water and I shake my head. He stares at me in shock. "You're next." I look at Emmett. "And then you. I want you all in my pussy."

"I think I'm in love," Knox shouts, garnering a chuckle from everyone. My laugh is stifled as Jax's hand moves over mine. He rubs my clit as his mouth brushes over my neck, causing my already pebbled nipples to harden even more, if possible.

Jax pumps harder and faster, the water slopping on all sides. Fortunately, the entire room seems to be designed as a wet room with tiled floors and drains, so no one's concerned about water getting out.

"Fuck me, Jax. Harder."

I can't get enough of him. I can't get enough of the boys watching me. It's so hot and erotic.

"My turn," Emmett shouts.

Jax pumps a few more times before he pulls me off him, then pats me on the butt, releasing me to Emmett. Still not believing I'm living this dream, I wade over to Emmett, climb onto his lap, and sink onto his cock. His cock feels different from Jax's. He moves slower, gyrating his hips more.

Popping up and down on Emmett's lap, I watch Jax watch us. His eyes are on fire, drinking up every delicious thrust and grunt, so I give him more. My fingers rub up my chest and roll my pebbled nipples between my fingers. Emmett's hand runs down my spine to the top of my ass, where his finger presses at my hole.

My eyes go wide with heady anticipation just as Emmett leans forward and bites my neck, sucking the skin into his mouth before his tongue swipes over his marks. "Good girl," he murmurs before slipping his thumb in. My core tightens and my clit throbs as a shot of pleasure courses through my body. "You like your ass being played with, don't you, Trouble?"

I nod, biting my finger.

"Good. Because I'm an ass guy too." He thrusts me up slowly as his thumb swirls around in my hole.

"Oh, God."

"No, Trouble. I'm just Emmett." He pumps faster and faster, causing my insides to clench and squeeze. I don't think I've ever had this many orgasms so close together. Each time they're more intense, but take longer to achieve.

My eyes stay focused on Jax. His eyes rake over me, over us, as his teeth set on his bottom lip and his arm pumps under the water ferociously. The tattoos creeping up his neck flex with every thrust, but my eyes land on the one over his pec, just above his heart. It looks like some sort of frog, but just the bones of the frog. I've seen it in pictures, but can't remember where.

Emmett pops me off, moving with precision as he rolls me over and lifts my legs over his shoulders and the edge of the tub so I'm floating on my back.

"You cheat," Callum teases. "Now she's definitely going to come."

Emmett casts a small wink, then brings my pussy to his face as his tongue darts in. My back arches, sending my head underwater. Super graceful. One point for the water. Zero points for me.

Jax is moving a second later, pressing his hand under my back while his mouth clamps around my breast.

"Dibs!" Knox shouts, moving to the other breast.

A low guttural moan escapes, like it's being pulled from the depths of my soul as he continues licking and sucking. Prickles are moving up and down my body as my orgasm edges closer. It's like I'm on the fucking merry-go-round of sex town! My legs clamp to his head and I ride his face hard, the sensations taking control of my body. "Fuck. Me. Oh. My. Ah. Shit." The orgasm is so intense, my toes literally curl as the muscles in my body constrict like the orgasm is sucking everything out of me. My muscles pulse repeatedly, then release and I sprawl out on the water, happy to have them holding my back.

"You're like a little sex fiend."

"I've not had sex in over six months and you all are putting me on a limit. So I plan on cramming as much of that six months into one night as possible."

"Why anyone would be stupid enough to lose you is beyond me," Callum says, stroking a piece of wet hair behind my ear. He grabs my arm and I float over to him as he pulls me onto his lap and cradles me. "Now for the pampering that was supposed to happen."

"But I haven't had your cock in me tonight."

"Later," he whispers, brushing a kiss on my forehead.

Knox reaches over the edge and grabs a bucket and dips it in the water. Callum places his arm under my neck so my head tilts back and the water pours over my scalp. It's relaxing. A moment later, they're working shampoo into my hair, lathering it around. My eyelids get heavy as relaxation settles into every fiber of my body.

"Are you falling asleep on us again?" Jax chuckles.

"It just feels so good," I mumble out.

Emmett and Jax both have washcloths lathered in soap and are wiping them up and down my legs, through my legs and around my feet, while their other hand gently massages and squeezes.

I'm in heaven.

I've somehow died and gone to heaven.

I'm in the bathtub with four devilishly hot men who have sexually satisfied me repeatedly, who are now washing and massaging me.

As the boys continue, my head lulls from side to side, getting a little swirly. I'm in that space between sleep and awake, because a second later, I'm being carried, but I'm too tired to open my eyes.

"I can't let her go, Jax," Callum whispers.

"You know the rules. It's why we put them in place. So no one gets hurt," he responds, his voice achy.

"What if we all vote?" Knox asks, before his words fall to a whisper.

"Now is not the time to discuss this," Jax says, his voice more stern, but still with a crack laced throughout.

"He's right. We have the club these next couple of days, so it will be hard to see her." I can feel his gaze on me, so I pretend as best I can to maintain my steady, slow breathing and not let my eyelids flicker. I don't want them to know I heard this because I don't think I was supposed to. "She's just perfect."

"You're infatuated."

"I don't know. You know I never get attached, but she's... the moment I saw her, I could tell."

Jax must give a look, because there's silence for a bit.

"We'll see you tomorrow morning," Callum says before walking away.

JAX - IF YOU CAN'T FIGHT IT, FUCK IT

I WALK DOWNSTAIRS AND see Callum sitting at the island talking to Emmett, who's standing in the kitchen. Callum knocks back the last sip of his drink and sits it on the counter, sliding the glass over to Emmett.

"Good afternoon, boys!" I say.

Callum nods his head, but doesn't speak.

I don't think mopey is the right word, but he's been quieter the last day and a half. I know he's feeling things for Everlee, which is unlike him, but he doesn't understand. We can't have a long-term relationship. We tried it once, and it blew back in our face.

Emmett casts a glance at me, but also doesn't speak.

"What is it?" I pull up a seat at the bar.

They both look at me.

"Fuck. Is it Everlee?"

"I just don't understand why we can't try..." Callum starts.

"You all know the rules. We made them together to protect us. You barely know her and you want to change them." My words come out clipped, not because I'm irritated so much at Everlee, but because they're making me be the bad guy to protect them. Callum's the one who usually commands the group, but right now...

I rub my hands over my face, trying to wipe the frustration away. "Look. I'm not saying that..." I sigh. "That there isn't something there, or can't be."

Emmett perks up and Callum shifts his body towards me.

"You guys. You're making me be the ass."

"Only you, can prevent you, from being an ass," Emmett says in a deep voice, reminding me of the bear that used to talk about forest fires.

"What's the purpose of the rules if we're just going to ignore them?"

"There's something about her, Jax. You have to admit it," Callum encourages.

Knox bounces down the stairs jovially, then quickly turns to walk back up when he senses the tension.

"Knox!" Emmett bellows.

"I didn't do it!" Knox shouts back, pausing on the step.

"Get your ass down here, Knox," I command.

"Mannnn," he elongates and whines.

"We're talking about Everlee," Callum chimes.

"Oh. Well, then." He finishes coming down the stairs and pulls up a seat at the opposite end of the bar. "I want to keep her."

"We've been over this before. She's not a pet," I drone.

"Stop. I was only teasing." He smiles. "Kind of."

"Look." Callum clasps his fingers together. "I think..." He huffs. "She's different. I've... I've never felt this way about the others and I know it hasn't been very long. I get that. But I don't know. I just feel... something different with her. From the second she looked up at me that first night. There was this look she gave... like she was daring me. She pushes and gives as much as she takes. Most of the girls we've been with aren't like that. They're needy. She's... not."

"Fuck," I say, realizing he really does like her and won't back down easily.

He rolls his eyes. "I know. Trust me. I didn't want to like her this much. I was curious about her and when I saw her running out of the bathroom... her eyes were a mixture of fire, anger, relief... like a girl trapped trying to get out. Then that man stumbled out after her..." he shakes his head. "This feeling bubbled up inside of me and I wanted to kill him."

"We're all glad you didn't," Emmett remarks. "Plus, that's more of Jax's style."

I cut my eyes at him and he holds his hands up in retreat with a mischievous twinkle in his eye.

"Just saying," he mumbles, washing Callum's glass in the sink.

"I want to see her tonight. It's been two days and I feel my body itching."

"You're like an addict." I laugh.

"She's like a drug." He sighs, blinking slowly.

I tap the counter, the sound echoing through the empty room. "Fine."

"Fine?" the guys ask with hope in their eyes.

"I'm not saying I want to change the rules, but we'll see. We can see if she wants to come to Vixen tonight. Sophie will be there, so maybe it will be good to get another set of eyes on the situation. Get her input."

"I bought Everlee something yesterday," Emmett chimes. "Maybe I should take it to her?"

I laugh. "You'd just end up fucking her. No. I'll go."

"You'll end up fucking her," Knox retorts.

"I doubt it."

"She has a way about her, brother," Callum warns.

"I think I can manage."

Emmett runs out of the room and comes back a moment later with a small purple silicone object.

I laugh, grabbing it out of his hand and put it in my pocket.

"It has a remote!" Emmett pumps his eyebrows.

"Dibs!" Knox shouts.

"Rock, paper, scissors." Emmett balls up his fist and holds it in the palm of his hand.

"Seriously? I never win these," Knox whines.

"While you all figure this out, I'm going to head over to her house."

"Don't fuck her," Emmett playfully chides.

"I'll try not to," I reply sarcastically. She doesn't seem to have the same effect on me as she does the others. But that's fine. I'm the hard ass of the group and I'm fine taking that role.

Twenty minutes later, as I'm walking up the front steps of Everlee's building, an older woman wearing a green dress, clutching her purse under her arm, is walking out. She smiles and holds the door open for me, letting me walk right in.

Straight in. She has no idea who I am or my intentions. She just let me in. What's the point in having security measures if old women are just going to let anyone waltz right in? I push down the thoughts creeping into my mind. Everlee is a grown woman. She can handle herself.

Because I don't care.

Well, I shouldn't care.

As I walk up the stairs inside the building, I hear her voice floating down the hall and I pause. She's upset. Angry.

My fists clench and I huff at my knee jerk reaction of wanting to run to protect her.

I stay on the stairs with my back pressed against the wall and continue to listen.

"I want to talk to you," the man whines.

"I'm pretty sure there's nothing that needs to be said between us." Her tone is razor sharp. She seems more angry than scared, but that's Everlee. Our little fighter.

No. Not our. Just her. *She's* a little fighter.

"What do you want?" She sighs.

"I broke up with Wendy."

Wendy? This must be that douche from the party Callum mentioned.

"Do you expect me to care?" she snaps back. Even though she's out of sight, I can imagine her hip jutting to the side, hand confidently resting on it, and a face full of sass. The thought brings a smile to my face.

"I broke up with her for you!" he nearly yells.

"Sucks for you, because this is never happening again."

I can't help but smile.

"Come on Ev. We were good together."

"We were so good, weren't we?" she says softly, like she's giving in.

My chest tightens with a small, involuntary twitch, making me feel uneasy.

She continues, "So good that you were sleeping with at least three other girls while we were together. It wasn't that I wasn't putting out. Because damn."

"It wasn't you. It was me. It is me. I have a problem."

"No shit, Sherlock."

I smile. She's a little firecracker.

"Stop. Will you let me in so we can talk?"

I roll my eyes. He's a whiny little twat face.

"No way in hell."

"You looked so good Wednesday night. God. I couldn't get you out of my head."

"I know I looked good. My date thought so too."

"Your date. So, you aren't serious?"

"It's none of your concern what we are or aren't. You need to leave."

"Come on Everlee. I'll do whatever it takes to make it up to you."

"Fine."

What? I nearly choke. She can't seriously be giving in to this jackass.

"Fine. Name it," he answers excitedly, equally as shocked as I am.

"Go without sex for a year. No sex, no oral, no jacking off."

"That's impossible."

"No shit. So is this."

Fucking hell. I shouldn't doubt her. I also should not be feeling this level of giddy excitement.

"But I dumped her for you."

"Well, at least you're breaking up with girls before you try to bang another one. That's progress and I'm proud of you. But when I say there's literally no chance in hell of us getting back together. I mean it. Zero. Zilch. None. Nada. Zip. Z-"

"Fine. But I'm not giving up on us."

"Sucks for you."

"I'll win you back."

Rolling my eyes, I turn around the corner. I don't have all day to listen to this little cum stain and he's clearly the kind of guy who can't take a hint.

As I walk down the hall, I notice Everlee with her head pressed against the door frame. My lips curl into a smile, because I can't help but think she's debating on whether to punch him or slam the door in his face.

"I think she said no, buddy," I say as I get closer.

Her head pops up and her eyes land on me, pulsing wide with excitement.

"Who are you?" Douche face asks.

Feeling a surge of anger, I stuff my hands into my pocket, resisting the temptation to slam his head through the wall when I see his cocky little expression. However, the slight quiver I see from him causes a pulse of pleasure to spread through me. I'm at least a head taller than him and muscle... there's no contest. I could flick him with my left pinky and he'd fall over. Probably crawl to find his mother's teat.

"None of your concern."

"Ev. I'm not going to leave you here with this stranger." He thumbs over his shoulder at me.

"Seriously, what the fuck?" she retorts. "He's not a stranger."

I wink at her. No, we're not strangers at all. I probably know her better than he does. He probably needs a fucking map to find her clit and then still couldn't find it. Fucking hell, this guy is just grating on my nerves standing here.

"I know most all of your friends."

"For the old me. But you know what I learned when you cheated on me? I learned that all *our* friends were really just *your* friends. I had to rebuild my life. But you know what? I'm good with that. I learned I don't need you or any of *your* friends. I'm happy now. I feel complete and, more importantly, I feel enough."

There's a slight ache in my chest at her words. The fact she didn't feel like she was enough before pisses me off and the fact it pisses me off... *also* pisses me off.

I push past douche face.

"I knew I should have never come here. Wendy is so much better than you."

I look at Everlee and feel my temper flare and my pulse quicken. I slowly turn my head to look at the little asshat. "You will not stand here and guilt trip her into feeling sorry for your weak ass. She doesn't need you and the fact you can see that is tearing you up inside to the point you feel you need to belittle and degrade her. If you don't walk your tiny timbuck, scrawny ass back down the hall, I'm going to help you and I can guarantee you don't want me doing that."

"You don't scare me."

I take a step forward. "I'm not trying to scare you, princess. I'm merely just giving you a heads up, so when I lay my hands on you, you can't say I didn't warn you."

He looks between Everlee and me. "You're going to regret this," he mumbles before storming away.

"Doubt it, dickweed," I call after him before slamming the door.

Everlee wraps her arms around me, catching me off guard for a moment. I swallow and wrap my arms around her, holding her there. Her scent of lavender and honeysuckle swirls in the air, and I can feel my arms tightening around her. This is not supposed to be happening.

"You smell good," she says, before pushing off me.

I don't tell her the same even though I think it because I need to draw a line in the sand and retreat. Seeing that little cumchummer set me off and made me feel things for her I don't want to feel. "I take it that was the ex, Callum met?" I ask coolly, pushing the emotion down.

"The one and only."

"Seems like a charmer."

"He could be. I fell for it at one point."

The pain in her voice pulls at something inside of me. I run my fingers down her cheek affectionately, staring into her eyes. Her lips part and her pupils dilate. Her responsiveness to me, to us, turns me on.

She swallows and blinks hard. "What are you doing here?" She walks into the kitchen to grab a glass of water.

I look around her living room and kitchen. It's small, but homey. "Just wanted to check on you."

"Wanted to check on me?" Her voice trembles with unmistakable doubt.

"Good thing I did since the *charmer* was here."

She presses her hand into my chest. "I'll have you know I don't need you or any other man fighting my battles for me. I'm a capable woman."

There's no doubt about that. Perhaps that's what makes her so attractive. "I've seen how capable you are."

"Don't you forget it." She casts a flirtatious look over her shoulder as she walks into her bedroom. My legs follow before I know what's happening. She flips the light, then turns around, bumping into my chest.

"What's that?" I ask, looking over her shoulder.

"What's what?" she asks with a hint of panic in her voice.

"On your shelf."

"Nothing." She throws her hand on the door frame, a feeble attempt to block me.

I chuckle. "That was not nothing."

A flush creeps onto her cheeks. "Pretty sure it's nothing."

I easily push past her arm and flip the lights back on. "Oh, baby," I say in a low voice.

"What? A girl has needs that need to be met."

"Yes, she does and if that's what you've been using... I mean, the green one's the only one that looks anywhere close to satisfying you, the others look like they'd just piss you off." As I walk over to the shelf, I carefully examine each one, mounted like silicone trophies, and feel her presence linger behind me. "Do you have any *needs* which need to be met right now?" The words escape my mouth before I can stop myself.

"Gah- what?"

I brush the few strands of fallen hair behind her ear. "You heard me."

Her jaw slacks. "Are you offering?" She squeezes her eyes shut and shakes her head. "Is that... allowed?"

I chuckle. "Do you ask that of Callum?"

"Fair point."

"So, I'll ask again... do you have needs?" My voice drops as I step closer to her.

She closes the gap, sucking her bottom lip in.

"You need to stop doing that."

"Doing what?"

"Biting your lip."

"Like this?" She teases, sucking her lip in again, letting her teeth slowly scrape across it.

Fuck me. I can feel what little resolve I have vanish. My hand clamps around her neck and I drive her back into the wall, staring at her. I know I shouldn't be doing this. Giving into these feelings, but damn it.

"If you're trying to scare me, it's not working. It's only turning me on more."

With a low chuckle, I watch her breath hitch, a clear sign of her anticipation. "I know." I take her mouth, pressing my tongue in, claiming her.

She whimpers out and her knees give the slightest buckle. Her hands nervously fumble with the buttons on my pants and I can't help but smile under our kiss. I give her another second before I unbutton my pants. She grabs them and pulls them down as she falls to her knees. I love how eager she is to take my cock in her mouth.

Without hesitation, she grips her fingers around the base and pumps it a few times into full erection. She looks up at me with those eyes. God. Those sexy fuck me eyes. She watches me watch her as she slowly presses her lips to the tip of my cock, almost like she's waiting for me to tell her to stop or that we shouldn't be doing this. I know we shouldn't be fucking doing this, but damn it, I can't- don't want to-stop it. I'm supposed to be the strong one. It's why I came.

I laugh to myself. Came.

After a second, she sucks me in fast and hard, without finesse. I draw in a breath and feel my muscles clench. Fuck, she feels so good around my cock. My hands press against the wall to hold me up as I watch her take my length in her mouth. A moan escapes from between my lips and it seems to spark something inside of her because she readjusts and gives more.

Her tongue runs down my shaft and back up again, coating it in her saliva, before she rolls it around the head and sucks it in. I hit the back of her throat and feel it tighten around me and my legs give a slight buckle. My hands tangle in her hair as a need flares inside of me. A need to fuck her face, to give her what she wants, but I don't want to lose control. I'm not like the others. "I don't know if you can handle me, princess."

She looks up at me and her cheeks hollow out around my dick like she's daring me.

"But goddamn, you suck cock so good." I lose control and thrust in, hitting the back of her throat. I watch her. Watch every part of her. Her eyes are watering, but she takes it. God, she fucking takes it. I pound into her relentlessly, waiting for her to stop me. But praying she doesn't. She feels so good. This feels so good. And I hate it. This was not supposed to happen. *She* was not supposed to happen.

I try to pull away, but fuck, it feels so good and she clamps around me tighter, not letting me budge. This can't happen. I have rules.

She closes her eyes, concentrating on taking my cock and sucks harder, like she's begging for my thrusts and I nearly explode in her mouth. She doesn't whimper or whine, but asks for more and that's what I'll give her. Rules be damned, I'll give her all of me. Her hand falls off, only momentarily, abandoning my cock as I fuck her face, but then, as if summoning the strength, she clamps her hand back on and gives small twists nearly making me come.

I raise on my tiptoes as my balls tighten. "Fuck, Everlee." I press my hands against the wall and let my body take over. Take what it wants from her and she gives it. Fuck, does she give it. I press in two more times, then feel the sweet release. Feel the tingle shoot down my spine as I explode into her mouth and she swallows. She fucking swallows and pumps, pumps and swallows, taking it like a fucking queen.

When I lift her from the ground, I wipe my thumb across her chin and take her swollen, just fucked lips with my mouth. I want all of her- her kiss, her pussy. I pull out of the kiss. "You made me break my rule."

"What rule is that?"

"You come first."

She shrugs apathetically with a smile curling her lips.

Heat races through me. "My turn."

Her eyes pulse with excitement.

As I snake my fingers between the opening in her shirt, I forcefully rip it apart. There are a lot of fucking buttons and I don't have the restraint right now to unhook them one by one. The sounds of little plastic pieces hitting the ground fill the air. I see a brief frown as she looks at the buttons scattering, but I don't wait. Her bra is off in seconds, sliding down her arms to the floor with her breasts on display. Perfection. Without waiting another second, I lean down and suck the right one into my mouth, letting my tongue play on her nipple.

I lift her off the wall and toss her to the bed like a rag doll. She tries to scoot to the center, but I grab her legs and pull her back to the edge. "Where do you think you're going?"

She looks up at me, panting. She likes to be controlled, but I don't think she realized it before. It's why Callum's praises set her off. The fire in her eyes. She wants to be submissive. My cock twitches with excitement, because until now, I don't think I realized how much I wanted to control her. Goddamn. The boys are going to have a fucking field day with this.

I shake my head to clear it and refocus on her. On her beautiful breasts and that delicious fucking pussy. With a swift motion, I tear off her pants and casually discard them, then slip my fingers into the top of her panties and gently pull them down, savoring the sweet revelation of her perfect body. The way her skin dips and curves. The way it erupts in a flurry of goosebumps, when she's excited or when the cool air hits her. She's a goddamn vision.

"I want you to finger fuck yourself. Show me how you do it when you're by yourself."

She looks at me for a second, then slowly glides her hand down to her clit where she pauses, no doubt surprised at how wet she is. Her fingers circles a few times, before she slips them in, arching her back off the bed.

I love watching her. The way she responds to her own touch. The way she nibbles on her bottom lip. "Keep going. I want to watch you come."

She circles faster as her other hand snakes up her body and rubs over her breast, pinching her pebbled nipple.

"Keep going," I command, walking over to her shelf of dildos. I grab a small bright pink one with a string on one end, and the large green dildo. "Which one should I use?" I hold them up.

She shakes her head, unable to concentrate. I can tell by the flush on her skin, the look in her eyes, and the way her fingers are moving, that she's getting close. She opens her legs wider as her fingers pump into her as far as they can go, her palm pressing to the outside of her clit.

"Good girl," I say in a low voice, my desire nearly robbing me of breath.

Her eyes flash wildly at the two words and a moment later her back arches off the bed, while she continues to fuck herself.

Not able to hold back any longer, I jump on the bed, grab her fingers out of her pussy and suck her release off them. I move to her breast, sucking and swirling my tongue around her nipple, then move to her neck. The overwhelming need to taste all of her consumes me, and a moan slips out. I rub my hand down her body and over her clit and she twitches under my touch. I know she's still coming down from her orgasm, but I can't help myself.

"Let's try this one first." I flip on the smaller light pink one, then look back at her. Our eyes lock as I slowly insert it in. A shudder of a breath escapes between her lips, followed by a moan. I pump it in slowly several times and then rub it over her tight hole.

Her eyes grow wide with excitement as realization hits. I lean over and place soft kisses on her neck, just under her ear, before gently sucking on her fevered skin. Her head falls to the side, granting me more access as I continue to suck. I want to suck harder. Mark her. Show the world who she belongs to, but I restrain.

Moving my lips over hers in a wide mouth kiss, I gently press the small pink vibrator in her ass, then swallow her whimpers of ecstasy. I drag it out, then push it all the way in, causing her hips to thrust up.

She grabs under my jaw with a firm grip, eyes on fire. "Give me your cock now."

"Yes, ma'am." I don't hesitate, lining it up at her entrance and slamming into her. A puff of air escapes as I fully seat inside of her, feeling the slight vibration from her ass. I slowly pull out, then punch in again. Her pussy feels fucking amazing, like it's made for my cock. "You told me to fuck you harder when we were in the bathtub."

She nods.

"I plan to fuck you so hard, you forget your name." As I slam into her again, I take her lips in an unforgivingly rough kiss. Needing to go deeper, I grab each leg and pull them in front of me and throw them over my shoulders. With her feet pointing towards the ceiling, she is fully open to me, allowing me to press in deeper–so deep that I hope her lungs feel my cock. Wrapping my arms around both her legs, I raise up on my knees, and fuck her. Hard and fast. After a while, I pull out and flip her over, pressing her stomach to the bed.

"You want more now?" I lean down and murmur in her ear.

"Yes. Jax. Give me more."

I smile. "As you wish."

Grabbing her hips, I pull her up onto all fours, then slide my hand up her back to between her shoulder blades and press down, so her ass is up in the air. My fingers dig into her hips, holding her in place so I can make her mine. She moans out as I press into her and fuck do I love that noise. She's moaning for my cock and no one else's right now and that causes sparks to shoot down my spine. I'm close again, but I refuse to come before she does. The first time, I was weak.

Snaking my hand around her waist, I find her clit and rub.

"Holy shit, Jax," she groans out.

The wet slaps of my body pressing against hers fill the room as I continue to fuck her. We aren't quiet and I couldn't give two shits. Let the whole goddamn apartment building know who's fucking her and making her moan and scream.

I can tell she's getting closer, because her pussy quivers just before her orgasm slams into her, so hard her chest bucks off the bed. I press her back down, pulling out the vibrator and tossing it across the room before grabbing both her hips and fucking her through the orgasm, pressing in deep. Her groans are so fucking loud it's pulling mine out of me and I explode. So hard my toes curl and the muscles in my thighs seize. "Fuck," I mumble out before collapsing on her back.

The sounds of our heavy breathing are the only sounds in the room, aside from the echo of the vibrator humming against the floor wherever it ended up.

After pulling out, I tumble onto the bed beside her, and she rolls over, her gaze landing on me. I pull her into me, feeling the warmth of her body against mine, and ask, "Had enough?"

"If I said no, would you believe me?" she smirks.

"Insatiable." I kiss her nose.

I roll over on my back and pull her on top of me, so she's laying on my chest. She lays there for a moment, catching her breath before she pops her head up and starts tracing my tattoos.

"What does this one mean?" she asks, running her finger across my chest.

I don't have to look down to know which one she's talking about. My frog. "I was in the SEALs and my buddies and I got them."

She props her head on my chest. "You were a SEAL?"

I nod, but don't elaborate. I don't talk about it much with people. It's not something I want to share because that was a time in my life that... I sigh. I was good. I was effective. But that's because there was a beast that was born which made me effective. A beast that I have to keep buried now. Fortunately, she doesn't ask more questions, but continues to look over my body. Tracing my tattoos, my scars, all of my imperfections.

After a while, she lays back down for an immeasurable amount of time, then asks, "So, why did you come by? Or was it to make up for the last time?" she teases.

I playfully push her off and jump out of bed, trying to fight the smile tugging on my lips. "Well, it wasn't to fuck you. That just sort of happened."

"It did, did it?"

I nod, feeling the cool fabric of my pants as I slip them back on. Reaching into my pocket, I pull out the small purple silicone vibrator and give it to her.

"What's this?"

"I think you know what it is."

"What am I supposed to do with it?"

"I think you know what you're supposed to do with it." I smile and toss it on the bed.

"The boys want to see you tonight at the club."

"And I'm expected to drop all my plans and come?"

"If you come is up to you, but we expect you to show up." I wink.

"I see what you did there."

"Just be sure to turn it on before you arrive. We'll tell the bouncer to be expecting you."

"And Lizzy, too."

"And Lizzy." I knock my knuckles on the door. "Try not to miss me too much."

"I've already forgotten you were here."

"I doubt that, love." Before I take her back to bed, I dart out of her room and out of her apartment and press my back against the wall to catch my breath. What the fuck was that? That was not supposed to happen.

EVERLEE - PPE, NOT PERSONAL PROTECTION EQUIPMENT

IF I DIDN'T KNOW better, I would say Lizzy somehow orchestrated this. I swear she puts things out into the universe and the Gods are like boom! Grant this one her wishes. She was texting me just before douchecanoe showed up, wanting to go out to Vixen tonight. It wasn't until she accused me of being an old hag with granny panties that I succumbed to her commands.

"This line is insane," Lizzy says as we walk up to Vixen.

"Good thing I know someone," I say, tossing her a wink. Tonight, I opted for a black sequin strapless dress with low heels. Much to my dismay, wearing the purple pussy eater required me to wear panties. I guess technically I didn't have to, but the thought of nothing to help protect it from falling out onto the floor made me nervous. Visions of me dancing, then birthing it in the middle of the room, played on repeat in my mind when I was getting ready. That would be awkward as fuck.

We walk up to the bouncer and before I can tell him who we are, he opens the rope for us. "They'll see you upstairs."

"Upstairs?" Lizzy shimmies her shoulders. "Look who's all fancy now."

"Stop." I bat as we walk down the hall. Standing midway down is another bouncer, who's standing at the base of the stairs and just waves us through.

"Are you sure Tony won't have a problem with you being here?" I call over my shoulder as we walk up.

"No. He's at a work dinner or something. He said he may swing by later tonight, depending on what time he gets done and where we're at."

It's already ten o'clock, and I know Lizzy said he was working on closing a big deal, which often means lots of late nights and expensive dinners. I can't imagine him wanting to come out to a club after all that.

The upstairs is a little quieter. There's a bar in the center and oversized booths scattered around the floor, with a small dance space in the middle. The second-floor curves around the downstairs so that whoever is up here can watch what's going on from almost every angle.

"There she is," a voice booms.

Callum.

He's on the opposite side of the room, walking towards us with his arms outstretched. Class and sophistication. Sex and Power. That is Callum McCall, and he's intoxicating.

"Hello ladies," he coos, sliding one hand into his pocket, causing the muscles in his arm to flex under his jacket.

"Hey," I choke out, trying to swallow the dam of drool that just released in my mouth.

"I wanted to formally introduce you to someone," Callum offers, pulling his hand out of his pocket.

I see her walking over out of the corner of my eye. She's sophistication bottled up in a petite little frame with a pixie haircut. She's wearing a spaghetti strap v-neck black dress.

Lizzy grabs my arm, recognizing her immediately.

"Everlee. Lizzy. I want you to meet my good friend, Sophie."

Lizzy is the first to step forward because she isn't tainted by the fact Sophie is Callum and the guy's ex-lover. She throws her hand out to shake Sophie's. "Oh my. I. What?" Lizzy glances at me, then back to Sophie. "I'm sorry. Just fan-girling over here. I bought your cookbook like two years ago and," she kisses the tips of her fingers. "Chef's kiss." She laughs out loud, realizing what she said, then continues excitedly, "And then I started watching your cooking show and your other at home show, then I saw you were in town." She pats the air down. "Needless to say. Huge fan."

Sophie chuckles softly. "Well, thank you. I love meeting fans."

Lizzy thumbs at herself. "Right here!"

I laugh because I haven't seen Lizzy this excited to meet someone since we got backstage passes at a Michael Bublé concert.

Sophie turns toward me. "Everlee. So happy I get to formally meet you." She quickly glances at Lizzy. "Callum has told me so much about you."

My eyes rest on Callum, wondering what in the world he could have said or if she's just being nice. He pumps his eyebrows, but I'm still uncertain.

"I've reserved the upper floor for us tonight," Callum says. "As well as the bar. Drink whatever you'd like." He directs us over to one of the large semicircle booths against the wall, out of sight from the floor below.

Sophie holds out her hand. "Lizzy, would you like to come to the bar with me to pick out a shot for the group?"

"Not me," Callum says, waving his hand.

Sophie glances at me, encouraging me to work on Callum. "Just one?" I pout, sticking my bottom lip out before mouthing, sir.

He glares at me playfully. "Fine. One. But that's it." He gives me a hard glare that tells me not to push it.

I grab his leg and squeeze, feeling his thigh muscles flex inside his pants, which causes butterflies to dance in my stomach. I have to look away to get ahold of myself and to hide the blush on my cheeks. It feels like there's a little sex fiend nympho inside of me who's been let out of her cage. I don't know if it's because I'd been celibate for six months, or these guys, but damn. It's like she's a scavenger looking for that dick, all bent knees, hands at the ready, flitting from one place to the other.

Lizzy and Sophie are at the bar and I can tell Lizzy is going on about something, judging by how fast her mouth and hands are moving and Sophie is just smiling, listening to it all. I appreciate she didn't use her past with Callum to sway him, but left it to me. Almost like she acknowledged me in their life.

His cheek brushes against my hair, before I feel his warm breath on my ear. "I hear you had a good time with Jax this afternoon." There's a playfulness in his voice.

When I look back at him, our faces are inches apart. "What are you talking about?"

He chortles. "Your poker face is getting better, but you have to understand. For us, we share everything. We can't afford to have secrets." His hand runs up my spine, causing a wave of goosebumps to spread across my skin. "Did you do as Jax asked?"

Excitement twists knots into my stomach as I slowly nod.

"Good girl."

A puff of air escapes between my lips. I live for his praises. It feeds into whatever this is inside of me, making me yearn for it. His head darts back to the girls, who are carrying drinks over. Sophie hands me a shot while Lizzy gives Callum his.

"To a good time tonight and a joyous trip to visit old friends," Sophie cheers.

"Here, here," Callum says before we all tilt the shot back. Lemon Drop shot, a Lizzy go-to.

"Oh, this is quite delightful," Sophie says with her soft French accent, wiping the excess of her lips.

"Oui!" Lizzy laughs.

"Here are your other drinks," the bartender says, arriving with a tray of three martini glasses.

"Pineapple Cosmo," Lizzy offers when I look at her.

One of my favorites. The cold sugar rim hits my lips at the same time a prickle vibrates from my pussy, causing me to nearly choke on the drink.

Trying my best to recover and not look like a complete idiot, I dab my mouth with a cocktail napkin and cut my eyes at Callum. He's leaning back in the chair looking every part the mafia king, with his hair slicked back, and one arm draped casually on the back of the chair and the other hand in his pocket, watching me with a knowing look in his eye. He has complete control over me with the tiniest of movements. A little press of the button.

The purple pussy eater- that's what I'm calling it - vibrates more against my clit and my g-spot. Trying to avoid completely losing my shit like a feral cat in the middle of the club, I lean forward and clamp my legs together, and attempt to place my drink on the table discreetly.

It doesn't help.

Not at all.

In fact, I think it's worse because a whimper trembles out of my lips and my eyes pulse with ecstasy. Fucking hell. My eyes dart over at him, still watching me, and a moment later the vibration slows to a point where I think he's cutting it off, but he doesn't. He leaves it on, slow and steady.

Lizzy and Sophie are engrossed in conversation when Callum leans in close, his warm breath tickling my ear as his hand firmly rests on my thigh. "So, tell me again. Did you have a good time with Jax this afternoon?" he whispers.

When I nod, the vibration picks up speed. My core is tightening and my nipples are pebbling as my fingers clamp around the edge of the chair.

"Use your words, Everlee."

"Yes..." I have to pause for a second as the wave is building.

"Yes, what Everlee?" he pushes.

"Sir," I pant out quickly, then the vibration dies.

As cliché as it sounds, I let out the breath I'd been holding, because it was the only thing keeping me from rocking in my seat and having a full-blown orgasm right here in front of everyone.

"Good girl." He kisses my cheek, then stands up. "You ladies have fun. I need to go check on some things, but I'll send Jax over here to keep you all company."

I huff as he walks away, because this thing is still inside of me like a ticking time bomb waiting to make me explode.

Why in the hell did I put it in? Give him this much power?

Jax walks over a moment later, looking as casual and sexy as ever, wearing a black suit with a black button-down. Fuck. These men in their suits. His dark eyes land on mine, watching me, drinking me in. I don't know if he's picturing me on his cock, but I am. Replays of this afternoon flicker through my head on repeat and I have to force myself not to grind my hips and take this orgasm that is dangerously close to pushing me over the edge.

He moves closer, his delicious scent swirling around me, and I try not to react. Try not to show how much I want to fuck him right here because Lizzy doesn't know which is really annoying. If they would have just allowed me to tell her and have her sign some sort of NDA as well, then I could talk to someone about this... situation. My eyes flicker to Sophie for a moment. I guess I could talk to her...

Would that be weird?

Sophie stands up, kissing either side of Jax's cheek. "How are you, darling?" she asks, grabbing both his hands.

"Doing well." He mirrors Sophie, nods a hello towards Lizzy, then moves to give me a hug. His large hands press into my lower back. "Glad you came."

"Not yet," I tease, causing him to chuckle.

"Not yet." He repeats before pulling away and taking a seat between Sophie and I.

I catch Lizzy looking curiously at us, but she doesn't say anything.

Sophie and Jax pick up a conversation talking about her new restaurant in France when I feel a vibration between my legs again. Fuck. Shit. Motherass. My orgasm is edging closer, becoming harder for me to hide. My eyes quickly dart around the floor looking for Callum, waiting to lock eyes with him so he can watch the torture he's executing on me, but I find him deep in a conversation with Knox, and both of his hands are visible.

The vibration stops.

Shit.

My eyes slowly turn to Jax, whose hand is in his pocket, coolly carrying on a conversation with Sophie.

He asks her another question, but I don't hear it because the vibration picks back up. He's toying with me.

"Are you ok, Ev?" Lizzy asks, clearly noticing my semi-panicked state and flush on my cheeks.

I nod. "All." It vibrates faster, causing the word good to be elongated, before the toy shuts off again.

Is there a range for this thing? How far can I go away from it to have it not work? Did I want to do that?

Jax keeps the vibrator off for a while after that, letting my body relax and ease into a false sense of security, but I know it won't last forever. The not knowing is exciting though.

After some time, Sophie suggests we go downstairs and dance, to which Lizzy and I agree. The music is pumping and with only the three of us up here- excluding the boys, of course- it isn't really a dance scene.

Jax stands up with us and casually buttons his jacket. "I need to check on some things, but Knox will check on you in a little."

Emmett is at Bo's tonight and is upset he can't be here with the three of us, but apparently Sophie spent the day there, working in his kitchen.

When we head downstairs, Lizzy grabs my arm gently. "What's with you and Jax?"

"What do you mean?"

"The way he looks at you."

"How?"

"Don't pretend you don't see it."

"I don't know what you're talking about."

"Like he just ate you for lunch."

Dinner, I want to correct. "That's just him."

"Well, don't let Callum see."

Callum would love to watch him fuck me. A flash back to Valentine's Day in the bathtub causes my stomach to tighten. I let my mind wander as the heavy bass from the speakers thumps through our bodies.

"This is great, no?" Sophie shouts back to both of us, grabbing our hands and guiding us onto the dance floor.

"So fun." She's impossible not to like. I literally tried not to like her, but she's this little ball you want to wrap your arms around.

A prickly feeling tingles on my neck and when I glance up, Jax, Knox, and Callum are standing shoulder to shoulder watching us. Wanting to put on a little show for them, I rub my hands up my dress and over my breast, then through my hair, never breaking eye contact.

Big mistake.

I'm dancing with the devil, and I don't even have a pitch-fork.

The vibration starts again, slower this time. Lizzy grabs my hand and starts swaying her hips from side to side, working her way down, wanting me to follow. I try, but sticking my ass out and swaying from side to side nearly sends me into convulsions.

The boys must have seen, because the vibration stops. They're toying with me. Bringing me to the edge, then cutting it off. My panties are a sopping mess now, but at least I'm standing and not sitting.

"You're acting really weird tonight."

"Sorry. I felt my hip pop," I lie. Seemed like it could be legit.

"Do we need to get your cane, grandma?"

"Shut up." I push her back and sway all the way to the floor and back up.

"There she is," Lizzy cheers excitedly.

The three of us dance in our little bubble for a while and when I look at the clock, it shows just after midnight.

"I'll be back," Lizzy calls over the music. She signs the word for bathroom.

As soon as she's gone, Sophie is by my side, holding my hands. "How are you doing with all this?"

"All what?"

"The four of them?"

I hesitate for a moment, because it feels weird. If I share, then would she share? Did I want to hear that? No, but the other part of me is dying to talk to someone about it, so I go for it and hope I don't regret it.

"It's tough."

She nods. "You may think you want it long term, but it's hard."

"How so?" We're still half swaying to the music, but anyone could see we're more interested in having a conversation than dancing.

"Callum says you've only had one group event?"

"Yea." I frown and she laughs.

"It's addicting, but then feelings become real. Attachments form. You will make yourself believe it can be a thing, all of you, but then you have to step outside of your bubble and the real world hits you. The world doesn't see love the same way the guys do. They are all, for the most part, one man, one woman. It's archaic. Sure, same-sex couples are being accepted more and more, but could you imagine showing up for Thanksgiving dinner with four men or going on a date? The world will put pressures on you." I can tell she's speaking from her own experience. Is that what happened to her? They thought they could be something more... I knew Europe is more free love and what not... did they get bit?

"Polyamory is a thing, though."

"Right, but they usually get away from city life, from the public, to avoid the daggers and swords being thrown."

I sigh because I agree with what she's saying, but I don't want to believe it. I want to believe we can make it work. They're all different and I can already feel myself getting attached. It hasn't been long at all, but it's easy to get swooped up in their life. Their world.

"I'm not trying to be a Debra Downie. I was you."

I chuckle at her mispronunciation of Debbie Downer.

"I always get it wrong. That's what you were laughing about?"

I nod. "Debbie Downer."

"Yes, that. But as I was saying, I was you until I wasn't. I had to make the choice to leave them. It was hard, but we were wrapped up in a cocoon for so long we fooled ourselves into thinking it was all going to be ok."

"The contract I signed limited our engagements to a few, but no more."

She smiles. "From what I've heard, you've already had a few and some, but one group..."

My lips tug to the side. "Maybe I can just have sex with them one at a time and never have a group play, and then we can go on?" I tease.

She gives me a hug. "I don't think they will let that happen. They have to protect themselves too. They aren't robots." She gives me a hug, ending the conversation just as Lizzy walks back.

"What did I miss?" she asks, jumping right back in.

"Oh, nothing much, darling. Want to go back upstairs and rest our feet?" Sophie asks.

"Sure."

We walk upstairs where the three men are waiting for us, looking as handsome as ever.

"We saw you dancing and were just about to come down and join you," Callum teases.

"You lie." Sophie boops him on the end of his nose.

"You're right. They weren't, but I was," Knox coos.

"We came back up to rest our feet," Sophie says, walking over to our booth.

"Everlee and I will get you all some drinks," Callum offers, placing his hand on my back as he ushers me towards the bar, but stops short. "What were you and Sophie talking about?"

His face is somewhere between playful and curious. Before this moment, I thought he'd instructed Sophie to lay the groundwork, but now I'm not so certain. "Nothing much."

"Everlee." His voice lowers and his head falls to the side.

"She was talking about you all and how I need to be prepared to let you go when this is done. Whenever it's done."

He looks down his nose at me.

"That's all. I mean, she said the world isn't ready for a relationship like ours- Sorry. Not to imply we're in a relationship. I know we're just having fun. But that's also what she said. That this needs to end before feelings get attached."

His lips harden into a flat line. "Yes, that is all very true."

His tone and the look on his face tell me there is a *but* coming, so I wait. Am I hopeful for a but? But we don't want to give you up. But we can find a way to make it work. But you've shown us we can have it all.

We walk up to the bar, and I'm too enthralled with all the ways that conversation could have gone that I don't even pay attention to what he orders. They may not be robots, but I feel like one right now. I want to be a robot, because whether or not I want to admit it, I'm getting attached. How could I not? I wouldn't call it love, but I know I don't want this to end. Whatever this is. It's all so new, but with them... I just feel... happy. At peace. Something I never felt with dickface. I feel enough for them. Which I know is stupid. But... I sigh out in frustration.

When we get back to the table, Callum hands out the round of shots and I knock it back, then sit the glass on the table and walk over to the bar and order another.

"What's wrong, jellybean?" Lizzy asks, meeting me.

"Nothing toucan Sam." Her brows furrow. She definitely knows something's wrong now. Anytime I add two things together that make little sense, it's a dead giveaway.

She grabs my arm. "Everlee. You tell me right now. Do I need to lay someone out?" She starts taking her earrings out.

I laugh, grabbing her arm. "Keep your earrings in. All is good. I just... I like them."

"Them?"

I shake my head, scrambling. "I like Callum and all his friends. They are just... they just seem great. So much better than dickface. You can tell a lot about a person, by the friends they keep."

"Is that why you keep me around?" She nudges my arm.

"The only reason. I'd have gotten rid of you a long time ago, but then people would think I'm super boring."

She throws her head back, laughing. "Yes. Yes, they would have." She Z snaps the air before we walk back over to the group.

Callum pats the seat between him and Knox, so I sit down, then lean over to give Knox a hug, and he manages to plant a quick kiss on my ear. "You look so hot tonight."

I put my hand on Callum's leg to hold up appearances we're in an exclusive relationship and guilt tears through me that I can't be like this with all of them. But they seem to understand their roles in front of people who don't know. If Lizzy wasn't here, would it be a problem? It doesn't matter because I wouldn't choose them over her. No matter how good the sex is.

EVERLEE - WHEN YOU'RE PLAYING HIDE AND SEEK, IT'S BOUND TO END IN A GOOD TIME

"YOU SEEMED QUIET DURING the last hour," Callum notes in the car ride back to his house. Lizzy called Tony, and we just dropped Sophie at her hotel.

"Sorry."

"What's going on?"

"Nothing. I mean something. But I don't want to talk about it right now."

"Do you want to do something else instead?" He closes the gap between us as his hand moves up my thigh.

I want to say no, but I can't. I just want to fuck and forget. "I'd love to do something else."

"Music, Brady. Make it something loud."

Were we really about to have sex in the back seat of a moving car, with the driver an arm's reach away? There's no way.

"I've been thinking about your pussy all night."

"I've been thinking about it too since you men thought it would be funny to edge me all night with the remote-control vibrator you gave me. You better be glad I was dancing on the floor that one time, because I would have definitely puddled all in your seat. My panties are a complete waste now."

"Then let's get rid of them."

"Already did."

He sucks in a breath before his hand slips under my dress and swipes over my glistening pussy.

"Fuck me, Everlee." He sucks his fingers, then reaches into his pocket and flips the switch for the vibrator.

Immediately the buzz clicks on and I try to close my legs, but his fingers grip onto my thigh and hold them open. "No, baby." Wave after wave pulses through my body, radiating from my pussy as my eyes lock on his. He's watching me intently, his eyes on fire. My fingers dig into the cushion of the seat and he comes in for a kiss, taking my mouth in his. Oh goddamn. A tear is trickling out of my eye because this is almost too much to take. His mouth expertly moves over mine as his tongue swirls around and my body begins to grind. I'm about to crest the top of my orgasm and all the sudden the vibration stops and a whimper rushes out along with a frustrated puff of air.

My body welcomes the brief reprieve, but it's almost turning into torture. For hours they've been playing with my orgasm, pushing it to the edge, then letting it back off. I'm so spooled up right now that the next bump or vibration could set me off on a cataclysmic orgasm that would probably show on the Richter scale.

When we get to his house, he scoops me up and carries me in. I'm fairly confident, once again, that my pussy is hanging out for the world to see, but we're on a private drive and Brady stayed in the car, giving us time to get into the house.

Callum walks us into the living room where the rest of the men are waiting. Emmett's hair is wet like he's just gotten out of a shower and is only wearing a pair of black joggers that are hanging low on his hips.

"I think she's ready, boys."

Fuck me. I go limp in Callum's arms.

I'm ready for Callum, but all of them?

Headline tomorrow reads: *Mysterious Seismic Activity reported last night. Cause still unknown.*

"Do you want to play a little game?" Callum asks.

I nod, not sure why. Because the last time they asked me to do something, I ended up with the purple pussy eater inside of me.

"Did you ever play sardines growing up?" he inquires.

"The reverse hide and seek?"

"Exactly."

I nod again, excitement robbing me of my voice box.

"Only we play naked."

My eyes grow wider.

"You hide first." He winks.

"How much time do I get?"

"How much do you need?"

"Ten minutes."

"Ten?"

"This is a big house and I want to make it good."

"Fine. Round one is ten minutes."

Round one? Thankfully, tomorrow is the weekend and I can sleep as long as I want.

All kinds of ideas fill my head as I think through where to hide. When I get to the kitchen, Knox shouts out, "Don't forget, no clothes!"

"And no orgasms unless there are two or more people hiding with you," Callum adds.

Oh shit.

My ten minutes are ticking away, but before I go upstairs, I watch the men strip out of their clothes.

The vibrator kicks on a second later, startling me and I squeal out, eliciting a laugh from the living room.

After a second, it turns off.

When I land on the top floor, I look around, having no clue where I'm going. I've only been in a few rooms up here and I know I can't go to those. The fun thing about playing sardines when I was a kid was to find the smallest space you could. Every time someone found you, they had to fit in there with you or they were out. Trying to see how many ten-year-olds could fit into a cabinet was something to behold. I'm doing the same thing now, only instead of hands and knees, it's going to be ass and cocks.

The floors barely creak under my weight as I move from room to room. They didn't say any room was off limits, so I pick a door at random and drop my dress in front of it, then hurry to the voyeur room where I drop my heels. The door at the end of the hall is calling out to me, so I sprint to it, knowing my time is running out and throw it open, only to find another set of stairs leading up. The door shuts quietly behind me as low-level lighting illuminates the stairway. Hand pressed on the wall for support, I walk up the stairs and push the door open.

I'm on their roof. But it's not just any roof. They have a rooftop bar with lighting, games, a pool, and a hot tub. I'm definitely going to hide up here, but where?

On the far end of the roof, they have a near perfect view of the downtown sky rises on the horizon. It's beautiful here, but still private.

A gentle breeze blows and reminds me I need to find a hiding spot, so I quickly settle on the green turf behind a row of chairs that overlook the cityscape. I can admire it while I wait.

The seconds tick by and turn to minutes as another cool wind blows, causing me to shiver.Why did I think it was a good idea to come outside on the roof of their house and hide in the nude in the winter? I didn't feel the air at first because of the excitement and anticipation, but now I've been outside for a moment, and the weather is starting to bite.

The steam rising from the hot tub and the gurgling of the jets call to me.

"Yea. Fuck this. A hot tub is an equally good place to hide," I mumble, pushing myself off the ground.

When I stand up, the purple pussy eater falls out and drops to the ground where I leave it. Probably not a good idea to take that into the hot tub. The water stings my skin, but only for a minute. By the time the water is at my neck, it feels like a warm blanket wrapped around me.

"Found you," a rough and deep voice calls.

JAX - FINDERS KEEPERS

THE MEN AND I are standing naked in the living room, and Everlee just ran up the stairs.

Ten minutes.

Ten long and agonizing minutes of waiting.

My head has been all sorts of messed up since I left her apartment this afternoon, and when I told the guys what happened, they gave me so much shit. I'm not a heartless bastard. I just follow the rules that we set forth. We put them in place for a reason and we need to follow them.

"I'm going to find her first," Knox nudges my arm, smiling.

"Fuck off!" I shove him back.

"I am," Emmett says, throwing his arm around my neck, tossing me a quick side eye.

I stare at him a minute without speaking, his look causing my pulse to quicken a bit.

"Or we can find her together," Emmett continues.

"No tag teaming," Knox whines.

"If they want to team up, they can," Callum adds.

I shove Emmett away playfully. "No thanks. I will get her on my own."

232 HEARTS AND ARROWS

"Shame. Because when I find her, I'm going to make her come before you even get a chance."

"Rules say three or more people," Knox retorts.

"Fuck the rules," Emmett challenges.

"You've been around Everlee too much." Callum laughs.

"Not as much as I'm going to be." He pumps his eyebrows.

"Fuck the rules!" Knox chimes.

I shake my head because I feel like this little mantra is developing into more than just an expression for the game. My eyes meet Callum's and when he shrugs, it causes a tightness in my stomach. Fuck me. It's up to me.

All the guys are looking at me and it feels like I have the weight of the world on my shoulders. Their looks are asking me to be ok with the change. Not in the game, but in this... whatever it is. They don't want to let her go, not yet. And I don't either, but this won't work out long term like they think it will. We tried it once with Sophie and it didn't work. It's why we created the rules. Fucking Knox... We almost lost him last time and I will not risk him again. He's an annoying little shit, but he's my brother in all sense of the word.

My jaw ticks as I clench my teeth, weighing all the options.

Am I the ass that doesn't give my consent, meaning we don't change the rules, or am I the ass for giving my consent, knowing I could have prevented the fallout and didn't?

Fucking Callum. I blame him. He's usually the one who is more grounded. Emmett and Knox are the dreamers living their life to the fullest because they don't have to make the tough decisions. Callum does, and I support him.

"This isn't a good idea."

"Things could be different," Knox says.

"And if they aren't?"

"Then we'll deal with it then."

My brows peak on my forehead as I stare at him.

"It will be different this time," he says.

Emmett claps. "Now is not the time to discuss this. Now is the time to find her and fuck her."

Everyone looks at him and nods in agreement.

This conversation isn't over by a long shot, but at least it is for now.

"Here pussy pussy pussy," Knox sings, tiptoeing through the kitchen.

"She's not down here, dumbass," I shout back, shaking my head. Stupid ass.

"You know you love him," Emmett says, shaking my arm.

"I love when the little shit is distancing himself from me. It's like a breath of fresh air."

Emmett's arm locks around my neck and pulls me over into a headlock. I sweep my leg under his, pinning him to the ground. We stare at each other without speaking and ignore the fact our cocks are touching right now.

"You two stay down here and play. It will give me a shot to find her," Callum chuckles, tossing me a wink before racing up the stairs.

I climb off Emmett and he quickly stands. "I'm fucking her first." He runs up the stairs and I'm left sitting on the floor with my arm resting on my bent knee. What the fuck was that?

Pushing whatever thoughts that are trying to creep into my head out of the way, I stand up and hold my ear to the air. Doors are opening and closing. Knox is efficiently sweeping and clearing the rooms. It's what we were trained to do in the SEALs.

She's not in a room.

I dart into the office and pull up the cameras on the rooftop and see her running to the hot tub.

"Caught you."

Shutting the screen off, I make my way up the stairs and down the hall without being seen. I want to fuck her first. I *need* to fuck her first.

Slowly, I push the door open and peek my head out. Her back is towards me as she moves around the hot tub.

"Found you."

Her body freezes, and she slowly turns to look at me, almost like she expected I would be the one to find her first.

Fuck me.

The look in her eyes, the way she drinks me in, it's addicting.

No.

Push those thoughts away.

With a gentle entry, I slip into the hot tub, barely disturbing the water, then slide next to her. She puts her hand on my thigh and looks at me with those fuck me eyes and it takes every bit of restraint I can muster. I can't very well be the one that said no to breaking the rules, only to fuck her without the others. Right?

"I was over there." She points to the chairs on the other side of the fire pit. "But you all took too long, and I was freezing my ass off."

"It would be a shame if that happened. Such a fine ass it is," I say, lifting her onto my lap, grabbing her ass in the process.

"How did you find me?"

"I looked for a bit, but when the others kept clearing rooms, I used the cameras."

"You cheat." She smacks at my chest and I flinch.

"I wanted to find you first."

"Why is that?" She flirts shamelessly, batting her eyelashes and twirling her hair.

"More time to play with you. I know you're ready to explode after how much we tortured you tonight."

"I'm glad you can appreciate the hell you all put me through."

"You liked it or you would have taken it out," I say matter-of-factly.

Our gaze lingers longer than it should.

"I guess you're right."

I smile. "Now be a darling and ride my cock while we wait for the others."

"I thought they said no orgasms with less than three people."

"There won't be."

"So you're going to continue to edge me?"

"Hopefully not, because I want to fuck that pretty little ass of yours."

Her eyes pulse wide with excitement and a second later, she's positioning herself over the tip of my cock. "So you want me to just ride you?"

I nod, raising my hips up a little, so my cock teases at her entrance.

"No, no, no." She bats her finger in front of my face and I can't help but laugh. "Payback is a bitch."

"Careful sweetie. One of us is trained in torture."

Her eyes pulse again. Her reactions to us and our words is addicting. She leans forward and presses her lips against mine, kissing me hard. Fuck, she tastes so good. My hands wrap around her back, pulling her to me, causing her breasts to press against my chest. She takes the moment and sinks slowly onto me, our breaths hitching as our lips part, breathing in each other's moans as that first thrust is all-consuming.

"Fuck, you feel so good," I whisper against her lips.

A low grunt dances in her throat as she lifts off me, then lower back down again. "Samesies." She smiles against my lips.

"I don't know if I can keep to the rules," I whisper, more to myself than to her. With need consuming me, I pull her hair back, until her head is hitting the water and take her breast in my mouth. She whimpers out and goddamn if it doesn't make me want to push further. She seems to like it when I'm rough with her and God knows I want to be. There's this restrained beast inside of me that wants to be let out of the cage, but I can't. Not yet.

The vibration from her silicone vibrator buzzes on the deck, grabbing both our attention. "Ooh cheater, cheater," I hum, grinding my cock into her slowly as my hand continues to tug on her hair. "Should we let your moans be the guide for the guys? I mean, technically, if they find you before you orgasm, we aren't breaking the rules."

"What if your neighbors hear?"

"Fuck the neighbors."

I take her breast in my mouth and run my teeth over her pebbled nipple. Testing her tolerance, I bite down a little harder and she moans, bucking on my hips.

"I don't think that was loud enough." I let go over her hair, lift her ass, then slam her down again, causing her to grunt out in hungry satisfaction. "Closer." I smile, then press a finger on her clit as her walls clench around my cock. "You're getting close. Maybe we should stop."

Her eyes set on me with fire. "Don't you fucking dare." She presses her elbows onto my neck as her arms wrap around my head and she kisses me hard, biting my lip as she rides me, grinding her hips into me.

With all the strength I can muster, I push her away. "Hold on a second." I push a button on the deck to pull up the intercom. "Found her boys. On the roof. You better hurry, because I'm about to fuck her right."

I lift her off me and push her to the other side of the hot tub so we're closer to the door. "I'm going to bend you over the edge of the hot tub and fuck you so hard the whole town will know you came." Running my hand up her back, I press between her shoulder blades until her chest is laying on the deck. She lets out a gasp when her nipples touch the icy cold surface, but it's quickly replaced with a whimper when I pull her arms behind her back, wrapping a hand around both her wrists. My free hand swipes up her center to her ass and I nearly blow my load.

"So fucking wet," I groan before pressing two fingers inside her.

Goosebumps spread over her skin as her body begs for more. I know she's close because she's not playing around anymore. She's eager and taking what she can get however she can get it. I pull my fingers out just as her pussy is clenching around them and she cries out.

"No. Please, Jax. Please."

"I want you to come around my cock and not until it's in you, will you come." The beast has gotten a foot out to play.

"Jax," she whines.

"The cries for my cock sound almost as good as your moans."

"Fuck you Ja-"

Her words fall away when I swipe my tongue across her clit, before I press it inside of her- tasting her.

"Fucckk Jax." She raises on her toes and tries to grab onto anything, but it's only flat decking.

The beast has another toe out, and need consumes me. She tastes like heaven and her moans are driving me. Driving every action. I want her. God, I fucking want her. Completely feral for her, I pull out of her pussy and suck on her clit before diving back in. Some sound between a scream and a moan works its way out of her body, and she tenses like she can hide her impending orgasm from me. She can't. I know her.

"Let it out Everlee. When you quiver, I know you're getting close."

Surprised, she looks over her shoulder. "You said not to come unless it's around your cock and they're watching."

"I said that, but I'm starving and I love the taste of your fucking pussy."

I press my face in, inhaling her sweet scent, and run my tongue along her clit. She clenches and I can feel all the muscles in her body squeezing tightly. We've been edging her for hours, so I am fairly certain this will be the most powerful orgasm she's ever had.

"Jax. I'm about to come so fucking hard."

"Squirt for me." I press my tongue inside of her, giving her something to ride, then pull out and suck on her clit as slip two fingers inside of her. I've lost control. For her. I want her to come all over me. I need it.

"Fuck!" She rears off the side of the decking just as the door bursts open and all the men are standing there watching her. Watching her fall apart under my touch. She explodes as her pussy gushes spraying across the water and her legs give out. She's trying to talk, to moan, but not a single sound escapes her lips. I dive back in, licking and sucking, slower this time, draining every ounce of pleasure out of her.

EVERLEE - SO LONG VANILLAVILLE

I'M BURSTING AT THE seams as I explode into the hot tub, pleasure pulsing through every inch, every fiber of my being. My pussy is gushing and my legs are weak as I try to catch my breath, unable to form words.

Jax dives back in, licking and sucking my clit, slower this time, draining every ounce of pleasure out of me.

"What took you guys so long?" Jax asks, standing out of the water, wiping the back of his hand across his mouth.

"How did you find her so quick?" Emmett growls, stepping into the hot tub.

"That's for me to know and you to find out, brother. Don't you say anything, Squirt." He pokes playfully at my side.

I chuckle, turning around. "Squirt?"

"Well." He tilts his head to the side. "Everyone else has a nickname for you."

"And you thought Squirt was the best one?"

"It's cute, and it fits after what you just did."

Embarrassment sweeps across me, so I bury my face in my hands because I've never done that before.

He pulls my hands down. "Don't be shy or ashamed or anything less than proud. That was absolutely amazing and exactly what I wanted." He gives me a delicate kiss on the tip of my nose.

"Who knew the SEAL had a soft side?" Knox chimes, climbing in.

"It's on my belly. Want to rub?" he teases.

"There's nothing soft about your belly," I say, rubbing my hands up his rippled edges.

He pulls me to him and murmurs against my ear. "I hope you're ready for tonight."

"You mean this morning?"

He shrugs. "You've come around my tongue and now you're going to come around my cock."

"I'm going to fix us some drinks and watch our girl get fucked," Callum says, walking over to the bar.

Knox starts to climb out, but I grab his wrist. "Not you." I point to the edge of the hot tub.

His eyes dart between Jax and me before he sits down. A smile curls on my lips as I slide over to him and wrap my hand around his hardening cock. He lets out a sigh as I run my tongue up the underside of it from bottom to top and swirl it around the head. I suck it gently like a lollipop, then pull the rest of it into my mouth, hollowing my cheeks until he hits the back of my throat.

"Goddamn Ali."

"She looks so good with a cock in her mouth," Jax says, lifting my ass out of the water so I'm standing on the two benches. "If you want me to fuck you, Squirt, we have to get out."

Torn between wanting to be fucked and wanting to suck Knox until he shoots down my throat, I hold up my finger to buy just a little more time. Knox's head rolls back as his fingers grip onto the side of the hot tub as the rest of the guys watch me. Damn, this is so hot. These men... the way they look at me. I feel like I can do anything around them and it will be perfect.

A few minutes later, I pull off and say, "I want to try something." I climb out of the hot tub, "but we need a bed. Can we go to the sex room?" All the boys look at one another, so I add, "According to your contract, this is our last time together. I want you all inside of me. At the same time."

They all quietly look around the space at each other, so I continue, "I want to take Jax and Emmett at the same time while Knox fucks my ass and I suck off Callum. I know how he likes to watch." I toss a wink at him.

"You had me at I," Knox jokes.

"You surprise me, Trouble," Emmett says, smiling.

Callum scoops me up in his arms. "I don't want you to slip and fall."

"My hero."

"I don't know about that." He looks at me, his eyes unreadable.

Mentally trying to prepare myself for what I'm about to do, I lean against his chest and let his heartbeat soothe me. Never in one hundred years would I have thought I'd be about to take four guys at one time. I've read about it in books when I was doing research, but this may be the last time I get to try it.

Callum pauses in the bedroom, holding me in his arms for a moment before standing me up. I wish I knew what he's thinking behind those beautiful blue eyes. Hell, I wish I knew what I'm thinking. Four guys? I've always been ambitious, but this is borderline scandalous.

No. It is. No doubt about it. I've leapt over the edge, leaving Vanillaville behind, and for the first time in my life, I feel great about it. I can do or say anything with no judgment. It's liberating.

Go big, before you go home, I suppose. And never see them again. Well, sexually anyway. Can I do that? See them and not want to fuck them? Not want to daydream about the could be's and should be's?

I need to stop dwelling about the future and focus on the now. Focus on the delicious men standing in front of me that want to help me live out the craziest thought I've ever had. Trying to muster up my sexy face, I crook my finger at Knox and motion for him to come over.

His walk is full of swagger, dripping sex. I wrap my arms around his neck and start kissing him softly. He seems to be the golden retriever of the bunch, the pleaser. His hands rove over my back as we enjoy each other's bodies.

Wanting to taste him again, I pepper kisses down his body until I'm on my knees in front of him. His hands gently glide through my hair and wait as I slowly take his hard length into my mouth. My fingers wrap around the base of his cock as I swallow him down, causing him to let out a stuttered breath. His hands massage my scalp while his hips rock back and forth slowly.

My gentle giant.

My little cinnamon roll.

After a few more strokes, I pull off because I don't want him to finish yet. Behind me, Emmett and Jax are slowly stroking their cocks, with beads of arousal glistening on the tip. These men and their bodies, and their cocks. My mouth is salivating as my eyes take in these gods.

Ready to take this to the next level, I walk over and grab Emmett's hand and lead him over to the bed, pushing him down. A small chuckle puffs out of his chest as he stares up at me.

"Your turn." I wink.

He's still pumping slowly on his cock as he watches me, and that alone is enough to get me off. His teeth scrape over his bottom lip as I climb onto the bed and straddle him. He grabs the satin sheet, fisting it in his hand, as I line up my pussy over his cock. Without conversation, without words, I lower onto his shaft and grab my breasts as I sink slowly onto him, taking his girth. My pussy pulls tight, stretching around his size. How in the hell am I going to fit both him and Jax inside? Nerves knot in my stomach, replacing the butterflies, but a moment later Emmett's hands are on my waist as he rocks into me. My body relaxes and stretches around him as we move faster, too fast, because Jax is behind me a moment later with his hand on my back.

"Emmett, you better not make her come right now."

With a smile, Emmett stops pumping and leisurely places his hands behind his head, tilting his gaze upwards to meet Jax's.

"Are you ready for me, you little sex demon?" Jax asks, wrapping his hand around my chin and turning my head to face him.

"Yes."

I slide off Emmett for a second as Jax lines up behind me. He runs his hand up my back between my shoulder blades and pushes me over onto Emmett. His nipple ring brushes across my nipple and we both make a noise, then look at each other, smiling. Emmett brings a comfort with him, like a big teddy bear, but with an edge.

Jax grips my hips and lines up, pressing in. He slides in faster than Emmett did, but his girth is a little wider, versus Emmett being just a touch longer. He pumps a few times until Emmett clears his throat, reminding Jax there are three other men who would like to participate.

"Are you ready?" Jax asks.

"Yes," I whimper out.

Jax pulls out, "Climb on Emmett, then I'll push in." There's something in his voice I can't place.

Nerves and excitement battle for dominance, but both rob me of my voice. I slide onto a waiting Emmett and a moment later Jax is there, the head of his cock pressed right at my entrance. My eyes lock on Emmett's and he just stares at me, his tongue running over his lips.

"Have you done this before?" I whisper.

He shakes his head without speaking. What is robbing him of his words? Is it the fact Jax's cock is touching his? My stomach clenches again.

Jax adds some lube to his cock and presses in slowly and I feel like I'm going to explode. It's so tight and I think he's barely gotten his head in. This will not work. They will not fit.

Emmett sits up, taking my breast in his mouth, causing his cock to slide out just a bit. Both Jax and I moan out, and Emmett's eye flick past my shoulder. He's watching him.

Jax pulls out, then presses his finger in, rubbing it around Emmett's cock as he tries to stretch me open. Emmett's teeth clamp down on my nipple, causing me to yelp out, so he retreats off my breast and lays back on the bed, hands fisting the sheets. He likes this. Jax touching his cock. And I like that he likes it. Holy shitballs batman.

Jax removes his finger and presses his cock in again. This time, he and Emmett push in together and hold for a second. My head feels like it's one hundred pounds and falls to Emmett's chest as I let my body relax and take both men.

"Hurry up, guys. I'm ready for her ass!" Knox whines, bouncing impatiently.

"Shut the fuck up," Jax grinds out. "We're going as fast as we can." The tone is his voice is low, sultry, like he's savoring every second, every sensation.

As he pulls out, Emmett also adds a subtle twist to his hips, easing out slowly. They press in again, this time a little faster. And my body likes it.

Loves it.

A tingle shoots from my pussy up my spine to my head, causing a guttural sound of pleasure to escape. Jax is moving in and out faster, fucking us both and Emmett looks like he's about to lose it. Jax's silent moans shake me to my core. It's like he's in a world of his own, just his cock and Emmett's, losing himself in the feel of Emmett while my pussy clenches around them.

"Fuck me!" I cry out.

Callum places his hand under my chin and lifts my head so I'm looking at him. "I can't wait to punish your filthy mouth."

My tongue forgets how to work so all I can do is smirk back at him.

A tantalizing smile curls on his lips before he drops my chin. "I think she's wet enough now," Callum calls out. His eyes look hungry, like he wants to get in on the action, but knows he has to wait. He's the last piece of the puzzle, the crème de la crème, the cherry on top. He continues to stroke himself, eager to plant his cock in my mouth, and I'm eager to have him there.

I want them to always remember tonight and remember me.

"Me. Me. Me!" Knox chimes, bouncing over. I don't see him, but I know him well enough now to know that's exactly what he's doing.

Jax pauses, leaving his cock inside of me while Knox grabs the lube and preps my ass. It feels like minutes tick by, but Emmett and Jax don't move. I clench my pussy a few times for good measure, just so I can watch Emmett smile. "I can't wait to sink my cock into this pretty little hole."

He pulls his fingers out, squeezes a little more lube on his cock, and presses it at my entrance. My eyes water with anticipation. He pushes in slowly and we all stop breathing. Why in the hell did I think this was going to be a good idea? *Because you're a kinky little fucker*, my subconscious chimes.

Knox presses in a little further and pauses. "Holy shit," he grunts.

My world goes dark as my eyes roll into the back of my head. When Emmett's face comes back into focus, I find him staring at me. Watching.

Knox slowly pulls out, adds more lube, then slides in again. All three men let out a collective sigh.

"I think watching her take your three cocks is going to make me come," Callum says, with his hand gripped firmly on his cock. It's like his hand and his mind are part of two different people right now, fighting for control.

As Knox moves faster, Jax and Emmett match his pace, moving and thrusting in sync with him once again.

"Oh my God. I can feel them inside of you," Knox pants out, hand gripped around my right hip.

The sensation is absolutely mind blowing.

See. Kinky fuckery.

"You feel so good," Emmett groans, but I don't know who he's talking about.

Feeling more confident in my body, I slowly rock my hips back and forth, moving faster and faster as the wet slaps of their cocks spur me on.

"You better get in here fast, Cal, if we want to give her all four of us at once, because I'm about to explode inside of her. This feeling is unfuckingbelievable," Emmett bellows.

Callum walks over and lifts my chin. "Give me your mouth, pretty girl, so I may fuck it."

I swallow hard and he smiles, happy with my reaction.

The King and his men.

"Feed her your cock, Callum. Make her choke on it, while she chokes our cocks," Jax urges.

These men and their words.

Callum grabs my head on both sides and guides his cock to my lips, and I open happily for him. If I wasn't already a dripping mess before, I am now.

"Emmett, don't let her fall," Callum commands.

"Never." He tosses me a wink and wraps his mouth around my hanging breast before his hands press along my ribcage to hold me up.

Callum presses all the way in until he hits the back of my throat and my gag reflex triggers.

Do. Not. Throw. Up.

Pretty sure that would kill the mood.

When he drags his cock out, I wrap my hand around the base to stop him from going so deep, praying that Emmett really won't let me fall.

He presses in again and the boys all move in the rhythm Callum sets. My body is like a cello that's being played by four bows at one time, each rubbing along the strings of my orgasm, working in perfect harmony. I take a moment to relish in this feeling of fullness. I don't know what's going to explode first. My orgasm or my head.

I suck Callum in hard and fast, my cheeks hollowing out around him.

"Oh baby girl," Callum hums, thrusting his cock in.

Screw it. I'm his tonight. He can do with me what he wants. My hands drop to the bed as I give my control over to him. His hands grip onto the side of my head and he unleashes. Tears sting my eyes, running down my cheeks and he owns me. But damn, do I love it.

I have them all, and it is glorious.

Wet slaps, grunts, and moans fill the room. Nobody speaking, only enjoying the sounds of our sex. It's erotic. If you could bottle this sound up and sell it, it would be worth billions.

"You are magnificent," Callum says, enunciating every word as he runs his fingers through my hair, pumping his cock down my throat. "You were made for our cocks."

"Yes, she was," Jax grunts.

The words hit me just the right way, and emotion wells inside of me. What did that mean?

Balancing on one hand, I wrap my hand around the base of his cock, squeezing as I suck harder.

"You want more? I'll give you more." Callum's hands clamp to the side of my head as he presses his cock in so slow, but so deep, I can't breathe. "Goddamn." He pulls it back out, allowing me to suck in a breath, then does it again, pressing his cock down my throat.

Knox bellows out. "Oh, shit. I'm..."

My hips rock just a bit as Callum pulls out.

"Don't you dare come before her," Jax commands.

"I'm trying, but goddamn. You try watching her take all of Callum's cock while you're buried in her tight ass. He's got a big fucking cock and-" he stops talking and only sighs as he tries to hold back his orgasm.

Jax's rough fingers brush across my clit and I let out a whimper around Callum's cock.

"Just a little further, boys, hold it." Jax's thrusts get sloppy as he focuses on making me come first. My clit is throbbing and is slick as butter. His finger keeps slipping off, but he doesn't give up.

Never give up, never surrender! My subconscious cheers, fist thrust into the air, standing on top of a hill.

I'm getting closer. This orgasm is unlike any other I've ever had before. My body is so tight and full that I don't think it knows what to do. But it's there in the shadows... building. Only Jax is coaxing it out into the light and my God, when it fully steps into the light, it's going to rip me apart. I've never had an oncoming orgasm scare me as much as this one does. This is going to wipe me the fuck out.

Oh no! What if I pass out? What if I die? Death by orgasm. Who would tell Lizzy? My parents? What would they say at my funeral? I shake my head. Why the fuck am I thinking about this right now?

I stiff-arm Callum, pushing him back, so he slides out of my mouth. "You need to come now, because when I do... I don't know what's going to happen and I don't want to bite your penis off."

A dark chuckle sounds as his eyes lock with mine. His fingers tilt my chin up. "Give me your mouth, darling, so that I may fill it with my come."

A fucking king.

I smile, just before he thrusts it back in, his moves erratic, needy. Jax continues to work my clit, and my hips gyrate, moving up and down without control.

"Callum," Jax calls, worried.

"I'm close."

Jax removes his finger from my clit, leaving me aching for his touch. He knows I'm a live wire. A bomb ready to explode and that's my detonation switch.

Eager to help him along, I latch onto Callum's balls, massaging them in my hand as he pounds into my face.

"Fuck. Here I..."

His back stiffens as his fingers clutch to my hair, holding me in place. A warm saltiness shoots down my throat as I continue to suck every ounce out of him. Callum pulls his cock from my mouth and I raise up like a hellbeast, who's had its fill. Jax rubs my clit and within seconds, I feel it. She's there. Lady Orgasm has arrived.

A noise, so low, so guttural, vibrates out of my chest and keeps getting louder and louder. My entire body freezes, muscles seize, my pussy clenches, and the world moves in slow motion as sounds fade, but not before I hear a collective 'Fuck', from the guys behind me. Seconds later, they all release into me, slowly pumping. My orgasm is still riding me, because there's no way I'm riding it. It's euphoric, magical, mystical. It transcends... everything. It's so intense I'm literally seeing stars and I'm having a problem breathing and then all the sudden, sounds return, as well as normal time. I collapse on Emmett, panting.

I am Jello. My limbs are mush.

"Everlee?" Emmett nudges my shoulder.

"I'm alive," I mumble against his chest.

Knox, followed by Jax, pulls out, and then I think someone pulls me off Emmett, but I'm not sure who, and I really don't care.

"Come here, Squirt." Jax cradles me in his arms.

"We're going to take care of you." He brushes a kiss across my forehead. Not because we're in a lust filled haze, but because he wants to. Jax cares for me.

Callum is standing in the bathtub waiting when we walk in. Jax hands me off, then grabs a towel to wipe himself before he steps in. These men. So rough with their cocks and their mouths, but equally gentle with their actions after. Exhaustion sweeps across me, so I lay my head against Callum's chest.

Will this be my last time here with them, like this? My contract is up. We've had our fun. I didn't care what it said before. I wanted Callum. I wanted the fun. I wanted the guys. What I didn't plan on was the addiction to the feelings of power they gave me, and now I want that.

I fight to keep my eyes open, but I'm so exhausted and satiated that it's damn near impossible. With the lavender scent, the gentle hands washing me, and the massages over my feet, legs and back, I'm out.

I'm jostled awake when they lay me on the bed and several warm bodies nestle in next to me. I take a deep breath and pass out again.

EVERLEE - GOOD 'OL BETTY FOR THE WIN

IT'S STILL EARLY IN the morning. I'm not sure what time exactly, because this room has no windows, but my eyes still burn and I feel the heavy sedation of much needed sleep still pulling on me, begging me to follow it down into the dark abyss.

Heat dances around me from the bodies in the bed. Knox is to my left and Callum is to my right, while Jax and Emmett are above me, with all our heads meeting in the middle of this oversized round bed. Someone must have changed the sheets to a beautiful dark purple, which is probably a good thing. It must have happened while I was in the bath with Jax and Callum.

I do a few kegels to get an idea of how sore I'm going to be and am relieved to find it isn't as bad as expected. The meticulous aftercare that the men are so focused on surely helps.

Last night was epic. Out of this world. It was our last hoorah together and while part of me believes they've changed their minds, the other part of me, the bigger part, believes that even if they all wanted to, they wouldn't allow it.

Rules are rules, and they aren't robots.

I laugh at myself since I've been notorious for breaking them, but after my conversation last night with Sophie, I understand why they have them. One, or several of us, will get hurt. It's inevitable. Society is not ready for a relationship like ours.

My throat constricts because I know what needs to be done. I have to leave. I can't stay. I can slide out of the bed, leave them a note, thanking them, and be gone before they wake up.

Damn it!

My eyes are stinging, and this time it isn't from the sleep. I try to hold back the tears, but one trickles out of the corner of my eye, down my cheek, onto the pillow.

Why did I have to let myself get attached? This was for fun. There were never any promises that it was going to be anything other than that. A montage plays in my head, Callum at the bar, Callum taking care of me, Bo's restaurant, Valentine's party, WendyDick's face, ice skating, all the delicious sex, the bathtub, the hot tub, Callum holding me in his arms and Jax kissing my forehead for no reason.

Fuck!

I'm in love with the attention and the feelings they give me. The feeling of invincibility and companionship. The feeling of power and control and vulnerability.

I can't say I'm in love with them because it hasn't been very long, but there is something. It's like those stories you read about where a look, a scent, or a moment frozen in time enlightens the character and they know. They know they are meant to be together. The yin to the yang. Only we aren't two... we are five. Is it a right place, wrong time sort of situation?

Maybe I have these feelings because they're my first group experience. It's like that first love thing... maybe that's what this is... my first fivesome love. Maybe it's the fact I had a complete dick of an ex who treated me like shit and I haven't been with anyone else in so long. My hormones are off the charts and making me feel things. Think things.

I need to get out of here before they wake up. I don't need them to see me crying at something that was always a temporary thing. I don't want to see the fight or the hurt in their eyes when I leave because that would give me hope... hope this isn't over.

Trying not to shake the bed too much, I press my heels into the mattress and inch my way down. Someone shifts, but I'm too scared to look. Or breathe. After a minute, I continue. When I get to the edge of the bed, I ooze onto the floor like a pile of mush, then stand up.

Knowing I shouldn't, but unable to stop myself, I turn and look at the tangled web of beautifully tattooed arms and legs. I want to remember them.

This.

Us.

My men.

Wiping the tears from my eyes with the back of my hand, I hurry towards the door and down the hall. I rush down the stairs and into the office, where I find a piece of paper and a pen and scribble a quick note.

What do you say? Thanks, it's been real? Thanks for the fivesome? Honoring the contract? I settle with

Thanks for the memories. You all have given me life! Goodbye.

                    -E

A tear falls on the bottom right corner and I try to wipe it away, but it's too late. The paper wrinkles up, but I don't have time to rewrite it. I don't want them to notice I'm gone and come looking for me.

I grab my dress and phone, and slip on my shoes, thankful they'd been moved to the kitchen at some point. I pray to God their alarm isn't set, because that would make my sneaky getaway super awkward.

The cool morning air makes the tears on my face feel like ice. I don't know how I keep forgetting we're in the dead of winter and here I am, standing outside a mini mansion in a t-shirt and dress shoes.

Hello walk of shame.

Needing to put space between the house and me, I walk down the sidewalk and duck into a small alleyway, out of sight of anyone who would be up at this freaking hour. I pull my phone out and look at it.

4:53. I'd only been asleep for maybe three hours.

I thought about calling Lizzy, but she'd have a hundred questions I can't answer right now, or maybe ever. Instead, I land on Betty.

Us non-hookers have to stick together.

Fifteen minutes later, she's pulling up at the curb wearing a shirt with ducks on it and has bright pink hair. She tilts her head down and gives me a look that I can't even begin to describe. It's a cross between excited and surprised to see me in my attire.

She waves me into the car. "Get in! What are you waiting for? You're going to catch a cold out there dressed like that."

"Hey Betty," I mumble, sliding into her back seat.

She throws her arm on the back of the passenger side headrest and turns around. "Everlee." She smacks her lips. "What have you gotten yourself into? You look well fucked and sad."

I let out a snicker. "Well, Betty, your observation is spot on."

She nods, not speaking for a minute, then pulls onto the road.

"What's got you so gloom and sneaking out of that mansion back there?"

"Mansion?"

"Oh child. This isn't my first rodeo."

I sigh. "I just needed to get away. I'm scared of getting my heart broken."

"Oh, I see. Tricky thing, the heart. You break your own heart to avoid them maybe breaking it."

She doesn't understand, and it's ok. No one can.

My phone dings like I'd been sent a message from cupid himself.

> **Sophie:** *Had a great time last night! Headed to the airport so I'm sure you won't get this until later, but if you ever need to talk, I'm only a phone call away!*

I look out of the window for a second, gathering my thoughts, then start typing.

> **Everlee:** *Had a blast as well. I'd love to chat.*

> **Sophie:** *Oh! Good morning! I didn't wake you, did I?*

> **Everlee:** *No.*

I type a long explanation, then delete it all.

> **Everlee:** *I was already awake. I just left them.*

> **Sophie:** *They don't know?*

> **Everlee:** *No. I thought it'd be better this way.*

> **Sophie:** *Better for who?*

> **Everlee:** *I don't know. I guess me.*

> **Everlee:** *Last night, per the contract, was my last night with them. Rules and all.*

Sophie: *I see. You're attached?*

Everlee: *I don't know how or why I let it happen. I know it's stupid. I knew this was temporary. And the conversation with you last night made it so clear why it has to be this way.*

Sophie: *Oh. I'm sorry.*

Everlee: *No. It was a good talk. I needed to hear it because I was trying to talk myself into how this could work, but you're right. We don't live in that kind of world yet. Family dinners, friends, dates, events… So many things I have to think about. I've been lying to my best friend in the world because I can't tell her what's going on with me and that's been killing me. I couldn't do that forever. She thinks I'm with Callum, but she's noticed the way the others are around me. The way Jax looks at me, the way we hold a hug for longer than normal. The lingering gazes and brush of the hands.*

Sophie: *This is for the best. I didn't think so when I left, but it gets better.*

Everlee: *You decided? You didn't have a contract?*

Three dots appear, then stop.

"Everything ok back there?"

"What? Huh? Yea. Just talking to a friend."

"At this hour? You young kids."

"She's catching a flight."

"You should give her my number when she gets back. Trying to build my portfolio."

I laugh. "I will, but she lives in France."

"Oh," she sighs.

My phone buzzes and I have to read her message twice.

> **Sophie:** *I think I'm the reason they have a contract. We thought we could all be happy together, and we were for months, but then things started getting more serious. Christmas was coming up and my parents wanted to meet the man who'd been occupying so much of my time. I brought Knox home with me and the others said they were fine with it, but I knew they weren't. And then, like parents do, they started talking about marriage and kids and it just put everything into perspective. I had always wanted those things, and I wasn't going to get it with them. It took another month for me to realize I had to make an impossible decision. So, I left. While I loved them, and they loved me, it just couldn't work. They didn't fight very hard, because they understood and they didn't want to keep those things from me.*

Betty stops outside of my address. "Home sweet home, darling."

"Home sweet home." I look up at the apartment building. If this was home, then why did I feel like that's what I just left?

"Fares on me this time."

"I can't do that. I probably woke you up to come get me."

"Darling. I get up before the birds every morning. I was just sitting at the kitchen table working on my book of crosswords. You've gotta keep a mind active to keep it young."

"I'll remember that."

Betty taps her nose. "You get on up there and get you some good sleep. See if it fixes your problems."

"Thanks Betty." I grab the fifty out of my purse as I get out of the car, then tap on her window. When she rolls it down, I toss it in before hurrying away.

She yells at me until I get inside of the building, but I don't turn around. Instead, I trudge up the stairs, unlock my door, throw my stuff onto the floor and fall into bed.

It still smells like Jax.

Fuck!

I rip my sheets off, throw them into a pile on the floor, grab the blanket off the couch in the living room, then fall onto my mattress, wrapping myself in the velvety softness of my reading blanket.

This is for the best, I repeat to myself as I drift off into the dark abyss.

CALLUM - THIS ISN'T GOODBYE

I CRUMBLE THE NOTE in my hand and toss it across the room as anger and pain sear through me.

Fuck!

"No. She didn't leave," Knox says, running across the room to uncrumble the note and read it.

My eyes meet Jax's and he just stares at me, lips pinched without saying anything. This isn't his fault, but we didn't get a chance to talk before we saw her last night to tell her we wanted to break the contract.

"Guys," Knox says, tossing the note on the counter. "We're going to go see her, right? This is bullshit. Fuck the contract and the rules."

"Damn it!" Jax fires out, slamming his hand against the counter. "What are we going to do? We've been down this road before and it didn't work out."

"You can't tell me you don't feel anything. I saw it on our face last night!" Knox lashes out, lunging after Jax.

Jax bats his hands away and grabs his wrists, spinning him around, and pushes him away. "I'm not saying that. Fuck! I did-do- feel something. Is that enough? I don't know?"

"So let's go see her then. Talk to her."

"And what if her mind doesn't change? Then what?"

"I know she feels something," Knox defends.

"She does, which is why she left," Emmett says just above a whisper.

"What?" Knox asks, confused.

"It's why she left. She fears getting hurt, too. All along, we have told her there is a contract and rules are rules." He holds his hands up to stop Jax from defending himself. "I get it. Rules are rules. We were saying that we were protecting her, but really we're protecting ourselves. We have a certain kink that not everyone understands, and that's fine, but we can't keep hiding behind a piece of paper. The rules were put in place to protect us."

"I don't... understand. What are you saying?" Knox asks, running his hands through his hair.

"I don't know what I'm saying. I know she's different. And I get it. It's stupid to think, feel, or say that. But I feel it. But what are we asking her to give up? We're selfish assholes, but not that selfish to ask her to give up all of her friends and family for us. Because that is what we're asking."

Knox bats the dishcloth onto the floor and yells out a garbled string of words followed by a very clear, "This is bullshit!"

I watch the scene unfold and my heart aches. Not for what could have been, but for these men. I don't know why Everlee is different. All I know is that she is. But is that enough?

"I want to go see her," Knox commands.

"I don't know if that's a good idea," Jax responds, catching an uneasy glance from Emmett. "Fine. Whatever. Let's go see her."

An hour later, we're all standing at her door. We knocked three times, but she still hasn't answered. We heard music when we walked up, so we know she's in there. Just as we're about to knock for the fourth time, she opens the door.

Her eyes are red, and her face is puffy.

Damn it.

My hand moves to cup her cheek, but I stop myself, pulling it back down. She opens the door wide and steps out of the way, saying nothing. When we get in, she closes the door and walks over to her couch and grabs a pillow and holds it on her lap. There is a box of tissues laying on the table in front of her. She looks at them, then us, then rolls her eyes, like she's ashamed we caught her crying.

We all take a seat around her living room, avoiding the couch she's on, while Knox ends up on the floor across from her.

"Hey," she says after a minute of us all staring at one another.

"Hey," we all respond in unison.

"I'm sorry." She straightens her back. "I shouldn't have-" her words get caught in her throat. "I just thought. I know it's stupid." A single tear trickles down her face before she wipes it away with the back of her hand.

My eyes catch on Jax's, and I can see his jaw tick.

"I know it was stupid for me to get attached, but I did." The guys and I just look at one another, not knowing what to say.

She continues, "But it's fine. I know the rules. There was a contract. I know why it can't work. You aren't robots and you have to protect yourself too. I talked with Sophie."

"Sophie?" I ask, a restrained irritation bubbling under the surface.

"Yes. She told me about the breakup you all had because the world had a hard time accepting you all. And I get it. It's fun while it lasts, but anything serious isn't smart. I've been lying to Lizzy about you all. Something that has made me feel..." she pauses, "this happy. Because of you all, I feel confident and... worthy. And I can't even share it with her. My parents, my brother, they are really important to me and I can't avoid them for the rest of my life."

She buries her face in the pillow for a second, then looks up. "I'm sorry. I shouldn't be crying. I've been trying not to cry, and I was doing good for a while and then you all show up... looking..." she waves her hand in the air. "And you just make it hard."

"We're sorry."

What was the sorry for? For making her cry? For letting her leave to begin with? For not telling her we want to tear up the contract?

The guy's eyes are nearly boring holes into my body as they look at me. Waiting for me to say something, anything. But I can't. I can't tell her about the contract because she's not wrong. We're making her choose between her old life and a new one. Her friends and family or us. We have no family, so it's easy for us, but her... we'd be taking that away from her. It's not fair to her.

"We just wanted to come by... and check on you."

Knox sighs and I see Jax lean forward and put his hand on his shoulder.

"I'll be ok. Because of you all, I'm in a good space right now. Not this second, but in general. I know more about me and what I want and don't want. I want someone who is going to look at me the way you all do. And I'm done with Dick." She laughs. "Rich. Not cock. You didn't turn me into a lesbian."

We all smile and I have to fight the urge more than ever to wrap her in my arms, lift her chin and take her in a kiss.

I could and she would let me. If we asked, I fear she would say yes and turn her back on her family and in months or years to come, she would resent us for it. It's unfair to her.

"You will have a standing reservation at Bo's every Monday at eight. No need to call. You will have a table," Emmett says, standing up.

Her lips pinch in a flat line. "Thank you."

Knox stands, followed by Jax, and we all meet at the door.

Jax turns around and looks at her. "This isn't goodbye." He walks out and stands in the hall.

"Ali." Knox sighs and I know he's fighting with saying what he wants to say versus what he knows he should say. He shakes his head and lets out a long sigh, balling his hands into fists, then turns and walks past Jax down the hall.

Shit.

I can see the tears welling up in her eyes and her bottom lip quivering. It is literally taking everything I have not to say fuck it all and comfort her. Even though she's hurting now, this is what she needs. She can't turn her back on her family. That's unfair. Maybe we can figure out a way...

"This isn't goodbye... just goodbye for now. We have to figure out how to make this work." My hand reaches across the distance, but I pull it back. "Please don't be a stranger." With that, I nod and leave, closing her door. Leaving her standing there alone.

Jax looks at me as I pass him, but doesn't speak. Emmett is by the car, looking down the sidewalk at Knox, who is about a block down.

"Let's go get him."

I get behind the wheel while Jax takes the passenger seat and Emmett jumps in the second row. We pull up to Knox, who looks at us, rolls his eyes, then gets in.

"This is bullshit!" he snaps as soon as the door is closed. "Complete bullshit. Everyone wants to throw away the contract. Everyone! And yet we're all fucking miserable because no one wants to say a goddamn thing."

Jax turns in his seat. "You aren't wrong, but it's not fair to her."

"Fuck the NDA too. Who cares? Lizzy couldn't give a shit."

"Her parents. Her family. This is the same thing we ran into with Sophie," Emmett counters.

Knox bats the air. "What the fuck are we even doing? I mean, seriously?" He looks out of the window, then back to us, his voice calm. "I'll give you some time to figure this shit out. Either way, I'm going back for her."

We'll figure it out. This is not the end of our story, just a hiccup.

EVERLEE - NDA for an NDA

TEN MINUTES.

That's how long I have until Lizzy gets here. It's been a week since I've seen her after I holed myself up in the apartment and she's getting antsy, and an antsy Lizzy is not a good Lizzy.

I spent most of yesterday scouring the internet for a non-descriptive NDA. I'm going to make her sign it, then tell her everything. I need to talk to someone that's local to me, and my best friend. Sophie and I have grown pretty close over the last several days as she was there to tell me the reasons this was good for me, while also playing go between with the boys.

When they showed up the day I left, I thought I was going to die of a broken heart. I wouldn't say I loved them, but I definitely loved the way they made me feel. The confidence they gave me. I loved being around them and seeing their smiles, their looks of desire.

They didn't try to convince me to come back and if they had, I probably would have said screw it all and left with them, but in the weeks, months, or years to come, there would be problems. I've been lying to my best friend, and it's killing me. What about the holidays and my parents? It's unfair that I have to choose the guys over my family and fortunately they didn't make me choose.

Emmett promised me a standing reservation every Monday at Bo's, but I can't go. I would see them there and I would find some reason to go back to them. The look in their eyes, the dimples on their cheeks. I would melt for them.

They've given me so much more than they'll ever know. After Dick, I didn't feel like the same person. I felt like a fraction of myself. I felt less than worthy. Dick was a... well, dick, an asshole, and if someone like that didn't think I was good enough, then it made me second guess myself. Near the end, when I asked him why he never complimented me, he said it was because he didn't want me getting a big head and leaving him. I should have known then, but I didn't. I think by that point he'd already pushed all my friends away, so he was my life, my breath. I'd broken up with him several times, but he would always apologize and I always went back because I was an optimist. I wanted to believe he had changed, or at the very worst, could and would change for me. But I always got my answer a month or so later.

He hadn't changed, and I was left feeling worthless and unlovable again.

The last time Lizzy stepped in. She didn't let me go back, and I have thanked her a thousand times since then, but there was still a hole. No matter how hard she tried to fill it, she couldn't. My confidence was less than non-existent.

That was until Callum stared at me in a bar. The look in his eyes, the way he watched me... the way Emmett flirted with me. It reignited a fire within me. A fire they continued to add fuel to minute by minute, hour by hour.

With them, I felt like my old self. I felt attractive. I felt worthy of love. I felt confident.

That is what they gave me. That and the most orgasms I think I've ever had.

I don't want this to be the end of us and I hope it's not. Hopefully, I can find the courage to explore what this lifestyle is and figure out a way to have it all. Them and my parents. My head wanders down paths, trying to figure out how I can convince my parents to love and accept me. They did with my brother when he came out to them... maybe there's hope for me?

My doorbell rings, bringing me back to the present.

Filled with excitement and trepidation, I race over to the door and see Lizzy standing there with a box of discounted Valentine's chocolate, a bottle of moscato, a new vibrator, a movie and a large clothing box. I laugh out loud, pulling her in.

"You don't have to always buy me a vibrator."

"Is that weird? I was in the store getting me a little something something and this caught my eye."

"You could have bought it for yourself."

She bats the air. "I did, and then I bought one for you. Twinsies."

"You're too much." I smile.

"But you love me." She touches the tip of my nose. "Now go plug him in next to your other boyfriends while I get us some wine glasses."

"I love you," I say, grabbing the vibrator from her and giving her a hug.

"I love you, too."

"Before we watch the movie, though, there's something I need to tell you."

"Are you a lesbian? Because that would explain a lot."

"What? No. At least I don't think so." I grab the NDA and a pen off the counter and hand them to her.

"What's this?"

"An NDA?"

"A what?"

"Non- Disc-"

"I know what is it... are you a spy? Do you work for the government?" Her face draws very long as shock spreads over her. "Oh my God. Is Everlee really your name?"

"Will you shut up! No, I'm not a spy. No, I don't work for the government and you have known me forever. Unless I was a spy when I was in elementary school..."

"So it is Everlee?" she teases.

"Lizzy!"

"Fine. Fine. I'll bite."

"I'm going to put this up and I'll be right back."

When I come back into the room, she's propped on the couch with two straws in the wine bottle, sitting with her legs crossed.

"Straws?"

"You're making me sign an NDA. Shits about to get real. Straws were needed."

I roll my eyes and smile. I should have done this sooner, because my heart already feels happier just being around her for less than two minutes.

"Oh, also, Jax got you something." She hands me the clothes box.

I look at her, confused, taking it from her.

"Also, why is Jax buying you things?"

Feeling like a soda can about to explode, I grab the NDA and make sure it's signed. I take a deep breath and peek inside the box.

My favorite shirt. The one he ripped off when he came to visit the day Dickface showed up on my doorstep. And there's a note.

Ev-

We're giving you space now, but it won't last. We will come back and get what's ours. But first we will let you figure this out, while we find a way to make it work.

- *Jax*

My stomach clenches at his words. Theirs. I am theirs. A tear falls down my cheek.

"What is it?" Lizzy grabs the box from me and tears the lid off. "Don't you already have this shirt? Why are you crying over a shirt?"

"Funny story..."

Ten minutes later...

"SHUT THE FRONT AND BACK DOOR! YOU WHAT?!" Lizzy shouts, climbing on top of me.

She jumps up and paces the room, hands running through her hair.

"I can't believe you didn't say anything to me."

"I couldn't."

Her eyes grow wide. "But still. I'm your bitch," she sighs.

"You are my bitch. But... I don't know." I take a big gulp of wine. "I think I was just scared... scared you'd not approve... or maybe you would. I wanted to do that on my own, see where it went. I think I needed to work through some things."

"Fuck yeah, you worked through things... on things... in things."

"Stop." I smile.

"I didn't know you were a little kink factory."

"Me either."

She sits down on the couch. "You're definitely not a lesbian. You love that dicky dick too much."

"I do love the dicky dick."

"Good thing I brought you another vibrator. If you're going to start taking four at a time..." She cuts her eyes at me with a sly smile spread across her face.

"Will you stop?"

"I will for now, but I don't want you thinking I'm anywhere close to done giving you shit for this. Four..." She holds her fingers in the air, trying to visualize everything, and I bat her hand down.

"What movie did you get us?"

"Oh, it's just an empty box that looks like a movie. I felt it went with the whole theme. But I did rent us the most classic breakup movie of all time. Legally Blonde."

"Bend and Snap."

"Yes, Queen."

"I need to connect to my account so we can stream."

Mentally exhausted, I rest my head on her shoulder and shove a chocolate in my mouth as Jax's note plays on repeat in my head. *We will come back and get what's ours.*

This isn't over.

We aren't over.

What's Next?

NOT ALL RELATIONSHIPS ARE easy. Everlee is close to her family and her best friend, so she needs to find a way to have her men without losing her family.

Bunnies and Bowties is next in the series and let's just say... It's Easter time and Everlee McKinley is two months post the worst decision she's ever made. When her best friend guilts her into getting back out there and going to the Bunnies and Bowties party at Club Vixen, she thinks she's prepared to run into her men, but when she does... she realizes things are still as hot between them as ever. Perhaps hotter...

Needing to clear her head and figure out what she's willing to give up, Everlee takes the long Easter weekend at her parent's lake house, but things don't go exactly as planned. Easter eggs aren't the only thing she'll be hiding.

Read Bunnies and Bowties here

About the Author

Hello lovelies! Follow me below for all the updates, behind the scenes and bonus content!

You can always email me at authorsnmoor [at] gmail.com or message me below. I do rely more on facebook, Insta and TT for most of my communication.

Websitewww.snmoor.com

Etsy Shop AuthorSNMoor

Tiktok@authorsnmoor

Instagramsn_moor

FacebookSN Moor Author — Author SN Moor Fan Group

GoodreadsS.N. Moor

Amazon

Made in the USA
Monee, IL
08 September 2024

64939906R00163